THE GREENING OF THE LAUREL

KATE RILEY

ISBN: 978-1-68046-892-2

Melange Books, LLC
White Bear Lake, MN 55110
www.melange-books.com

Published in the United States of America.

Cover Design by Lynsee Lauritsen

Dedicated to my Aunt Irene Doyle, 1935 - 2019
whose smile is dearly missed.
And to my grandchildren who at least attempted to patiently listen to my
WW2 history lessons at the dinner table.

"At the end of seven hundred years,
the laurel will be green once more."

ANON. TROUBADOUR, 13TH CENTURY

PROLOGUE

1937
Languedoc, France

THE MOUNTAIN VIEWS FROM THIS HEIGHT WERE BREATHTAKINGLY beautiful. Dense, misty clouds clung to the mountain sides, offering the occasional glimpse of wild rocky gorges as they dissipated into ghostly vapour.

Sophie lightly stroked away a stray hair from her eyes and looked over towards Victor, quietly watching him concentrate on his driving. What a strange friendship they had forged. Not at all like the type of men that she usually hung around with. Victor was different and being friends with him meant that she had to look at herself differently. Take her life more seriously.

A self-taught archeologist and writer, he was passionate about the local history here in the Languedoc. He even looked like an academic with his short, slight build, frizzy hair and wire-rimmed glasses that he continually shoved back up the bridge of his nose.

He owned four shirts, all the same shade of blue and two pairs of pants. When she asked him why, he looked surprised as if it was obvious. He liked the colour blue and didn't want to be bothered with decisions he didn't care about. It was functional.

She was a pretty, fun-loving Parisienne with long legs, blonde hair and dressed in the latest fashions. She loved jazz. What brought them together though and cemented their relationship was her family history. Sophie had grown up in this area and came from a long line of Cathar ancestors. He, strongly suspecting that the Grail legend was true, spent years researching and exploring this area for the treasure and anyone connected to it. This is what drew them together.

Lightly touching his arm, she smiled, took a deep sigh and softly said, "It's become quite complicated hasn't it?"

Taking a quick look in his rear-view mirror, he furled his brows and looked irritated, making Sophie wonder whether she should just stay quiet. His recent conversation with his German patrons had not gone well. He had not said a word since they had left.

"I'm sorry Victor—I just keep thinking how crazy this is."

He looked back at her and then stole another quick look in his mirror.

"You're right but it's not that. It's the car behind me. I keep making room for him to pass us, but he doesn't and he's driving too close."

His dark brown eyes briefly caught hers before he looked and focused on the slick mountain road ahead. "What if we're being followed?"

"What? That's crazy!"

"Is it? Considering what they want from me and where we've just been?"

About to turn around to check on the car behind, Victor snapped, "Don't turn around! I don't want to let them know that we know something's up."

"Victor this isn't funny."

"I agree. If you want to check, take out your compact and see if you recognize who it is."

"You think that it's the SS?"

"You tell me."

Pulling her compact out of her purse, she positioned it so that she could get a good look at the car that followed closely behind. It was a large black Mercedes with two people in the car, a driver and someone in the back that she couldn't make out.

Snapping the compact shut, she shook her head. "I don't know, but you could be right. It's an expensive car."

Suddenly, a heavy bump from behind jolted them both forward.

Victor swore, "What the hell?" Pushing the pedal harder, he gained some speed and distance from the menacing vehicle.

Clutching the seat, Sophie, tensed. "Be careful, the roads are wet."

"I know, but we need to lose them."

Checking his rear-view mirror again he relaxed a little having put a little distance between them and the Mercedes.

The mountain roads spiraled around making excessive speed dangerous, but he knew the area well, as well as the hairpin turn ahead. His plan was that he would continue with this speed until he got close and then would take the turn slower. But that was not to be.

As they approached the turn, the car behind sped up, force-fully pushing their bumper forward and over the cliff. The car crashed through the barrier, arched high into the air and then plunged down the mountain ravine.

In the minute before it exploded into a fiery mass of twisted metal and charred bones, Victor thought of the treasure and a lost opportunity. Sophie thought of Meli.

———

Once the car had gone over the edge, the black Mercedes pulled over and came to a stop. The chauffeur stepped out and opened the back passenger-side door where a smartly uniformed SS Officer, anxious to stretch his long legs, leisurely stepped out into the rain. Holding a large black umbrella over his head, the pair walked to the edge and craned their necks to see below. Black smoke billowed from the tangled wreck, leaving no doubt as to the fate of the two occupants.

The Officer rubbed the scar on his face, looked to the chauffeur and nodded a job well done.

"You are sure that there was nothing of value in the vehicle, correct?"

"Yes, sir."

"Good. I think it's time for a glass of that lovely Chardonnay they served me last night at the hotel."

"Very good, sir."

"Oh, and Klaus? Drive carefully. These mountain roads can be quite dangerous in the rain."

CHAPTER ONE

Unoccupied France
The Languedoc,
June 5, 1940—Three years later

A DISTANT ROOSTER CROWED AS THE SUN, STILL LOW ON THE horizon, poured brilliant streams of yellow and orange warming the ancient, provincial landscape.

Stepping out from the shadows of an ancient stone barn, 15-year old Melisende Durand prepared to take on her chores for the day. *Mamina* had long said that the old ones polished and shone their hot *solelh* so brilliantly that it cured everything. Meli hoped that this was true.

Placing her bucket down, she unlatched the door to the chicken coop and opened it wide before grabbing a handful of seed. Leading them out with a scant trail of food, she cooed gently to entice the five hungry hens into the yard. Her grand-mother's girls were regular layers and sure enough, four warm eggs awaited her inspection when she stepped inside. Placing them gently in her basket, she scattered a few more seeds in their path, then wiped her hands on her pants before she began to slowly walk back towards the house, taking in the warm summer air.

Drifting past a small patch of flowering wild thyme, she inhaled its sweet scent, then swept a lock of her shoulder-length, mousey-colored hair away from her eyes and looked around. Although close enough to town, their stone cottage was safely nestled in the embrace of the hills, rocky outcrops and thick chestnut forests, just as it had been for hundreds of years.

The village itself was less than 200 souls at best, with one main street and a row of staggered half-timbered houses with red clay roofs. A few little shops, strategically positioned near the Catholic Church, bordered a grassy square where elderly men played pétanque and old women gossiped on warm summer evenings. Despite the war, there was still a sense of safety and permanence here.

The cottage and the land were a juxtaposition of natural beauty and endless decline—in constant battle for control. With a war on and only a few able-bodied men around, she and her grandmother did their best with the repairs, but there were always things that needed to be done.

The wooden door and indigo shutters that struggled to fit their frames were badly in need of paint, while portions of the fence had been cobbled together to keep in the goats. But despite the rotting wood, paint chips and downed fences, there was a haunting beauty to be found everywhere she looked.

Worn slate slabs, each framed with soft moss, marked out a path to the front of the cottage, while a pink rose bush climbed the stone walls and prettily framed the main entrance. A large thistle that had grown through a rusted and corroded hole from an old paint can, stood resolutely by a lavender bush that gave off the most intoxicating scent. Bunches of aromatic herbs hung from an outbuilding's low ceilings to dry, while an old basket on the dirt-hardened floor was filled with drying, papery onions.

Today was Wednesday, which meant that Mamina would be doing the laundry, an endless all-day chore that involved boiling clothes, sheets and towels to within an inch of their threads. Meli, meanwhile, would take care of feeding the chickens, milking the small herd of rove goats, then letting them out to pasture while foraging grasses for the rabbits. Tomorrow she would do this all again and more. There were, however, lots of other things that she'd prefer to be doing, but what choice did she have? It was just her and her grandmother now to do all the work.

Meli wanted to be a writer and as she saw it, her own story was a simple one. Orphaned as an infant by a distant family relative, Mamina and her daughter, Sophie, had generously adopted her and given her the only home she had ever known. Isabel Durand became her grandmother and Sophie her big sister. The end. Or it would have been, had Sophie not been killed in a tragic car accident three years ago.

To Meli, Sophie had been so much more than a big sister. She was what Meli aspired to be. She was glamorous and wonderful—everything that one day she hoped she would be, and everything that her grandmother would forbid. Much to Mamina's chagrin, Sophie was never afraid to be herself. She laughed louder than anyone else and dressed like a movie star—red lipstick, tight skirts and silk stockings. The works.

Meli was nothing like Sophie. Her petite figure had not yet blossomed into the woman she hoped she would one-day be and worse, she was far shorter than most girls her own age. Her dull, brown hair, not nearly as blonde as Sophie's, constantly fell in a limp, tangled heap on her sun-browned shoulders. Her nose, although small, was sprayed with freckles that Sophie had promised she would grow out of, but so far had never happened.

Her world always brightened when Sophie returned for short visits from Paris—always bringing her a little something special.

She was like the mother that Meli would never know and she loved her for it.

Mamina on the other hand, seemed to save up all her frustration for Sophie's visits and they fought endlessly. Why did she need to live in Paris? What sort of friends did she have there? Why couldn't she stay here and help out more? Take off that red lipstick!

When she was five, Sophie had taken her by the hand and shown her where the original stone cottage had started hundreds of years ago and then where it was added to over the centuries until it stood as it was now, a hodgepodge of heights, out-buildings and crumbling stonework. She told her that the *bonnehommes*, good people, had lived here and their spirit would always watch over her.

Mamina had inherited the farm, an unusual situation at that time, but only because there had been no male relatives left. This cottage would be their future too, and then she smiled her special smile.

Thinking of Sophie made the lump in her throat begin to throb and before tears began to fall, she pursed her lips, swallowed and blinked away the pain. Now it would be just hers.

She knew that Mamina loved her, but when every room, every stone echoed of Sophie's presence, they both tended to curl into the comfort of silence. In the three years since her death, each of them found solace in different ways, Meli in her books, Mamina in work and the church.

Her parents, other than being told that they died, were never discussed. There were no pictures to compare her looks. No warm memories of when she was born. They simply ceased to exist. Before Sophie died, she had asked about them, but her grandmother's silence was deafening. Her questions were even shooed away by Sophie who was always too busy to discuss anything to do with her parents. After a while, she just stopped asking, but secretly she imagined herself to have a royal lineage or even a movie star parent which would one day be revealed.

When Meli had complained to Mamina's oldest friend, Berthe, that her grandmother seemed to be always angry, she had explained that a part of her grandmother's heart had been broken when Sophie died and work was the only way she knew how to relieve her pain. So even though there were days when she too felt angry and heartbroken and just wanted to give up, she read, walked the dusky hills, did her chores and carried on. Mamina was the only family she had.

To Isabel Durand, productive work centered around food. The six goats produced enough milk to make Banon cheese which was then wrapped in chestnut leaves and finished in a cave high up on their property. These she sold in the village which provided a small but necessary income for the farm. Why waste money and time on painting window frames when it was best spent tending to their goats, the chickens, rabbits and the garden, growing and preserving what they could to help them through the winter—perhaps longer. Her daily mantra: "Do whatever we can, because who knows what the future holds."

A small knot of sparrows flew over Meli's head and her gaze followed until the birds landed side by side on the cottage's ancient wooden rails, when through some trees a small movement caught her eye. That would likely be Berthe. Shading her eyes and squinting to see if she too had been noticed, she smiled warmly.

As usual, Berthe's hefty girth was clad in her old black dress, white apron and dark stockings; her snowy white hair pulled neatly into a tight little bun. Her small eyes were almost lost in the soft folds of wrinkles and rosy, sunburned cheeks.

Meli waved as she drew closer but noticed that her usual awkward gait wasn't due to being winded. Berthe was limping and using a sturdy pole as an improvised walking stick to support herself.

Quickly placing her egg basket on the ground, she ran to her side and gently tried to provide further support by holding on to her arm.

"What's this? What have you done?"

Berthe smiled but her eyes couldn't hide the fact that she was in pain. Berthe's soft shoulders leaned heavily on her makeshift cane as she stopped to catch her breath. "Oh, it's nothing. I think I've just twisted it."

Meli shook her head and clearly disagreed. "Lean on me and let me help you inside."

Wincing as she took another step, Berth replied. "No, no, I'm fine. I just need to stop for a moment. It hurts, but I got this far."

"Then I will help you the rest of the way." Meli waited patiently until she was ready to carry on, then slowly guided her towards the kitchen door. Once there, Berthe hobbled carefully over the uneven flagstone floor and deposited her heavy frame in a chair at the old wooden table. Letting out a long whoosh of air, Berthe closed her eyes and visibly relaxed. "Ah that's better."

Calling Mamina from the base of the stairs, Meli looked back at Berthe and smiled. "It's Wednesday."

"I'll be down in one minute!"

Berthe stretched her neck upwards and yelled back. "Take your time, Isabel, I'm not going anywhere."

While they waited, Berthe chuckled as she watched the cat, swishing her tail back and forth, intently stalking a small bug in the corner.

"That cat has to be at least eight years old now," she mused. "I remember the day that I brought her over for you. She was just a little kitten, a little ball of white fluff with a single black splash on her face, in need of a home. Oh my goodness, how Isabel and I laughed. She looked like she had spilled paint on herself."

Meli chuckled. "Well, Minoux must be happy, because she

always brings us little treats of dead mice and small birds to prove her worth."

Isabel stomped down the stairs carrying a basket of dirty clothes and looked first at Meli, and then at the make-shift pole beside the table. Wearing her usual plain cotton dress and full sleeveless pinafore over the top, Isabel's petite but sturdy figure always seemed larger than she actually was. Her greying hair neatly tucked into a bun, she shook her head and turned to her friend.

"What's this for? What have you done now?"

Berthe, looking a little sheepish, replied. "Oh, it's nothing. I twisted my ankle moving some things from upstairs."

"Why do you do these things by yourself? You should have said something. I would have sent Meli to help you." Isabel reprimanded.

"Well, if I knew I would have tripped over such a simple chore I might have, but what's done is done."

Putting her basket of laundry down on the floor, Isabel retorted. "Well, someone needs to scold you and since there's not a husband between us, I consider it my job. You are too much on your own. You need help."

Berthe waved away her scolding with a flick of her wrist. "Psh, I've only come for coffee and gossip, not a lecture. Look, I've even brought my knitting bag so I can be productive."

Looking around, Berthe nodded pointedly towards the blue paint chipping from the old cupboards. "And as for needing help, it's no more than you, I see."

Isabel, recognizing that she might have a point, conceded. "Hmmm, we'll see. After I start the coffee, I'll look at that ankle for you."

She quickly wiped her hands on a damp cloth before reaching for the coffee tin from the cupboard. Carefully scooping a measure of her own blend of rationed coffee, roasted chicory and acorns into the moka pot, she set it on the gas stove to boil.

Having already lived through the Great War, they had been acutely aware of what items would be scarce. There were another four large tins of the mixture stockpiled in the larder.

Isabel walked over to the table and bent down. "Now, let's have a look at that ankle, shall we?" Gently rolling down her black stocking, she softly pressed the tissue around her foot, causing Berthe to wince and pull her foot away.

"Well, you can obviously move it. I'm guessing you've badly bruised it, is what you've done."

As Isabel gently lifted her foot onto an empty chair, she looked over to Meli. "Run and get me a pillow from the salon for Berthe to rest her foot on."

Meli, anxious to be helpful, dashed into the front room and was back immediately with a soft blue floral pillow. "Here you go."

After she placed it underneath Berthe's foot, Isabel orchestrated what needed to be done. "You'll stay with us for a few days. Meli can tend to whatever chores you need done—right, Meli?"

Meli scooped up Minoux, scratched her ears and sat down. "Yes, of course."

Berthe however, shook her head. "No, don't be silly. I can manage."

Isabel simply snorted her reply. "I don't think so and don't give me that look that you've been giving me since we were teenagers. You would do the same for me."

Turning to her granddaughter, she was where she was most comfortable-in full control. "Meli, were there any eggs this morning?"

"Four." But suddenly realizing they were still outside, her eyes widened. "I put the basket down to help Berthe. I'll go get them right now."

Isabel nodded her approval. "Perfect! We'll save those for

supper and have a nice omelet." She turned back to Berthe and smiled. "There, it's settled. You're staying."

As Meli walked out the door, Isabel, added, "While you're outside you might as well grab a couple of tomatoes from the garden as well."

Berthe watched her go and once she knew they were alone, quietly nodded to Isabel. "She's looking more and more like her mother every day."

CHAPTER TWO

THE MOKA POT BEGAN TO BOIL, DEMANDING ISABEL'S ATTENTION. Getting up, she placed her hands on her hips, leaned back to stretch out her aching bones, then busied herself with wiping three cups for the table. Taking the pot off the stove, she poured her wartime brew and sighed. Not quite coffee, but it would have to do.

"It won't be long before they start more rations. Coffee, sugar and flour are already impossible to get."

Looking at Berthe, she shook her head. "What news from up North?"

"Françoise, the Baker's wife, delivered what she dared to call 'bread' yesterday and said they were talking about it in town. Isabel, you have to get your wireless fixed! The Germans bombed Paris on Monday. They've killed hundreds of people, most of them civilians and children. Everyone is terrified and fleeing."

"No! This can't be true. Are you sure?"

"Yes, it was on the wireless last night! The situation is getting worse and things are not looking very good."

"But everyone says that they will eventually just give up. They won't get past the Maginot Line."

Berthe slowly lowered her head and took a small sip of coffee. "I disagree."

Isabel tilted her head, the better to look her friend directly and said quietly, "And what makes you so sure?"

Berthe's guilty eyes lowered. "I might have just taken a quick peek."

Isabel gave her friend a stern look. Tapping her finger on the table in front of her to make her point she continued. "You need to put those tarot cards away once and for all! Father Pelletier says..."

At that moment, Meli came through the door, basket in hand and having overheard the word 'cards', she looked excitedly towards Berthe. "Did you bring your cards? Can you read mine?"

Placing her basket of eggs and two tomatoes on the counter, she pulled up a chair, entirely missing the dirty look that Isabel gave Berthe that warned, *don't you dare!*

"Please—pretty—please. For my birthday?"

Berthe raised her eyebrow and simply gave Isabel a long look back. "No. Father Pelletier wouldn't like it."

"So, I'll say an extra prayer for forgiveness at mass on Sunday. Can she Mamina?"

Isabel's response was abrupt. "Absolutely not! You're too young to be asking about silly things like boys."

Meli looked down and pouted. "What boys—there are no boys around to like. They've all gone to war. Besides, I already told you I want to be a writer!"

Isabel sighed, then gave Berthe another dirty look.

"Meli, that's the end of it. I'll need some of that dried lavender we've got hanging in the shed for a poultice. Scoot outside and get me a handful—enough to fill a small bowl."

Looking back at Berthe she asked, "Do you need her to do any chores at your house?"

Shaking her head, Berthe replied. "The house will survive until tomorrow."

Isabel then faced Meli. "After you get the lavender, you can have your coffee."

Meli, knowing that this wasn't the time to push, got up to find a small bowl, then turned to head outside, frustrated at yet another chore. "Yes, Mam-i-n-a."

Isabel seethed at Berthe through her pursed lips. "You'll burn in hell playing with those things. Our men beat the Germans before and they can do it again."

Berthe shook her head and then snidely commented. "Strong words for someone with your family history."

"You know as well as I do where that's led the women in my family and before you say another word, no, I will never tell Meli of that infernal myth. It's passed her by and that's the end of it!"

"Pfff—You're touchy today. I never said a word and what makes you think it's passed her by?"

There were only two things that they ever fought seriously about. The first was Meli and how much of the truth she should know and the second was Isabel denying her family history and the 'gifts' that went with it. She rubbed her neck, then brushed away a wisp of white hair along with the thought. There were some things too painful to remember.

In truth, she had a strong suspicion that her granddaughter was someone who embraced both worlds like her great-grand-mother before her. Like her mother. Like herself. A dangerous gift to have in these uneasy times.

Berthe sighed and gently placed her palm on top of her friend's. "Relax Isabel, Meli's a good, obedient girl. It's been three years since Sophie died and no one has come looking."

Isabel nodded, took another sip of coffee, then got up to pull a small jar of dried chamomile flowers off the shelf. Placing it on the counter, she then reached up to carefully pull down an old book, its fragile spine broken, and cover frayed and torn with use.

"I suppose you're right. Sophie was certainly my wild child. But then a young, spirited, pretty girl who grows up without a father will always be susceptible to the charms of a young man's eager words of love. If I chased them away, I was a horrible mother. If they never returned it was always my fault. I was rude. I was sharp. I scared them. You remember the fights we had. In the end, I had to let her go and let her learn." Isabel winced. "But in the end, letting go is what killed her."

Angrily fighting the tears that would inevitably come, she thought about her gawky grandchild and the history that she must protect her from at all costs. After Sophie, she wouldn't have the strength to lose her too.

"There, there, Isabel. I told you, there is nothing that you could have done differently. You know this. Meli is too smart for boys and besides what she says is true, all the young eligible men are at the front. Now, give me a smile. She's probably on her way back."

Isabel was lost in thought. *She's too young to know the truth that no longer matters. Family secrets best laid buried in a long, forgotten cave.*

As she entered, Meli looked suspiciously from one to the other as Isabel wiped her eyes with the corner of her apron. Looking determinedly to Meli, she took the bowl of dried lavender from her and said, "Right, now let me get started on that poultice."

Gently opening the book, Isabel flipped through several pages until stopping midway through. Flattening it as best as could, she squinted to read the thin, hand-written script.

"This was my grandmother's remedy. Still works like a charm." At the word *charm*, Berthe raised her eyebrow catching Isabel's attention.

"Don't read anything into that."

Berthe simply smirked her reply.

Placing one teaspoon each of the dried chamomile and lavender flowers in a cup of hot water, she covered it to steep. "There, we'll bathe this bruise several times over the next day to take that swelling down."

Isabel turned to Meli. "Have you milked the goats yet?"

Meli sulkily replied. "Can I have my coffee first?"

Her grandmother chuckled. She knew that she was irritating her granddaughter, but she couldn't help it. Things needed to be done. "Of course. You know I was thinking that since tomorrow is your birthday, we can celebrate with a rabbit stew."

Meli looked up over her coffee cup, mid-sip and gave a grateful, crooked smile. "You remembered."

Her grandmother tilted her head in response and sighed. "Of course I remembered, Meli. I remember a lot of things."

Seeing the disappointment in Meli's eyes, Berthe quickly interrupted. "Isabel, did you say Jeannette Dupuis' daughter got married?"

Looking towards her friend, she raised her eyebrows and gave a little nod. "Oui, and you can guess why."

Berthe gave a little smirk. "How far along?"

"Two or three maybe?"

"Suits her mother right after what she said to you about Sophie."

Isabel widened her eyes to be quiet.

Clearly understanding that their current gossip was not for her ears, Meli took one last gulp and headed towards the door.

Opening a drawer, Isabel pulled out some long strips of used, but clean linen and lay them aside until the liquid cooled enough for them to be dipped into. Busy with her task, she thought of Meli, and then of her own self at that age. Tomorrow she would be sixteen and she knew well enough what the echoes of the past could conjure up.

Desperately trying to focus on her task, she worked in silence until she just couldn't keep it in anymore. Her voice breaking,

Isabel slapped her palm against the counter. "Berthe, I can't do this again. I tell you, the women in my family are cursed. This medieval myth of my ancestors needs to be buried forever. It no longer belongs in our world."

"I know, Isabel, I know."

CHAPTER THREE

THE NEXT DAY STARTED AS IT ALWAYS HAD. THE SUN HEATED THE landscape, a wren warbled, the cicadas sang, and Isabel rose to drag in the cold water from the pump outside the house.

Lost in her thoughts, Isabel looked around and in a single glance took in a lifetime of changes that had happened here. The farm was as it had always been and her tidy cottage with crucifixes hung in every room was a safe haven from all that was going wrong in the world.

Isabel had grown up here, her room where Meli's was now. She had seen saplings grow into trees, seasons of rain and heat and unbearable cold, but the cottage and mountains had endured, protective against the world gone mad.

Her father had worked hard here, repairing, building and making improvements where he could. She missed her parents. Most of all she missed their guidance and her father's quiet ability to fix everything with a single nod and a puff of smoke from his pipe. He didn't say much, but was always intently listening and by that alone, you knew he could solve whatever problem was bothering you.

Her husband Pierre was like that as well and was what drew her to him in the first place. She always knew that when he was around, he would take care of them—her and Sophie. When their daughter was born, he held them both in his strong arms and swore that he would be the man her father was. Until he died.

It had been twenty-six years since Pierre had been killed in the Great War. Twenty-six years that a part of her heart was buried alongside his battered and burned body in the ravaged fields of Verdun. Twenty-six years of being angry with him for leaving her alone with a daughter to raise. And now Meli.

She was young when she married Pierre, but they had known each other all their lives and had liked each other for just as long. He was her first crush, her first kiss, her first everything. Her best friend Berthe had married his best friend. Their lives were supposed to be perfect, but all this was before over 400 thousand of good French men were killed by the German army. Was that not enough?

She looked over at the small copse of trees next to the house and listened to the cicadas. The garden path still echoed the ghosts of his gentle teasing. "Isabel, in my next life I will come back as *le cigale* and completely pass my summer days as a raucous lay about, singing endless love songs to you." And she in turn would scold him that everyone knew that the cicada was sent by God to disrupt the peasants' endless siestas and stop them from growing too lazy. How she missed those days. How she still missed him. She listened again, tried to single out just one, lowered her head and smiled. It would be like Pierre to do just that. The bastard.

She could hear the tap, tap, tap of Berthe's cane upstairs and knew that she would soon be ready for a cup of coffee. Berthe and her had been the best of friends since childhood and their families had lived in these hills even longer. She the serious one and Berthe the more adventurous of the two. Or was it the other way around. Who knew anymore?

Many nights Berthe had regaled Melisende with endless stories of their escapades and secret recipes. That was so long ago now that it felt like another person. Was she ever that young?

Non-stop talkers, one would swat the other if a story was incorrectly told or related in a way to tease the other. The ongoing competition—who made the better cassoulet? Berthe insisted that duck and paprika be used and she insisted that aged goose and pepper, and lots of it, was the traditional and therefore correct version. She could still taste her mother's recipe, handed down from her grandmother and her great-grandmother before that. When this war was over, the first thing she would do is gather all the ingredients and teach it to Meli.

As she put the moka pot on the stove, Berthe slowly hobbled down the stairs taking one step at a time. Tap, step, tap, step. Spilling herself into a kitchen chair, she rubbed her eyes with the flat of her hand. "Morning, Isabel."

"How's that ankle?"

She shrugged her shoulders. "Still sore, but not too bad."

Footsteps and a sharp rap on the kitchen door alerted them to a familiar face. Already smelling the brew, the postmaster had a smile of anticipation on his face. Boasting a handlebar moustache already white with age, Henri Bouchard poked his head through the open kitchen door. Henri and his wife Rose ran the local post office, a position that held important benefits; plenty of coffee, cigarettes and a wealthy source of information, both local and afar. Isabel liked to point out that no secret was safe, no gossip unnoticed as long as the Bouchards' were near.

A veteran from the Great War, he still carried pieces of shrapnel in his leg, a fact that he proudly and repeatedly shared with anyone to explain the cause of his limp and various aches and pains. He took his position seriously and explained in hushed tones to his veteran friends that postmasters were the eyes and ears of France. "*Ca va*, Isabel, Berthe. How goes it for you?"

Isabel opened the door to allow him in.

"You know me, Henri, I don't like to complain, but my arthritis is getting worse and making me grumpy."

Staring at their cups, he continued. "I have a letter for you Isabel, and given the current situation, I of course, felt obliged to deliver it immediately." Swinging his brown leather satchel around to the front, he opened the flap, pulled out the letter and held it out to her. Nodding an acknowledgement to Berthe he added apologetically, "Nothing for you."

Isabel smiled back and took the letter from his hand and placed it on the counter. She had a good idea as to what it was, but she'd be damned if she'd open it now.

Berthe looked over to Isabel. "Coffee, Henri?"

Henri looked at them both. "For sure, don't mind if I do." Taking off his cap, he placed it on the table, revealing a balding pate with wisps of snow-white hair. He then lifted the strap over his head and placed his weathered leather satchel by the side of a free chair.

As he sat down, he took out a hand-rolled cigarette from a packet in his pocket and a box of matches. Offering one to Isabel and then to Berthe who both declined, he proceeded to light it. Inhaling a deep satisfying pull of smoke, he looked at the both. "You've heard of course what happened in Paris and the latest news."

Isabel gestured towards Berthe. "She told me yesterday about Paris being bombed."

"Have you not been listening to the radio?"

"My wireless is broken, Henri," Isabel clipped, "and I just haven't had the time to get it fixed."

"It's not good. Not for them. Not for us. That's why I brought the letter so promptly."

Isabel expected Henri to continue, but he sat in silence as if he was considering giving her a lecture on responsibility.

Berthe, noting Isabel tapping her fingers in frustration, turned to Henri, and nodded towards his cigarette. "Henri, I can't stand it. Give me one of those things, then tell us what you've heard?"

Reaching for his packet, he pulled one out for Berthe, then lit it for her. "You sure you don't want one Isabel? It's real tobacco, not that god-awful blend with sunflower leaves." She simply shook her head.

Tapping two ashes into the ashtray he continued, obviously enjoying his superior position as the bearer of important information.

"They say German bombers are bearing down on the villages in the North, killing everyone. Pétain himself went on the radio. Placing his hand on his heart, Henri proceeded to repeat the old Marshal's words. 'It is with a heavy heart that I tell you today that we must cease hostilities. The fighting must stop.' Rose and I, we heard it ourselves."

Wide-eyed the two of them could only shake their heads in disbelief.

"People are flowing down the highways like molasses. A trail that is endless they say, as far as the horizon."

"Oh my God, is this true? Where are they going?" Isabel asked.

"Pffff! Where do you think? South towards us. Ladies, as much as Paris has been invaded by the Germans, we too are being invaded by the North. They think we have room for them, food for them, tender warm hands waiting to welcome them. You know as well as I do, we don't."

Taking another long drag of his cigarette, he inhaled and paused to let that information fully sink in. "Of course, there's adequate food for those who can afford to buy it for now, except of course for butter lovers, as we know most Parisians are, but how long can that last?"

Berthe turned to her friend. "Perhaps it's time to get your wireless fixed."

Isabel gave her a worried look and nodded in agreement. "You may be right."

Henri lifted one eyebrow towards the letter. "Your letter seems to be from Paris, Isabel. It could be important."

Isabel, knowing that he was dying of curiosity, simply got up to refill her cup.

"Probably birthday wishes for Meli," she replied.

As if on cue, Meli stumbled into the kitchen, yawned deeply, then rubbed her eyes and stretched. Grateful for the interruption, Isabel smiled. "Our birthday girl awakens! Bonne fête ma petite!"

Berthe opened her arms and gave her a big hug. "Bonne fête, Melisende."

Meli smiled, then nodded to the postman.

"Bonjour, M. Bouchard." Walking over to pour herself a cup of coffee, she cut off a wedge of cheese then joined the others at the table.

Henri tilted his head in respect and said. "Bonne fête, Meli. How old are you now?"

"Sixteen, Monsieur."

"Sixteen—can it be? Seems impossible. It feels like only yesterday that you were a just a baby."

While they chatted, Berthe couldn't help but notice that Isabel had taken the letter and quietly slipped it into a drawer.

Having taken one last deep pull from his cigarette, Henri squashed the stub into the dish and stood up to leave. Lifting his strap over his head he put his hat back on and straightened out his uniform.

"Mark my words, ladies, this sluggish river of people will suffocate us. They'll raid our gardens and steal our food. Consider yourselves warned and get that radio fixed. Take it over to Roman Kowalski. You know him. That big Polish fellow, good with his hands—he'll sort it out for you."

After Henri had left, Meli nervously looked to her grandmother. "Are we in danger, Mamina?"

"Of course not," she replied with more confidence than she actually felt.

"Our tiny village is worth nothing. Why there are barely enough shops for us as it is. This crazy Hitler man and his war will never reach our town. Where will his soldiers stay? Why would he even bother?"

Nodding to her friend for confirmation, she continued. "Berthe and I have been through this before. If we keep our heads down, make do with less, the war will never reach us, and all will be well. We'll carry on as we always have."

Turning to Meli, she carried on. "You know, it just occurred to me that there's a good sturdy cane of my grandfather's in the attic. Your bones are younger than mine Meli. How about you go up and see if you can find that old hickory cane for Berthe. It'll be much easier than that old pole of hers and it should have a proper handle."

Meli simply sighed the deep sigh of an over-burdened teen with endless chores and no fun in her life.

"Mind the dust and any rotting boards."

"Yes, Mamina."

"I'll bet you don't even know what's up there," Berthe muttered under her breath.

Watching her go, Isabel suddenly got up to wipe the counter. Berthe was right, she hadn't been up there in years. The last time anyone had been up there was when a local handyman had stored some of Sophie's things after the accident.

After Meli had left the room, Berthe wasted no time in grilling her friend. "So, a letter from Paris? Are you going to tell me what's it about or do I have to beg?"

Isabel gave her a quick glance, sighed and rubbed the back of her neck. "It's nothing of any importance."

Berthe was not one to be put off. "Of course, it's none of my business, but as your closest friend…"

"It's a birth certificate for Meli. There! Now you know." Berthe knitted her brows, but before she could ask another question, Isabel sighed.

"Okay, okay. I know you won't rest until you know it all. It's a *new* one and a *Carte d'identité de Français*, without *his* name as the father."

"And Sophie?"

Isabel barely spoke above a whisper. "That's been altered as well."

"But why, Isabel? Why can't you just tell her?"

"What's done is done, Berthe. Sophie is dead. Why bring up the past and smear her name now? Besides, what she doesn't know won't hurt her. Let's face it, considering the circumstances, it may even save her life."

"But that means the document is false. Isabel, however, did you manage this?"

If you must know, Sophie's friend Helene arranged it all in exchange for food. I sent off a large box to her last month, eggs, potatoes, carrots, vegetables. She was having a hard time getting by with just the rations.

Berthe stared at Isabel's back. "The best friend? She's the one who introduced Sophie to *him* isn't she?"

Isabel stopped, wiped her hands on her apron and turned around to face her friend. A simple nod was all she could manage.

"How much do you think she knows?"

"Well, certainly about Meli's father. I don't know how much more. But she and Sophie were close, so who knows?"

"Isn't she the one who married that butcher?"

Isabel leaned back into her chair and smirked. "She did, but I

27

guess he wasn't good enough for her because she left him, took the baby and married some banker."

"Oh, really?"

"Uh huh, an Austrian. But who knows who the father is? I know she has some big fancy apartment in Paris, but we hadn't spoken in years. Not since Sophie…"

"Then how?"

Isabel rubbed her shoulder. "She contacted me last month. I guess the rations are hitting the Parisians pretty hard. She mentioned there was things being disclosed in her circles about Jews, especially the rich ones and that she had made a promise to Sophie. In the end, she had the connections and I have food."

"It's a bit odd though, don't you think?"

"I thought so too, but she always did have an anxious temperament, so I thought what could it hurt?"

Berthe sat back and took a sip of her coffee. "Why didn't you tell me?"

"Truthfully? Because I felt ashamed. Because I don't want to think of this anymore. If Sophie wanted this done, then who am I to argue? It's a harmless document that will sit in a drawer."

Berthe shook her head, "There's more to this Isabel. You know it and I know it."

CHAPTER FOUR

THE ATTIC WAS ACCESSED BEHIND A SLENDER UNASSUMING DOOR towards the back of the house. Almost hidden, it looked like it might contain a small closet or something equally as trivial. Long forgotten and easily bypassed, Meli tried to think of the last time she had actually been up there and although she was sure that she must have, she couldn't remember when.

The passageway was dark, the stairs steep and so narrow that she had to keep her hands against the walls in order to steady her balance. Slowly creaking her progress upwards, her shoes barely covered the center of the treads worn down from centuries of use.

In the dim light she continued until the stairs reached a small landing and stopped. To the right was a closed small but heavy ancient door and on the opposite side, a more modern, modest entryway lay slightly ajar. Peeking through into the room on the left, she was surprised to find a small bed and desk—obviously not the attic, but worthwhile of an exploration at a later time.

Turning to the right she hesitated for a brief moment, then lifting the latch, she gave a gentle push. The door resisted.

Suspecting that it had been closed far longer than anyone realized, she gave a hefty push. As she applied her weight, the wood and wrought iron fittings groaned in protest and suddenly gave away. Assaulted by a rush of stale and musty air, trapped for who knows how long, she coughed, immediately covered her nose, then took a moment to catch her breath and her bearings.

As her eyes adjusted to the light, she stood in awe, for before her lay a room where time appeared to have simply stopped. Large wooden beams supported an ancient tiled roof and bare pinewood planks, un-swept for years, were coated in a thick layer of dirt and dust.

In the dim light, she took in small hints of the attic's long forgotten past. An antique wooden dress frame stood forgotten in the corner with a moth-eaten fox fur wrapped around the neck. There were wooden crates, boxes on top of boxes, a large ancient steamer chest, and a large dark antique dresser. Off to the side was a variety of chairs whose cane and fabric seats were in various states of decay. Everything was covered in a thick blanket of dust and in that brief heartbeat of a moment, she had the oddest sensation that she had been expected, that the attic itself had been waiting just for her.

As she took in the room, she noticed a small casement window against the far wall and although it was a poor source of light, it would at least bring in some much-needed fresh air. Picking her way to the other side of the room, she stooped to pick up a broken chair spindle to use to get rid of any cobwebs and noticed some rotted planks in the corner. Mamina was right, she would have to be careful of where she stepped.

After swiping away the cobwebs around the casement, she twisted the wooden latch to open the shutters and to her relief, they opened easily. As if waiting for their chance, trapped dust motes immediately broke free and danced in the sunlight and gentle breeze. She smiled as she looked out towards the distant hills and valleys.

How many of Mamina's ancestors had gazed out from this very window to the very same enchanting view, she wondered? Would they have seen the same hazy purples, the same ochre horizons? Down below, the chickens pecked away at juicy bugs. Further on, the rove goats nibbled at the taller grasses that grew next to the fence, a small pond shimmered in the pasture and the sun kissed her cheeks. Turning around and scanning the room, she smiled to herself. Happy birthday Meli; your own treasure trove of marvelous things with stories to tell.

Towards the left side was a few chests, another dresser and an old wooden hobby horse as well as hodgepodge of old clothes piled high and spilling out from an old cardboard box. Heading in that direction, she figured that this was the most likely area to rummage through. At least it was a place to start.

Trailing her finger through a layer of thick dust on the dresser, she wondered to whom all these things had once belonged. Would Mamina even know what was up here or what their stories were? What more treasures could be found?

Her curiosity heightened, she temporarily forgot about the cane and slowly opened the top drawer to the dresser, disappointed to find it empty except for an old faded piece of Christmas paper used to line the bottom. The middle drawer though, looked deeper and after closing the first, she pulled at the second. It was heavier, obviously full and with a few good solid tugs, she managed to slide the reluctant drawer out enough to examine what was inside.

What caught her attention first was a small open box laying on top of a sheet with several loose pictures laying inside. Picking them up she looked at each one individually, curious as to what she found. She smiled.

The first one was of Sophie looking much younger, perhaps even the same age as herself. She was sitting on some steps, legs curled to the side, her shoulder-length hair gently blowing in the wind. Her head rested on the palm of her hand, while her eyes smiled directly at the photographer as if in that moment, they were sharing a secret. She was beautiful. This one she would keep.

The next two pictures were of people she didn't know and were obviously very old. Sepia-tinted and fading with age, one was a man standing in a soldier's uniform and the other was of a peasant woman sitting on a stone wall surrounded by sheep. In the background was a large hill and at the craggy top, the ruins of a citadel. Laying the pictures of Sophie aside, she put the other two back into the box and poked around some more.

The old sheet folded over lengthwise, covered the length of the drawer and as she lifted the one corner, she was surprised to find what looked to be a pile of foxed pages tied up with string. The top page appeared to be water damaged, but she managed to make out the name 'Victor' hand-written lower down. Making a mental note of this, she put the corner back down and lifted the other side. She grinned with excitement! The rest of the drawer was filled with books, which certainly explained the weight.

Picking one up, she looked at the cover. Tauchnitz Publishers translations of Wuthering Heights and Little Women. She loved books that transported her into another time and place and the way Jane Austen made her understand how someone would have thought at that time. She even liked the thought that maybe there would be a Darcy in her future.

Opening the book, she saw Sophie's name scrawled across the first page. Not small and neat the way she would have done, but loud and boldly as if she herself had taken ownership of the book's very existence. That was Sophie.

Meli had a little library started of her own, so to find books on her birthday was more than just a coincidence. These books were Sophie's gift to her.

She always wanted to write her own romance story, but she could never nail down a plot. One day she decided that her heroine would happen across a handsome pilot that needed her help. The handsome man would be impressed by her bravery and fall in love with her. When the war ends, he asks her to marry him and he takes her to his family's estate in England, a place that Meli had always wanted to see. But then she would change her mind. Perhaps the handsome pilot wasn't British but a brave and handsome Frenchman. France needed strong men and instead he would build them their own cottage. Of course, that would require her actually writing the story.

As her fingers lingered on the book, she suddenly felt heavy. She felt foggy, not herself and much older. Feeling sleepy, she tried to widen her eyes, but then her gaze softened, and time seemed to slip. She imagined herself wearing a long dress, could feel the weight of the fabric and the warmth of the shawl around her shoulders. The air around her smelled wet and even though a distant part of her knew it was a warm sunny day, she felt cold as the rain beat hard on the casement window. Shivering in the damp chill she reached for her shawl, but in that moment, the spell was broken by the faint sound of someone calling a name that seemed familiar.

"Meli. Meli, what's taking you so long?"

It took a moment to realize that it was her grandmother calling from the base of the stairs. A little shaken as to what had just happened, she weakly replied. "I'm coming." Then repeated it, much louder in order to wake herself fully. "I'm coming!"

Still somewhat disoriented, she looked down at herself, half expecting to still be in a long dress but instead found herself in familiar dungarees and a white blouse. Quickly closing the book, she placed it beside the picture she intended on taking downstairs, then closed the drawer.

She then regained her focus and poked around for where a cane might be stored and within a few minutes had found an old copper umbrella stand filled with a variety of sticks, canes and dingy, moth-eaten umbrellas. Grabbing a cane that she thought would be the sturdiest, she walked back to close the window.

Taking a last quick look outside at the hens pecking away in the sunshine she tried to shake off what had just happened, but she felt different and this tiny shift in perspective made the green leaves of the trees shimmer and the mountains in the distance change colour, deepening into purples and dark grey. Shutting the window, she focused only on the light from the door ahead and made her way downstairs.

Not once did Meli notice the spectre in the corner who watched her every move. The misty form, that by the time the door had closed, had dissipated back into shadow. As Meli hurried down the stairs, she didn't know it yet, but her life had already changed. Her path committed.

CHAPTER FIVE

LATER THAT AFTERNOON, ISABEL WALKED THROUGH THE WOODS to the village, the canopy dappling her way with delicate streams of sunshine on the dusty path ahead. Dragonflies buzzed around her while birdsong lured her deeper into the thick forest. She could feel the stirrings of magic around her—tugging at her senses, pestering her to pay attention, demanding to be acknowledged.

If she kept silent, relaxed her breath and allowed it to continue, she knew it would swirl, flutter inside her thoughts, inviting her to play, perhaps even tell her things and for a brief instant she was tempted. But in that moment, she thought of Sophie and stubbornly focused on the path ahead to shake it off.

"Stop!" she yelled, raising her hands in protest. Looking around to ensure no one else had heard her, she scratched the back of her neck, ran her hands through her hair and took a deep breath.

Focus, focus, focus. It was the little things in life that mattered— the scent of lavender from her kitchen window, the joy of fresh eggs, planting seeds in the egg shell halves that would turn into sturdy tomato plants, digging up potatoes, turnips—having enough to feed yourselves. The predictability of it all. You plant things, you water them, and they grow. This is how she wanted her life—simple and uncomplicated. Mentally pushing it all away, she raised her chin and carried on down the path.

Enough of this nonsense. Willpower and prayer would see her through this. Hard work was what was needed here. Keep your head down. Take care of your own. Plan ahead. Ignore the feelings. Ignore the magic. Tuck them away. They have only caused you grief and will only cause you more.

As she finally stepped from the path onto the village street, she could see everyone out in the warm summer sunshine. A group of women were huddled together chatting in their cotton dresses and crossover aprons. Familiar faces looked up, nodded and smiled at her as she slowly walked down the street listening to snippets of conversations on the latest news about Paris.

The effects of the war were most noticeable here in the village where the lack of young men left the old ones sadly remembering how it was in the Great War. Wordless nods and fearful looks were testament enough to the devastation that took friends, neighbors and relatives. They had lived all this before.

The village today was a sea of worried faces and non-stop chatter. It was all everyone and anyone was talking about and it didn't surprise Isabel in the least to see Rose Bouchard, the post-master's wife, in the thick of it. Ruddy-cheeked and as wide as her husband was tall, she proudly held court to several others as she waited in line at the bakers. As she staged-whispered her information, Rose looked around to see who else was acknowledging her importance. "My husband said he heard it straight from another colleague who said that the railroad stations are filled to capacity. The police are even stopping cars in the streets and requisitioning them for military and government use. And now there's a curfew in effect from nine in the evening until five in the morning. Everyone in Paris is frustrated with the shortages and humiliation of it all."

The moment she saw Isabel she waved and tried to call her over, but Isabel could see her nodding to others as she spoke. "Isabel...letter...Paris."

Instead, Isabel quickly turned right towards Berthe's little home at the other edge of town. She would get Meli's present and the jar of blackberry jam now; the bread could wait until she was ready to walk back home.

As she walked along, she couldn't help but overhear a tête-à-tête from two young mothers who tightly held their children's hands, "...hundreds of thousands of people on the move. Surely, Marshal Pétain has the right idea. Don't antagonize the Germans. Work together and just wait it out."

In the centre of the market, a small table had been set up under the shade of a small chestnut tree where two old men played chess. As she walked past, one of them aggressively pointed his finger at the other and continued his rant "...not enough troops to hold off the German advance. The British aren't doing enough!" Nearby, two grizzled old veterans sat together on a bench and while one tapped tobacco into the bowl of his pipe the other carried on. "I would have done things differently—shown them what's what. Why aren't the Americans helping out? Is the world watching? Do they even care?"

Stopping in front of a store window, she looked at herself reflected in the glass. An older, tired woman stared back, and she carried on.

Finally reaching the end of town, she passed four women who shaded their eyes and stared off into the cloudless sky. "German and Italian aircraft...machine guns... bombs thudded and exploded all along the road."

Isabel sighed and looked towards the sky with them. If Sophie were alive, she would have been there. She would be escaping like all the others. But sadly, not even that would have kept her safe.

Reaching into her apron pocket, she unlocked Berthe's door,

and entered into the coolness of the house, then slowly shut the door to the world outside. Leaning against the wall, she pursed her lips, put her hand over her mouth and shut her eyes. *Were they really safe here in the free-zone?*

In truth, they were all holding their breath, hoping that the German's would ignore the South and let them carry on. Just stay quiet, keep your head down until everything returns to normal. Vichy France, already bled of its husbands, brothers and fathers from the Great War, was in no mood for a fight. These ancient hills still smelled of the stake.

CHAPTER SIX

MELI'S BIRTHDAY DINNER WAS A QUIET EVENING OF RABBIT STEW and fresh vegetables from the garden. Mamina had made a small blackberry tart from Berthe's preserves. They had wine with their meal and Meli was delighted when Berthe handed Meli her gift —a blank notebook to write down all her story ideas. Berthe smiled as her present was met with big hugs. Even Isabel had a smile on her face.

After dinner, as Mamina and Berthe tidied up, Meli trudged back from locking up the chickens in their coop. She stopped for a few moments and took in the scents of wild mint and thyme. Time seemed to stand still as she stared at the starry night sky. There was a change in the air, she could feel it. Something was different. The cottage was always magical to her, but this was the first time that there was weight in that word.

Later, as she snuggled herself into bed, she opened up her notebook with the intent of writing down the beginnings of her story, but instead her focus once again became soft and fuzzy. Feeling suddenly exhausted, her writing hand seemed to take

over and in a tidy neat script she wrote, 'and so it begins'…
before turning out the light and falling immediately asleep.

Meli fell deeper and deeper into the abyss of darkness and time. Her senses alive with the fear of being hunted and the knowledge that should she be discovered, it would mean instant death.

Disguised as a boy, she knew with absolute clarity that should anyone recognize her these would be her last moments. What she didn't know was why.

Instinctively she held her breath and squeezed her eyes shut amid the roar of battle cries vibrating through the deep bowels of the fortress. Willing herself invisible, she plastered herself against the clammy, damp foundations. Heart pounding, she could barely breathe so afraid was she at being caught.

Just ahead, the yellowing flicker from torches indicated that another tunnel crossed to where hers ended. As she crept forward, she could see that the left side of the tunnel floor appeared to ride gently upwards and likely led outside to where a clamor confirmed that a battle had already ensued.

To her right, the frenzied roar of an army of male adrenaline was getting closer and closer to where she stood, running towards her direction, obviously to join their comrades in combat.

Pressing herself further into the wall she considered running in the other direction but had no idea as to where or what she would run to. The clash of metal on stone and the rush of soldiers as they raced through the halls was getting even closer.

Terrified and exposed with nowhere to run, she flattened herself even further against the walls in hopes that her small frame would blend into the darkness. Then in an instant, they were there. Like a deafening train they stormed through the tunnel. Hundreds and hundreds of them ran in unison yelling, howling, in their rabid heat to join in the onslaught, cudgels, spears and broadswords brandished high above their heads.

Her eyes strained through the darkness, desperately seeking a safer niche, anywhere but in this open passageway and then she found it. Just a short distance away in the opposite direction she spied the dark outline of an archway.

Her legs rubbery, her heart pounding, she edged towards the door, hardly daring to move lest she attract attention. Just then, from the darkness at the end of her hallway came single confident, heavy footsteps in her direction. The decision was made. It was now or never, and she ran.

With no time to see anything clearly, she caught only shapes and colors. The room was small, dark and shadowy, empty, except for a long table with a large white linen cloth draped over it. The footsteps were now dangerously close and without further thought, she dove underneath the table, minimizing herself into a fetal position and squeezed her eyes shut.

Terrified, she could hear that the footsteps stopped at the archway door. Whoever it was, was now in the same room. As step-by-step they came closer, her heart pumped wildly. Too frightened to look, she frantically prayed to God to make them not see her and leave.

The footsteps slowly walked towards her until she knew he was beside her. She could smell the sweat of him, the mud from his boots. Rivulets of sweat trickled down her forehead. She knew he could smell her fear. Then silence. Unbearable silence…and in the next moment, a rancid breath that was far too close.

Slowly she opened her eyes and turned her face towards her fate. Deep coal back eyes held her gaze. There would be no escape.

Meli woke sweating, shaken, still dazed and disoriented. The veil between the past and present felt sheer—misty. Where was she? The dream tugged at her soul to return, when suddenly she heard a deep, firm male voice from inside her head. "Wake up and hear my words." Groggy, she struggled to return to her room, but she was still wavering between the two worlds when she heard the man's voice again. This time he sounded urgent and strong. "No matter who you are now…"

As she opened her eyes, the voice had one last sinister message. "I will find you."

Shaken, she lay awake scanning every dark corner of her room until completely exhausted, she finally closed her eyes and fell back into a deep dreamless sleep.

———

The following morning Meli rose early as usual and began to get started on her day. She couldn't shake the feeling that something significant had happened even though it was just a dream. *At least it must have been just a dream, wasn't it?*

Later, she came into the kitchen carrying a small basket of eggs to see Berthe quietly knitting at the table. "What are you making?"

Berthe smiled back. "Just socks for the boys at the front."

Meli looked around, half expecting her grandmother to walk in from the other room. "Where's Mamina?"

"She left a while ago to go into town, so she shouldn't be long. Do you need something?"

"No, but I thought I could keep you company." She ventured, "And maybe ask you a little question?"

Berthe stopped her mending but did not look up. "What is it that you want to know? If this is about your parents, you'll have to ask your Mamina."

"No, no it's nothing like that. It's just that I had this strange dream last night and it hasn't left me. It didn't feel like a dream at all. It was like it really happened but a long time ago. So, I wanted to ask you, do you think that dreams can be real?"

Berthe's face blanched and for a moment she just stared back. Finally, putting down her knitting on the table, she quietly replied, "What kind of dream, Meli?"

Meli shook her head. "It was all so strange, more like a nightmare but it was so real. In my dream I was disguised as a boy and I was in danger. There was some kind of battle going on and I had to hide. Some man found me and before I woke up, I heard his voice telling me that no matter who I am now, he'll find me."

Berthe licked her lips, took a deep breath and looked out the window. "Dreams can be funny sometimes, but I'm sure it's nothing. Best to forget it."

"But that's just it. I can't. It felt real." Meli then gave a little chuckle. "I wonder what Mamina would say? She'd probably make me go to confession."

Berthe barked out her reply, "You are not to tell her."

Surprised at her outburst, Meli started and her eyes widened. "But why? It was a strange dream, but it was still just a dream wasn't it?"

Berthe looked shaken and refused to look back at Meli. Her head down, she continued her knitting and in a low voice she replied.

"Listen to me, Meli, it will upset her. There are things that I can't say."

Frustrated, Meli put both hands on her hips. "What things and why can't you just tell me?"

"Meli, it's more complicated than me just telling you something."

"But…"

"No buts. For now, think of this as a strange dream, but promise me you'll tell me if this happens again. Promise me."

Meli raised her hands in mock surrender. "Okay, okay, I promise." Then suspecting an opportunity, she smirked and gave Berthe a sheepish look. "Can you read my cards then?"

Berthe frowned, sighed and looked over to Meli. "You know, your grandmother and I disagree about this, but you are sixteen now, a young woman, what do you say? And before I break a promise I made to my oldest and dearest friend, tell me why this is so important to you?"

Meli took a deep breath then put her shoulders back.

"Because, as you say, I am now a young woman and need to figure out who I am and my future."

After what Meli had disclosed about her dream, Berthe was curious as well, but she wouldn't let Meli know that. "You know it's funny, Sophie was sixteen when she came to chat with me one day. She wanted a reading too. Sat right where you are now."

"What did Sophie want to know?"

"Oh, about boys, or more to the point, about one boy in particular. The heart is a funny thing, it wants who it wants, and a young girl in love is like a thirsty horse heading for the barn. Nothing else exists."

Meli sighed and rolled her eyes. "It's not about a boy."

Berthe gave her a sly look, smiled, then looked down at her cloth bag. "Alright, alright. I do happen to have my cards with me and yesterday was your birthday. But this must be our secret! Do you promise?"

Meli smiled and practically jumped into her lap giving her a huge hug. "Yes, yes, I promise, I promise!"

"Let's do this now then, before she gets back." Reaching into her bag she pulled out a well-worn deck in her hand. "Remember, not a word."

"They look really old. How did you learn to do this, Berthe?"

"They are very old. See the pictures? These are all hand-painted from woodcuts. It's called the Tarot de Marseille and they were my grandmother's. She's the one who taught me."

Placing the deck in front of Meli, she sat back in her chair and closed her eyes. Briefly thinking how much Isabel would kill her, she said a Hail Mary for good measure then looked at Meli. "I want you to think about a question that you want answered, then shuffle the deck."

Meli looked down at the cards in her hands and concentrated on shuffling and not dropping them at the same time. Try though as she might to think about being an author, her mind kept going back to the dream. When she couldn't shift her mind, she gave up and placed the cards in a stack on the table.

Berthe took a sip of her coffee. "Okay, now place them in three stacks."

Meli picked up the deck in front of her then cut it into three places. She then folded her hands in her lap and waited in anticipation.

Berthe thought back to Sophie. Her element had been fire. She was passionate about life, charming and spirited, always looking for a good time, easily bored and switched from one love interest to the next.

Meli's element was water. Often quiet and peaceful, water people did not mind spending time with themselves, in fact, they preferred it. They were often lost in a world of their own. Serenity came easily to them and they tended to be imaginative and calm. It would take a lot to irritate a water element person because they went with the flow. Water she knew, helped people of this element obtain knowledge, and they were more likely to listen than to vocalize.

Satisfied with the shuffle, Berthe stacked the piles back into one, placed ten cards in position and then turned over the top card. The Empress.

The reading was a strong one and indicated change, challenges, a young man, an older man and good over evil. The paranormal. Uncovering the path and a truth…a dream realized.

She frowned and held her breath. She had seen this exact spread before.

Just then, they heard footsteps outside the door. Fearful that Isabel had returned, Berthe quickly packed up the cards and hid them back into her bag.

Just before her grandmother opened the door, Meli leaned forward and whispered, "What about my cards? What did they say?"

Berthe looked back and gave an anxious smile. "They say

that you will be a famous author and write many books that people will love to read."

At this point Isabel walked in and noticed that they instantly stopped talking. Giving Berthe a pointed look she said, "You look pale. Are you all right?"

Berthe simply nodded guiltily.

Something was brewing—she could feel it. And if she knew, then Isabel did too. Too many strings kept in a tight little ball had started to unravel and once loose would be impossible to roll back up. She knew her friend well, knew all her secrets so she understood only too well that it wasn't just the truth or the future that Isabel was afraid of. It was the past that haunted her.

The problem as she saw it was that Isabel had not prepared Sophie enough about the consequences of sharing the family secrets. How could Sophie have realized how dangerous what Isabel had presented to her as a myth, really was.

The prophesy was awakening before their very eyes and this was not the time for Isabel's self-pity or anger. The time for secrecy was over, but Isabel was adamant she would protect Meli from their family history at all costs. Borne out of guilt, Isabel vowed that Meli would never follow the same path, despite the ancient mark on her shoulder blade that stated otherwise.

Isabel looked kindly towards Berthe. "You're quiet this morning."

Staring back at her friend who slowly sipped the last of her coffee, she simply patted Isabel's hand and smiled. "Just tired."

How can I tell you that Meli has exactly the same last cards I dealt for Sophie before she died?

CHAPTER SEVEN

At 6',4" Lieutenant Wolfgang Koch cut an imposing figure. A hulk of a man, he used it at every opportunity to his advantage. Adding to his intimidating size, was a deep angry scar that ran all the way from his mouth to his ear. A jagged lightening slash that matched his mercurial temperament.

By contrast, the man sitting across the table from him was anything but. Soft-spoken and bespectacled, his short stature and narrow shoulders were hardly an example of superior Arian genes, but it was he who had the power and had demanded the meeting. By 1940, Koch had already distinguished himself in the Nazi party and as Hitler's most loyal devotee he was keen to complete whatever mission Reichsführer-SS Himmler chose to give him.

Tipping back a glass of schnapps, Himmler ordered another round from a plump young waitress, then turned to the giant across the table.

"It would appear, Lieutenant, that you have a tendency towards some rather unorthodox methods."

"Sir?"

"I have been following you for a while Koch. You shot down a portrait of Prince Bernhard of the Netherlands from the wall of a Dutch café after the owner refused to remove it. You got caught stealing equipment from other divisions, and as I understand it, even took tires from a depot at gunpoint."

"I prefer to think of it as being resourceful, sir."

"Precisely why I used you back in in '37."

"Sir?"

"Victor Schreiber, the archeologist grail writer. Unfortunately, a young lady was with him at the time, but these things happen. A little matter of wet mountain roads as I recall, and I was very happy with the outcome."

"I'm glad to hear it, sir."

"I understand you speak French?"

"Fluently, sir, as well as seven other languages."

"And you have an Engineering background." This was not a question.

"Yes, my father owned an engineering firm and I graduated from the University of Vienna with an Engineering Degree."

"Excellent and exactly the skills we need. The Führer himself has sanctioned a pet project of mine and one that I think you are uniquely qualified to handle."

"I'm intrigued."

"I am very interested in hunting down important historical relics. You need to understand that these relics are necessary in order to support that our Aryan race, from which all true Germans are descended, is superior to all others. When they are found, I intend on establishing our own religion to rival and replace Christianity. Needless to say, they will be Germany's shining jewels once we have won this war. In fact, I believe that once they are in our possession, their powers will aid our quest."

Himmler suddenly stopped talking, then sat back in silence as the waitress returned with their schnapps, as well as a small plate of pretzel buns to snack on.

"Will there be anything else gentlemen?" she asked.

Himmler was quick to answer. "No, this will be fine, thank you."

The waitress nodded. "Very good, sir."

After she had left, Koch's superior continued. "Yes, where was I? I have teams all over the world looking for these artifacts, but I want you to go to France."

"France, sir? What would you like me to find there?"

"Victor Schreiber, the young man you so creatively disposed of, was in my employ to research the Cathars' in the Languedoc area. He had already been studying this area on his own for many years, so our meeting through another acquaintance of mine was very fortuitous."

Taking one of the buns from the basket, he proceeded to tear a small morsel off and popped it in his mouth. Nodding to Koch to do likewise, he finished chewing, rubbed his fingers together and continued.

"Let me give you a little history lesson, Lieutenant. In 1244, 220 Cathars descended the mountain fortress of Montségur and voluntarily walked into a burning pyre."

Koch's eyes widened and his eyebrows furled in confusion. "Voluntarily? But why?"

"They believed in a dualistic religion where God ruled heaven and Rex Mundi ruled the earth, which they considered to be hell. To leave this earth was to be reunited with God and so they did so willingly. So pure of thought were they, that they were reputed to be the Keepers of the Holy Grail.

"In fact, legend has it that four believers escaped Montségur the night before everyone died with the Cathar treasure containing valuable books, documents as well as the Holy Grail. The hunt to eradicate the Cathars continued for decades after, but the treasure was never found.

"As I mentioned before, Schreiber had been researching the area for years and uncovered substantial evidence that this was more than a myth. Personally, I was firmly convinced that the Grail and the other treasures were hidden away in a church at the Rennes-le-Chateau, but Schreiber was certain that it's still in the Montségur area. Apparently, he even had proof.

"Unfortunately, Herr Schreiber, it turns out, embraced the Cathar dogma to a degree that he believed that he was a reincarnated Parfait, and subsequently refused to disclose its whereabouts. In short, he became a traitor to our quest.

"In '37, when we requested your 'prior' services we had understood one of two situations. One, the treasure was at either Montségur or Rennes-le-Chateau, and Schreiber had not discovered its location. Or two, he knew its exact location and had purposely misinformed us.

"Through further contacts, it was also our understanding that he may have warned a local woman who shared his Cathar beliefs as to the need of its removal to a place of safety. Your timely intervention killed 'two birds with one stone' shall we say."

Himmler shook his head in frustration. "Such a brilliant mind wasted on such misguided ideas. We did warn him but sadly, he was unable to see the error of his ways. You understand then the necessity to remove him from the project.

"What has not been found, is the manuscript he was in the process of writing which outlines the exact whereabouts of the grail. This we know exists.

"We do know that he had planned a return trip to the Languedoc, intent to search certain specific grottoes near Montségur and then perhaps 'retire' from society. We have also since learned that this woman friend of his, Sophie Durand, was not just someone with a casual interest. Apparently, she came from a very long line of Cathar believers and may have even played a key role."

Koch sat up straight and nodded. "I see, sir. How can I help you with this endeavour?"

"It would appear, Koch, that very shortly the French will ask for armistice terms and Marshall Pétain will order all French troops to stop fighting. Within a matter of weeks *all* of France will be under German jurisdiction. What this means is that we will now be in a position to remove the treasure of Montségur to German soil, with little fear of interference.

"The war is going so well that I see no reason for haste in recovering these artifacts. The important thing is to do this properly.

"We have a number of excavation expeditions currently running in Biskupice, Poland; Olympia, Greece; Slovakia; the Croat fortress of Surval; Serbia and Caucasia. I've also recently initiated a second expedition to Tibet related to the origins of our Aryan race, so I'd rather wait for any excavations until France is fully occupied.

"We are in possession of many of Schreiber's papers and believe that we have an idea of where the grail is hidden, but we'll need to find the missing manuscript to be sure. What I need from you is to follow in Schreiber's footsteps. Listen to the locals and find out where he's been, what he knew, who he spoke to. Leave no stone unturned.

"What I want for the Reich is the Grail, so ultimately an expedition will need to be organized and you will be heading that up on my behalf. Once it is found, it will be brought and stored at Wewelsburg Castle."

"Of course, sir."

Himmler reached down for his glass of schnapps and took a sip before continuing.

"As for me, my tastes run elsewhere. I presume, Koch, you have heard of my *H Sonderkommando*, my witch's library?"

"I have heard of it, sir, but not enough to discuss."

"Then let me enlighten you. My library focuses on witches and their persecution in medieval Germany. I am gathering as much information on mysticism, dark magic the occult and the supernatural. As a matter of fact, I have recently learned that one of my ancestors was burned at the stake for witchcraft. Did you know that the Roman Catholic Church attempted to eliminate our Aryan race with their witch hunts?" His eyes were cold as his face grew dark. "For this I assure you they will pay…but I digress.

"This brings me to my last request. As I mentioned, the Cathar treasure from Montségur, was not only the Grail but sacred books and documents. Some, it is rumoured, are about elemental magic. I want those books. I want them found and I want them in *my* possession. Understood?"

"Absolutely, sir. These books—I presume they are likely to be found with the grail?"

"I have left no stone unturned, unexplored and have mastered several, shall we say, unorthodox methods in order to determine this."

As Koch stared at him, the smaller man seemed to grow in height as he spoke. "I am not without my own powers."

Himmler's eyes glazed as he seemed to glow with an unnatural passion. "During an intense séance, my ancestor came through and took over the body and voice of a colleague of mine, in order to give me a message. I was told that they are together and that the books are guarded to this day by the Grail Keeper.

"So, Lieutenant Wolfgang Koch, find the Keeper, find the grail, and find the books. My best suggestion is to familiarize yourself with the material. You may also want to start with that woman, Sophie Durand's family.

"Oh, and Koch? Do well and I'll see to it that you are recommended to meet with Walter Schellenberg, head of the SS foreign intelligence service. Schellenberg needs someone to take charge of the schools being organized to train special agents in sabotage, espionage, and paramilitary skills. I might also add that you will be welcomed as one of my SS Knights of the Round Table at Wewelsburg. Any questions?"

"No, sir. Thank you and may I say, I am honoured to be trusted with this mission."

Himmler downed the last of his schnapps, then looked at the giant of a man who sat across from him.

"I have one more question, Koch. Where did you get that scar?"

"I fought my first duel during my freshman year, and in 1928 earned the coveted 'scars of honor.' I carry that lesson within everything I do. Through my sabre, my knowledge of pain taught me not to be afraid.

"In dueling you must concentrate on your enemy's cheek, so, too, in war. You cannot waste time on feinting and sidestepping. You must decide on your target and go in."

CHAPTER EIGHT

EVERY SUNDAY, ISABEL WOULD FAITHFULLY ATTEND MASS WITH Meli. Together they would walk (more like march, Meli thought) to Sainte-Madeleine Catholic Church in the centre of town, where, dressed in their Sunday best, Isabel would smile and nod a pleasant hello to Father Pelletier as they entered.

Always early, they sat up front and centre, where Meli was expected to be attentive, earnest and eager to recite the ecclesiastical Latin phrases drilled into her head.

This Sunday would be no different, unless of course, she could use staying home with Berthe as an excuse. The key to this of course would be establish concern for Berthe's wellbeing in Mamina's mind.

As they sipped their morning coffee at the kitchen table, Meli gave it her best shot but the attempt would be short-lived.

"Perhaps I should stay behind today in case Berthe needs help."

"Why would Berthe need help?"

"What if she falls again?"

"She's got her cane and she'll be fine until we get back. This wouldn't be an excuse to get out of going to church would it?"

While Isabel stared down Meli, Berthe looked at Isabel with a hint of a smile. *The apple didn't fall far from the tree with that one.* "Thank you for being so thoughtful, Meli, but I'll be fine. Say a prayer for me, won't you?"

Defeated, Meli drained her cup then headed upstairs to change.

Arriving at the church, they both dutifully dipped their fingers in the holy water fonts mounted on each side of the door-frame and made the sign of the cross on themselves.

Isabel smiled warmly to Mme Voisin, as she asked how Berthe's foot was doing. "She should be more careful." To which she assured her that she had advised Berthe of the exact same thing.

As they walked up the aisle to her grandmother's usual preferred pew, Meli looked at the Stations of the Cross. She always wondered about all the little details, what they meant and who got to paint them. In fact, she wondered why they bothered to go at all. Mamina had only taken this up after Sophie had died. Prior to that, church hadn't been instilled as something important.

Arriving at the front of the nave, they genuflected towards the altar and then knelt for a few minutes of prayer in the pew, before sitting down. At least that is what most people did.

Mamina went one step further.

Pulling out her rosary from her pocket, she began to pray holding each tiny wooden bead between her fingers, while Meli kneeling, head bowed, was expected to join her. Instead, her mind wandered as it always did.

The pews were never designed to be comfortable, so she was relieved to finally be allowed to sit down after Mamina's oblig-atory 'Hail Marys'. Mass began and was said in Latin that as far as Meli was concerned, was a language that only Father Pelletier seemed to understand. Dressed in green vestments, the color of life, he stood at the pulpit and began his usual sermon with themes that supported Pétain's views of family and sin.

Father Pelletier droned on. "It is, therefore, desirable...that all the faithful should be aware that to participate in the Eucharistic sacrifice, it is their chief duty and supreme dignity, and that it should be done not in an inert and negligent fashion, giving way to distractions and day-dreaming, but with such earnestness and concentration that they may be united as closely as possible with the High Priest, according to the Apostle, 'Let this mind be in you which was also in Christ Jesus.' And together with Him and through Him let them make their oblation, and in union with Him let them offer up themselves."

Swinging his incense, the altar boy stood, model of attention while his proud parents looked on in hopes that their son would one day follow in the church's footsteps.

It was the same thing every Sunday—step and repeat. *Dominus vobiscum, Et cum spiritu tuo.* Light the candles, kneel, genuflect, pray.

The smells of others in the close quarters of the summer heat, mingled between the mix of perfumes and the acrid smell of M. Donal's urine-soaked pants who sat directly behind her.

As she looked around, she caught the eye of Mme Dupuis with her heavy red lipstick and turban style hat covering her old head, handbag glued under her arms. She smiled pleasantly back at Meli who wondered if she had ever been sixteen or if her back had ever been straight or if M. Donal had ever been a dashing young man who didn't pee his pants.

As the blood-red vigil candles fluttered away under the statue of Mary and baby Jesus, the smell of incense floated by heavily, mesmerizing and softening her focus. Struggling to stay awake, her head jerked forward a few times and more than once she nodded off. Suddenly the man's voice from her dream jarred her in her seat. *"I will find you!"*

Surely Mamina heard that, but when she turned to look at her, she was face forward intently listening to Father Pelletier. *What did it all mean?*

After Mass they gathered outside in little clumps of friends, briefly chatting with one another. "How's your daughter this week? Have you heard the latest?"

Everyone had on their very best clothes and children were scrubbed within an inch of their lives. The younger boys wore suspenders holding up their cropped pants that showed off skinny legs too thin to keep up socks that puddled at their ankles. Their hair slicked back, they stood around, their hands in their pockets, joking with each other while eyeing a group of young girls their age.

Little girls were dressed up with bows almost the size of their heads in their hair, while the women with their best hats and freshly ironed dresses missed their men. Old women in their traditional black dresses with their hair neatly tied back gossiped with their friends, while another woman grabbed a stick out of the hands of her young son and threw it away scolding him as he pouted the loss of his prize.

Everyone complained about the rations and the war. Everyone knew someone who knew something and someone who had died. They prayed to keep those they loved safe and prayed to end the war before it found its way to their doorstep. It will be over by Christmas was constantly repeated.

Meli looked around and felt lost within the rules of who she was supposed to be. Smile, be polite, answer when spoken to. Don't get yourself dirty. Don't think bad thoughts. Concentrate. Is it over yet?

She thought about the dream and the voice and what it could mean. *Who was she? And why was this man hunting her down?*

———

The next morning the swelling around Berthe's ankle had gone down considerably and although she swore that she was much better and able to go home on her own, Isabel insisted that Meli walk her back and do whatever chores needed to be done. As usual, she brooked no disagreement with her decision.

Before they left, she placed the radio in Meli's bicycle basket saying, "On your way back, you might as well take the wireless over to M. Kowalski to get fixed. Get back here as soon as you can so you can finish your chores and no gossiping with anyone do you hear?"

Directing her no-nonsense stare to her friend, she added, "Berthe, no more doing difficult chores that Meli can do."

Both Meli and Berthe smiled and tossed a, "Oui, Mamina," back at her grandmother as they slowly walked down the path. As they turned the corner and no longer in sight, Berthe blurted out, "She is my oldest friend, but goodness that woman can be bossy!"

Shocked at her outburst, Meli took one look at Berthe's wicked little smile and broke out in laughter.

"Was she always like this?"

Instead of a witty retort, Berthe looked straight ahead and grew silent as if collecting her thoughts. Finally, after a few minutes, she barely spoke above a whisper. "No, Meli. She was not always like this, but there is far more to your grandmother that you will ever know."

They continued on in silence until they reached the edge of the village where Berthe insisted that she could carry on from there.

"Ouff! Look at the sky. It's getting late. Off you go before she worries that something has happened. Go straight back from the Kowalski's—no dawdling and remember not a word!"

Resting her bike against a large tree, Meli leaned in for a big hug. Berthe suddenly grabbed her face with both her hands, stared at her for a moment or two, then closed her eyes and planted a kiss on her forehead. "Go, give your Mamina a hug for me and be safe."

———

Riding her bike to the Kowalski farm, Meli's mind raced with details and unanswered questions as she bicycled past huge plane trees that lined a narrow lane leading to the house. As the path widened, an old farmhouse with several old outbuildings for animals and equipment came into view.

The main building was small and sturdy, but like their own cottage, had seen better days. Neither the building nor the shutters had been painted in years and ivy had overgrown and covered one of the smaller buildings.

As she rode up to the house, she could see that the front door was open and a few chickens were pecking away at some tasty treat that a girl, about eight years old, was tossing to them. A slightly younger boy was leaning over a small pool of water at the base of the well. Small and wiry, a rope kept his shorts up, while his knee-high stockings that didn't quite fit his skinny legs slumped loosely around his ankles. Poking at something with a stick and obviously too preoccupied to look up, she well imagined a dirty face to go with his rumpled hair.

Laying her bike against an outbuilding, Meli started to walk towards the house. The children, hearing her approach, shielded the sun from their eyes to have a good look, then ran to the open door to announce her arrival to their mother. "Maman, maman, come quick, someone is here."

Running back towards Meli, they smiled and danced their hellos, then suddenly bolted, having spotted their father walking up the lane behind her. "Papa, papa," they cried as the children jumped into his arms. Meli smiled, wishing that she too had a sweet memory of a father's embrace. Getting down on one knee, he gave them a hug then released them to catch up to Meli.

"Bonjour, Meli, isn't it? How can I help?"

"Hello, M. Kowalski. We need our radio fixed. It stopped working a few weeks ago and Mamina is worried about the latest news."

He nodded. "We all are. Come in, Meli. I'll have a look and see what needs to be done. This is my wife Halina."

As they walked in, Meli noticed that Roman gave an odd look to his wife in the doorway, as if to say, 'We'll talk later.'

Placing her hands on her belly, Halina Kowalski nodded a hello, then led Meli into the kitchen. Obviously very pregnant, her apron, printed with miniature pink rosebuds, was barely able to wrap around her belly. Her dark hair was pulled back, but rogue loose pieces fell into her face. She wiped her hands on her apron and then used her palm to wipe her face with the back of her hand. She gave Meli a quick smile as a barefoot, curly-haired little two-year old in a dirty cotton dress ran behind her mother and grabbed her leg. Peeking out from her safe position, she smiled shyly then retreated back to the folds of her mother's skirt.

The kitchen was modest with a large wooden table and mismatched chairs in various condition. A worn painted cabinet with three open shelves held neatly stacked piles of chipped bowls, dishes and cups while an old wood stove occupied the centre of the room. Several smaller tables were hobbled together to act as a counter and were filled with bowls needing to be washed.

Roman pulled a chair towards Meli. "Have a seat while I look at your radio." Then nodded to his wife. "Halina, maybe we could have some tea."

Pulling out a handkerchief from her apron, she wiped the little one's nose while looking towards her oldest daughter. "Anna, take the kettle and get me some water."

Scrunching up her face, the little girl wiggled to get loose and followed her older sister outside to watch her pump water for the tea. They could hear her giggle and squeal as water splashed on her toes.

Moments later, Anna hustled in and put the heavy cast iron kettle on the stove and reached for a tin on the shelf.

Feeling a little guilty watching this obviously busy family serve her, Meli asked if she could help but Halina shushed her back down. "No, no you sit. It's good for them to be helpful."

Shooing the children outside, she retrieved three cups from the cupboard. Giving them a quick wipe, she placed them on the table.

"I am sorry we have no biscuits to serve with the tea."

Meli watched as Halina dipped the tea bag into all three cups, keeping the last and weakest for herself. She smiled an apology then shrugged. "War rationing."

"Thank you, but this is fine. When is your baby due?" Meli asked.

Halina smiled and placed her hand on her belly rubbing it as she replied. "God willing, sooner than later. But at least we are safe here in France."

"You weren't safe in Poland?"

Halina looked down at the table for a moment, then back up and deeply into Meli's eyes. "How old are you, Meli?"

"I know I don't look it, but I turned sixteen yesterday."

"Halina raised her eyebrows. My little sister in Poland is sixteen. I pray that one day I will see her again."

"Maybe she can come to France too," Meli offered.

Halina simply gave her a pained looked and stared down at the table.

Concerned that she had somehow offended her, Meli could only think to keep talking. "Is it because of the Germans? Because Mamina thinks that we will all be safe here."

"Meli, there is more going on in the world than your little corner. In Krakow where we are from, I have already lost my older brother and Roman's uncle was beaten to death outside his shop. Every day the situation gets worse and worse. I fear for my family and my little sister."

Meli's faced paled. "Why was his uncle beaten?"

Halina had tears in her eyes as she patted Meli's hand across the table. "Because we are Jewish, my dear. He was murdered for the crime of being Jewish."

"I'm so sorry. But that would never happen here. The government would never allow it. Besides, you are now French."

At that moment Roman returned with the radio in hand. "All fixed. It was just a loose wire, so it was easy."

"Thank you, M. Kowalski. My grandmother will be very relieved. She is anxious to listen to Radio Paris with the latest news. She said if you like, we can give you some Banon in exchange for your time."

"That would be very appreciated. Tell her thank you, but perhaps I could make a suggestion?"

"Of course."

Halina gave Roman a funny look and for a moment he hesitated, before he spoke. "Radio Paris is now entirely under German command so you will only hear propaganda and not the truth. Radio Vichy is Marshall Pétain's and perhaps a better choice for your grandmother. But many people now are listening to Radio Londres on the BBC. You seem like a smart girl, but you'll need to be careful.

"I think you would like the mysterious coded sentences that they slip into the personal messages programme. Escapees from France who wish to reassure their families that they have arrived safe, let them know in coded words. Many of them are quite amusing, like 'the purple giraffe flew to the moon' or 'the gardener's dog is crying.' No one knows what they mean except, of course, whoever they are meant for."

"Thank you, M. Kowalski. Halina, I'm sorry about your family but I am glad that you are here where it's safe."

Both husband and wife nodded and smiled but Meli had the

distinct impression that they saw her as a little girl rather than a young woman. She felt embarrassed at her naiveté. Protected by Mamina her entire life, she didn't even know what was going on in the world. It was time that that changed, and it would start with the BBC.

CHAPTER NINE

Summer spilled into fall with a morning that started with a fog so dense that Isabel and Meli could barely make out the path ahead. Prodding the goats up the rocky incline, Isabel turned to her granddaughter. "I'll take the goats to the high pasture and you can carry on to the cave to collect the Banon. If you can fill that pail with chestnut leaves on your way up, we'll use those to wrap the cheese with later."

Meli laughed, "That is if I can find my way there."

Isabel smiled back. How long had she been doing this? It had to be at least fifty years now, starting as a little girl with her papa. Of course, they had more goats back then, but there were also more people to help. Her whole life had been nothing but work, sun-up to sundown—supporting the family, supporting the farm. She had no expectations of doing anything else. No designs for anything else other than the lamps and the refrigerator—the only modern conveniences that had been added to the farm.

Not like Sophie. She had been caught up in the excitement of Paris, the cultural capital of the world. How could farm life compete with the vibrancy of the city? In a country where women didn't have the right to vote or own property, Sophie and her friends showed their contempt with bobbed hair, dancing till the wee hours, drinking, smoking and pre-marital sex. No, Pétain was right. There must be a return to traditional values.

"You know, it may be wise of us to make a big batch of soap while we can."

Meli, who was busy prodding one of the goats back onto the path, had to ask her to repeat what she said.

"I was just thinking of things that may be difficult to get later on. During the Great War we went without so much. Soap was hard to come by and I never want to experience that again. It wouldn't hurt for us to use the cave as extra storage."

"Do you really think we will need to, Mamina?"

"Maybe not, but I think it's best to be prepared."

Once they had reached the fork in the path, Meli turned and continued her climb towards the cave. "I'll see you in a bit Mamina—I won't be long."

"I'll meet you back at the kitchen and we'll get started wrapping the Banon. Mind your step in this fog."

"I will."

It took only a minute before the heavy fog enveloped her tiny frame into the mists until she too became part of the spectral landscape.

The hills felt different today. Nothing that she could put her finger on, but again something felt out of place. Stepping carefully up the worn path, she looked around at the misty shapes of trees and boulders and couldn't shake the feeling that she was being watched. Looking around, she stood still for a minute to listen for the crackle of footsteps on the forest floor but heard nothing.

Pulling her cardigan a little tighter she continued her climb until she could make out the cave entrance ahead. With a quick sigh of relief, she hurried to the entrance.

Ever since the Germans had taken control, she was anxious

about everything, which didn't make sense because Mamina said there was nothing to worry about and so far, that had been true. Their home, their food, their farm was all safe and she had yet to see a German.

A soft breeze played with a loose tendril of hair and she raised her hand to wrap it behind her ear. Reaching into her pocket, she pulled out an old heavy key to the iron-gated door installed generations ago. The heavy gate groaned from its rusty hinges and she stepped inside to the dark coolness.

Relieved to no longer be in the woods, she carried on through the cave's narrower entrance until it suddenly opened into a modest-sized cavern. The curved stone walls had been chiseled smooth over generations to enable wooden shelves to tightly fit every which way along the sides. Many of the shelves were already weighted with discs of aging cheese.

The roof of the cave, although low, was smooth giving a sense of a vast ceiling of flowing rock, while wooden boards replaced the cave floor, giving the cavern a sense of a proper room. Six large oaken barrels of eau-de-vie were stacked to the ceiling at the very back along with several bottles of wine, some left over from when Mamina's father had produced them many, many years ago.

In the centre a solid hewn oak slab had been fashioned to serve as a table where crocks of young Banon, seasoned with salt and pepper then doused in vinegar and eau-de-vie had been left to ferment. These were what she had come to collect.

After retrieving the lantern from the corner, she placed it on the table, then proceeded to light the wick. Plunging her hand into the crock she deftly pulled out and placed the pungent three-inch discs into her pail to be wrapped later. Having emptied the crock, she made a mental note that the earthenware jar was getting low and would soon need to be refilled with more cheese and left to cure.

Walking over to the shelves, she then began the routine of

turning each round of the rinded wheels, one-quarter turn. Mamina had explained that this ensured that the milk solids were evenly distributed throughout the cheese. Concentrating on her tasks, she worked quickly to ensure each wheel had been turned, noting any mold that needed to be wiped off.

Satisfied with her work, she wiped her hands on a clean cloth and prepared herself for the walk back down, when suddenly she again felt as if she was being watched.

Reaching for the lantern, she held it high, scanning the room, its dim light barely reaching into the dark crannies of shelves and cave walls. Turning to the back where the barrels were stacked, she shivered and sensed, rather than saw, that she was being watched, but the back of the cave ended behind the barrels and clearly no one was there.

Not wanting to stay any longer, Meli picked up the pail and lantern and walked the short distance to the entrance. Extinguishing the wick, she left the lantern on the hook by the entrance gate and proceeded to lock up.

The fog had begun to dissipate leaving only a light mist as she made her way back, grabbing chestnut leaves as she went. Unsettled by her feelings of being watched, she hurried as fast as she dared, not slowing until she reached the lower pasture's gate. She felt better now but wasn't sure that she wanted to be alone in the cave again.

When she arrived back at the kitchen, Mamina took the leaves from the pail, added them to the ones she collected and began the process of softening the chestnut leaves in boiling water and vinegar.

Meli lifted the pail to the table. "We'll need to make more Banon after this batch."

Isabel nodded in agreement. "I thought we might. Did you turn the wheels?"

"Yep, I got them all. I felt weird though."

"What do you mean you felt weird?"

"I don't know, like someone was watching me. Does the cave wall end where the barrels are?"

Isabel suddenly turned and stared at Meli. "Why would you ask that?"

"No reason. Just because I felt kind of strange."

"Of course it ends there. Why would it not?"

As she wrapped the fermented discs in chestnut leaves, then tied them with raffia, Meli nodded in agreement. Maybe she was right, but there was something about how her grandmother answered her that didn't quite sound like she was telling the truth.

"Mamina are you sure we are going to be okay?" She sounded irritated. "Meli, I told you, Marshall Pétain is in charge of what is left of France and will guide us accordingly. He has our best interests in mind and after all he was a decorated war hero. Moderation is key and he will see us through this war safe and sound. You heard him on the radio.

"He is grieving just like us, even more so, because he is our country's loving father. Paris was too free—too much alcohol, too much sexuality—they needed to rein all this in and instil solid family values, French values, keep our heads low and pray."

Meli nodded. This wasn't the time to bring up the BBC.

CHAPTER TEN

HENRI GAVE TWO QUICK KNOCKS ON THE KITCHEN DOOR THEN
quickly stepped inside to get out of the pouring rain. Noting
Berthe sitting at the table with a warm cup of coffee, his eyes
widened in obvious envy. "Bonjour, Berthe, Isabel. Ca va?"

Isabel, puttering away at the counter, simply turned and
nodded in his direction.

"Coffee?" asked Berthe.

"I wouldn't say no. It's a wet one out there and getting chillier
every day."

Isabel grabbed another cup from the cupboard, gave it a
quick wipe, then poured him a cup. "Tell me, Henri, do you ever
say no? Be honest now—how much coffee do you drink every
day? Surely you have no need to buy your own."

Henri's moustache twitched while his eyes glared back at
Isabel. He was not amused.

Berthe quickly intervened.

"Now, now Henri, you know how Isabel likes to tease. Have
some coffee and give us the news. Not quite placated, he formally

69

announced his reason for being there. "Isabel, I have *another* letter for you from Paris."

Isabel looked up and for a brief moment there was fear in her eyes. *Could he see it?*

Walking over to the table, she took the envelope from his hands, quickly looked at the address then put it down over on the far counter. "Thank you, Henri. It's likely relatives just letting us know they are safe. Please, drink your coffee and tell us the news."

"Well, as you know I'm not one to impose, but a small cup would be appreciated. My injury that I sustained from the war has been acting up lately especially in the rain, and having come all this way to deliver the letter myself…"

"Of course, of course. Please, sit. Is it true what they say about food prices in Paris?"

Henri made a point of looking at the letter she had put on the counter and nodded his head towards it. "You may well be about to find out on your own. The food stamps they receive is not enough to feed anyone and they are relying on relatives to supplement their rations.

"I heard that North of Paris scores of towns are largely destroyed, villages deserted, farmsteads empty. Crops are rotting on the ground. The first wave of the German Army consumed everything and now the first pick goes to them, the second to those who work for them and the scanty crumbs that remain are left for those who can pay.

"They are paying ridiculous prices for food—eggs, potatoes, carrots, meat. The '*marché noir*' is making everyone rich. To be honest, we were the poor cousins for so long that in my humble opinion it serves them right. Everyone knows that occupied France is in much better shape, in spite of all the devastation, than us. Why shouldn't we make a little profit? Let's face it, they would be doing the same if the situation was reversed." Henri pointed his finger to the letter. "Open it and see if I'm not right, Isabel. Could mean a little extra money for you."

Isabel looked over to Berthe and smiled. "You could be right, Henri, and if it is, I'll be sure to ask for your advice. I wouldn't want to do anything illegal."

"I don't know how you do it, Isabel. My hat is off to you for managing all these years. It's not been easy for you."

As Henri sat for a few minutes in silence savoring the warmth of the coffee in his hands, Isabel looked out towards the barn where she could see Meli running hunched over towards the house. "She'll be soaked through," she said to no one in particular.

Moments later, Meli burst through the door, water dripping from head to toe. Grabbing a tea towel from the counter Isabel tossed it to her. "Here, take your coat off there and wipe your face. I'll get you a cup of coffee to warm you up."

"Thanks, Mamina." Turning to the old postman, her ruddy cheeks brightened into a smile. "M. Bouchard, has Mme Kowalski had her baby yet?"

Berthe put her cup down then turned towards him. "Yes, Henri, you must have heard something."

"As a matter of fact, I have. I understand she had a healthy boy, but you haven't had anything more to do with them though, have you?"

"No, why would you ask?" asked Isabel. "You suggested that he fix my radio and he did a good job. I'm happy for them though. Perhaps I'll get Meli to bicycle over with a round of hard cheese."

Henri looked up over his glasses to Isabel. "I presume then that you are not aware of the recent law from our Vichy regime? If not, then I consider it my civic duty to inform you that a law has been passed calling for the re-examination of the citizenship status of immigrants.

"In short, the citizenship of all French Jews has been revoked and as a matter of fact, in Paris, they are starting to round up these foreigners. As you know, the Kowalski's are Jewish so you may want to be careful. I'm sorry for them of course, but what's to be done? It's the law and certainly in line with Pétain creating a more stable France."

Meli stared hard trying to make sense of what he had just said. "But M. Bouchard, what does that mean? Will they have to go back to Poland? Halina said that they murdered M. Kowalski's uncle because he was Jewish."

"No, no, no, nothing like that. I think for now, they will simply have to wear a yellow star to identify themselves as such. Perhaps they will be sent to a work camp at some point, but I am told by the Malice that they eat better than we do. Besides, we must support Pétain with his vision of a better France and controlling immigrants is just a part of that. This does not mean that they are not very nice people, Meli, but we need to support France first. And with that, I must go back out into the rain and continue my duty. We postmen are the lifeblood of France! Bonsoir ladies. Stay dry."

After Henri left, Berthe and Isabel looked towards the letter laying on the counter without saying a word, then turned to look at each other.

Isabel snapped, "Meli, it's too wet outside for Berthe to walk home. Could you please put some clean sheets on the bed for her? She'll stay here tonight with us."

Taking her cue, Berthe patted Meli's hand and smiled sweetly. "That would be so kind of you to do that for me. Thank you, Meli."

Unsure of what had just transpired, Meli eyed them both with reserve but taking the last sip from her cup, she rose from the table and headed up the stairs.

Isabel whispered to Berthe as Meli exited the room. "Look out the window to make sure he's really gone, but don't let him see you!"

Walking to the front room, Berthe parted the curtains, then waited a few seconds until she confirmed that he had finally left. Hurrying back to the table she joined Isabel and sat so close to her that she couldn't help but chuckle to give her some room. "It's from Helene. I'm sure she just wants more food."

Ripping the envelope open, she carefully pulled out two sheets of scented, expensive paper. Helene's handwriting was small, neat, controlled, but as Isabel read the first line, her eyebrows knitted together in concern. She turned to Berthe and quietly read aloud.

"My dear Isabel,

I have left Paris with my daughter Nicole and desperately need to impose on your kindness for however long as we can. I am so sorry to ask this of you, but we have nowhere else to turn. My husband Hans travelled ahead with the bank to Zurich, and we were to follow by train, but there has been no communication since he left. Train tickets are now impossible to get, and the situation is desperate. I am afraid of what will become of us if we stay. We are trying to make our way by car with some friends and God willing we will arrive sometime next week. We have taken only what we could. Please pray for us.

Helene."

Both women simply looked at each other, not sure what to make of it.

"What will you do?" Berthe asked.

"Well, I hope she's not bringing trouble with her," Isabel replied. "Best not to say too much to anyone. I'll tell Meli that Sophie's friend will be staying with us for a short period and that's that. No mention of what went on before. That's the last thing we need."

"There's nothing you can do but sit and wait to see if she shows up," Berthe offered.

Isabel stood up, putting the letter back into the envelope. "You're right, but we'll have to prepare in case she does.

"From the sounds of it, their journey won't be easy, if they make it here at all."

Isabel sat silent for a few minutes then turned to her oldest friend. "I never liked her and truthfully I wish she had somewhere else to go. She's far too flighty and knows too much."

CHAPTER ELEVEN

THE DREAM SLIPPED GENTLY INTO MELI'S SUBCONSCIOUS THIS time. Like floating on a slow meandering current, it carried her downstream taking her back, back into the past, where she found herself dressed in the ancient clothes of another time. There was a familiar narrative to the dream that lapped at her subconscious, taking her deeper and deeper into a story.

She was not a Parfait of the Cathar faith like her grandmother, (for whom she was named after), but she was a believer.

Raised by an enlightened father, Jordan Le Tardif, taught her the gift of words, of forward thinking and of faith, and for this she would be forever grateful. It had been two years since he had passed, at the ripe old age of 83 and she missed him dearly. India attempted to echo his teachings with her own daughter, but her love of learning was nowhere as keen as hers. Her daughter was instead, teaching her mother patience. In abundance.

India looked on over the landscape. Another summer had passed, and the fresh, sweet air held the promise of another autumn.

At 36 she had been blessed with a life of love and learning. She had had the love of a good man and had known the joy of a child stirring in her belly. Her father and he would be together now along with her grand-mere India. All of them together hopefully watching over them—over Sophia in the years to come.

Looking over the landscape, she watched her little daughter work away in the garden tending to the last of the turnips and cabbages for the season. Already at eight she had a gift of growing things, as if by magic.

She always knew that one day she would be called and now the time was upon her. Decisions needed to be made. Actions taken. Sophia would need to be protected along with a secret that would outlive them all. She would miss her dearly, but God willing one day they would be reunited at least in spirit.

She fingered the amulet around her neck and smiled. It seemed not so long ago that she herself was Sophia's age digging away in the same garden. She remembered the day she found the amulet like it was yesterday—poking in the dirt with Papa not far from where her daughter worked now.

How excited she was. "Papa, come quick. I have found something." So many years ago.

She had always felt a strong connection to that amulet, a hand-carved dove flying over the distant Pog, the ruins of Montségur at the top. She had been convinced as a child that it had been a gift from her grandmother to keep her safe and she still believed it. Which is why it would now belong to her daughter in hopes that it would keep her safe as well. She could only hope.

Once again, the hunt was on to rout out any semblance of what they considered heresy no matter how simple or innocent the belief. There was in their area patches of the Good Christian's teachings, but what harm could innocent shepherds cause by such beliefs? So far no one had been sent to the stake, but this is but a matter of time only. What she guarded could not wait. She already knew what Fournier the chief inquisitor wanted, and it would be only a matter of time before he found her.

Benoit and his wife Marie-Ange would arrive in the next few days and then it would all begin. There will be no turning back once she left.

Her good friends and followers of the Catholic faith would take over her cottage and her land. They would become parents to her daughter, but most importantly these good people would raise her and keep her safe. She trusted them with her life, for there were other things that they were charged to teach, to protect and to keep hidden.

Closing her eyes, she sighed deeply as two errant tears escaped and fell on her hand. How was this possible that this was happening again? This tiny, insignificant corner of the land was still not free. Wiping away her tears, she stood resolutely looking at their stone cottage surrounded by hills, forests and caves. What she was about to do was for her daughter and the generations to follow. They must never forget.

The dream began to fade and dissipate, but before she reawakened to a later time, the woman in her dream spoke one last time to another version of herself. *"You Meli Durand, must never forget!"*

CHAPTER TWELVE

Meli arose earlier than usual to find Mamina already sipping her coffee as she entered the kitchen.

Smearing soft goat's cheese on a slab of bread, she nodded to Meli. "You're up early."

Shuffling to the counter, Meli picked up a cup and poured herself some of the hot brew. "I know, and I didn't sleep well last night either."

"How come?"

"I don't know. I had a weird dream."

Isabel flashed a look of concern, but suddenly stopped, sat up straight and listened to what could only be the sound of wagon wheels and the dull plodding of horse hoofs on hard ground.

Wiping her fingers on her apron, she rushed to the front window to see Helene and her daughter being handed down off the wagon.

Turning back to Meli in the kitchen she whispered as loud as she dared, "They're here. Quick-tidy up the table before they come inside."

Still watching from behind the lace curtains, Isabel took the moment to gather herself together. She recognized the driver as Gaston, a local farmer, and as he fumbled with their two dusty and worn suitcases, the two of them simply stood and stared at the cottage as if they were uncertain of what to do next.

Helene's stylish blue suit hung off of her thin body like a rag. The wrinkled, dirty creases seemed to mirror her face, extenuating the deep lines under her eyes from lack of sleep. Her hair was covered in a dusty travel-worn scarf that had obviously been used for more than head cover and she wore heels that Isabel knew wouldn't last longer than a week. She shook her head in disgust. Where did she think she was coming to, a resort?

Her daughter Nicole looked to be in no better shape. She appeared to be slightly older than Meli, but then her granddaughter was smaller than most. Her blonde hair hung in greasy strands and framed a pouting face that had never known a day of hard work. Undernourished, her dark tweed skirt hung loosely at her hips and her pink sweater set, filthy from travel, was blood-spattered across the bottom. Both women looked as if they were ready to drop or cry but didn't know which one to do first.

By the time Gaston deposited the suitcases at the door, Isabel had already opened it wide with Meli by her side. Seeing them face-to-face though was a shock. Between the two of them the smell of smoke and filth and body odour was overwhelming.

"Come in, come in."

Helene immediately reached out her arms and fell sobbing into Isabel's embrace while her daughter just stood there staring at Meli in her blood-spattered sweater. As Isabel held her breath and hugged Helene back, she stared at Nicole's blood stains and wondered whether they would ever come out.

Isabel shooed Gaston away with a brief thank you, knowing that he would be annoyed, but no matter. She was quite sure that he had more than enough gossip for his wife to be satisfied. Having not spoken a word, she quickly looked at Nicole and just as quickly turned away. She was clearly unhappy. *I've seen that look before.* No wonder Meli just stood there silently smiling and awaiting orders.

Now that they were in the house, Isabel took a deep breath, then quickly sized up what needed to be done. "Meli, grab the suitcases and get some water from the well. They are going to want a bath."

Grabbing her daughter's arm, Helene started to pour out her gratitude, but Isabel shushed her quiet. "Plenty of time to be grateful. First there are practical things to be done. Let's get you both cleaned up and out of those clothes."

———

Meli glanced back at Nicole and quickly determined how helpful she was going to be. Nicole clearly didn't want to be there, and she looked just the type to ensure that everyone was as miserable as she was. After having a lousy night's sleep with chores to still be done, she didn't relish the idea of also having to play maid to some fancy rich girl from Paris.

First Helene had a bath, but the water was so filthy it had to be emptied and refilled again for the princess who refused to bathe in anything but fresh clean hot water. What did it matter to her that the water had to be carried in and heated on the stove? Next time she could do it herself.

From the look of disdain on Nicole's face, the clean clothes she had brought for her were obviously what she would consider rags, let alone the three-inch height difference between them. The dress was too short and would need to be lengthened and it wouldn't surprise her if she had to do that as well.

While they bathed, Meli was sent to the kitchen to warm up some vegetable soup while Mamina went out to the henhouse to gather some eggs.

From the kitchen, it was not hard for Meli to overhear the explosive argument that ensued once Nicole found her voice.

Nicole, clearly unhappy with the arrangements, let loose on her mother. "We should have stayed in Paris instead of coming here. At least there was restaurants. We could have stayed in our apartment where I still have all my things."

She could hear Helene telling her to keep her voice down, but Nicole would have none of it. "There's nothing to do here. Do you even realize these people are communists? What am I supposed to do?"

Meli rolled her eyes as she strained to listen. Having them here was going to be hell.

Stomping down the stairs Nicole walked into the kitchen and looked around, then stared at Meli. "You actually live here? How do you stand it?"

Meli looked back and could feel the air prickling around her. "It's not that bad. It's safer than Paris is right now." Then feeling a little guilty, added. "Travelling here must have been awful for you."

Nicole pulled out a chair and sat at the table. "It was. There were people everywhere and our car was so crowded I had no room for my things. And then we ran out of gas. You should have seen the clothes that I had to leave behind. I don't know what she expects me to wear. If papa were here, he wouldn't let her treat me like this.

"When the Germans arrive, I'll be sure to let them know that I am half-Austrian, you can be sure of that! I'm starved and need to eat. I don't suppose you have any jam, croissants and some butter? Everyone knows that *you're* not suffering."

At that moment Isabel walked through the door and was more than ready to put this young lady in her place. "I'm afraid you'll have to do with far more rustic fare than you are used to around here which for us means extra work. We'll be glad of the extra help."

"You mean like chores?"

"I mean exactly like chores."

Nicole raised her chin and stared back hard. "I don't do housework. I never have and more importantly, I don't know how."

A slow smile spreads across Isabel's face. "You do now."

Helene, who had been making her way slowly down the stairs, snapped at her daughter. "Nicole Angeline Moser, you apologize right now! Isabel, I am so sorry. My daughter has been through a lot and forgets her manners."

"Nicole. Apologize this instant!"

"I won't! I hate it here! If papa were here, he would put us somewhere safe and at least sanitary!"

"Well, he's not. He left us."

"He left *you*. He would never leave me and one day you'll see. He'll come back and take me with him. We'll have everything and you'll have nothing." With that, Nicole ran out the door slamming the door behind her.

Isabel took a deep breath. "Meli, go after her and make sure she doesn't get into trouble. Helene sit down and calm yourself. She's just angry."

"I know." Helene sat at the table and watched Meli leave. Looking back at Isabel she shook her head. "It's incredible. She looks so much like Sophie."

———

As Isabel spooned her coffee blend into the moka pot, Helene raised her elbows to the table then lowered her face in her hands.

"Do you want to talk about it? What happened in Paris?"

"I don't know, Isabel, it was just all so crazy. So terrifying. The artillery fire could be heard even from where we lived. The constant bang, bang, banging all the time was terrifying. By the time everyone decided to flee, the train stations were filled with thousands of people not even caring where they were going. The station didn't even bother announcing destinations they just filled the trains and left to who knows where. Towards the end, the stations were so crowded that there was no point in even making the attempt.

"To make matters worse, thousands of people took to the roads, filling the routes out of Paris with anything with wheels… automobiles, buses, trucks, wagons, carts, bicycles, and hundreds of others just on foot. Everywhere you looked it was chaos.

"I called everyone we knew with a car, but either they had no room or had already left. I was in tears, worried what we would do. We were finally able to get out at the last minute, due to the kindness of an older couple in our building, but the routes were so congested that it took ten hours just to cover thirty kilometres. Their car was already loaded with their own things, so we could only bring a few suitcases each." She sighed. "Even then, we had to abandon two of those as well."

"The British urged the men to defend Paris street-by-street, but Pétain dismissed the idea. He said he didn't want to make Paris into a city of ruins. I suppose we can be thankful for that.

"We met people on the road who said they woke up the next morning to Germans entering the city with loudspeakers instructing Parisians not to leave their buildings. By the end of the afternoon, they hung a swastika flag at the Arc de Triomphe, and organized military parades with a marching band on the Champs Élysées."

Helene's hands began to shake as she stared straight ahead, reliving what she had seen. "The route out was horrendous. There were hundreds of cars that had been abandoned by the side of the road. They had been shot at by German planes and everywhere we looked there was blood and dead bodies… mothers and children, just left lying in the ditches. I've never been more frightened in my life. I broke down…I, I couldn't stop crying, but Nicole, she saw all of this and just stared. She was numb."

Isabel could only pat her hand and assure her that she was

now safe. "Does Hans know where you are?"

Helene, with a guilty look, replied in a soft voice, "No."

"Well, you can contact him from here. I imagine he must be beside himself with worry. Once he knows you're safe, I'm sure he'll make all the arrangements so you can be together."

Helene visibly became fidgety. Rubbing her arm with the palm of her hand, she replied. "Maybe we could wait a month before contacting him and making any arrangements. Would that be all right?"

Isabel knitted her brows, then gave her a look that demanded some kind of an explanation.

"It's just that I...I don't really know where he is."

Isabel didn't know what to say. *This was the last thing she needed.* Getting up to take the moka pot off the stove, she began to pour two cups. Placing a cup in front of Helene, she sat down then took a sip of hers. "What's happened?"

"The thing is," she stumbled, "Hans and I were having problems for a long time, problems of a personal nature. You understand?"

Isabel understood only too well what she was trying to say and nodded.

"The embarrassing truth is that two months ago he left me...left us."

"He left you? I don't understand. You said in your letter that he left with the bank in Zurich. Where did he go?"

Helene's voice was petulant. "Where indeed. Apparently, he took his mistress and her daughter and went somewhere, who knows where, probably somewhere warm and expensive. She's welcome to him, but the bastard left us high and dry! There's no more money in the bank. Nothing. What kind of a man does that? I gave him my best years. My best years!

"We tried to have children, but it was obvious even to him that it was his fault. After a while he couldn't bear to even look at me, let alone touch me. Better I suppose to have other women and hide his lack of virility behind affairs. With Nicole, Hans could at least pretend that she was his, that he had fathered a daughter and the problem was therefore mine. He spoiled Nicole terribly, buying her love with the latest dress designs and jewelry."

Helene flashed a quick look at Isabel and then lowered her head. "They would laugh at me…at the silly things that I said or the ridiculous things I thought or did. I became the outsider in the relationship. Then about a year ago, he started to look at her in a different way. You understand? Like a man with intentions would look at a pretty girl in the street. And the more he spoiled her the less she needed me…her own mother.

"I of course blame myself. I hid behind a façade of smiles and drinks and fashion and parties for so many years I didn't realize how ridiculous the situation was. But what else could I do? I don't care that he's gone, but I hate him for leaving us penniless."

Isabel, who was clearly seeing the writing on the wall, simply shook her head. "Does Nicole know?"

"No. Not all of it."

"Well, you're going to have to tell her soon enough."

"I know, but not yet. Please let me do this in my own time. She's so angry right now. She reminds me of Sophie." Realizing the faux pas, she tried to back-step and apologize.

"I don't mean…"

Isabel waved her hand to stop. "It's fine. I know that Sophie and I had a difficult relationship. I'm sure you can appreciate that even more now with Nicole."

Helene, stared ahead, then slowly took a sip of her coffee. Purposely placing it on the table she turned to Isabel. "I'm sorry I didn't know what else to do, so I contacted you. I figured with the birth certificate…"

Isabel's voice went cold. "What do you mean?"

"No, no I don't mean that. That part is real. It was good that we did that, for Meli's sake. I only thought that you would be more inclined to help me that way. I know that you didn't approve of Sophie and my friendship."

"Helene, I simply thought and still think, that you were a bad influence on each other. I didn't like the parties and the men and the flashy lifestyle."

"I know. I know but we're a different generation than you. Sophie and I were like the sisters neither of us ever had. The more Hans ignored me, the easier it was to forget him and go to the cabarets with her. It was her friendship with Victor that killed her, not me."

Isabel glared. "Yes, and had she not become friends with that writer she met at one of *your* parties, maybe she'd still be here."

Helene's eyes began to water, and her face turned red. She could only look at Isabel and nod. "I'm terrified, Isabel. Forgive me for bringing all this to your doorstep, but I have nowhere else to go. Sophie was my best friend and I was there for her. I have no parents to go to. Please say we can stay with you. We'll help out. We'll do anything you say."

"I'm gathering then that you could conceivably be here a while."

"Isabel, I have come to you not knowing what else to do, because I don't know what to do. You and Sophie may have had your differences, but she knew you would care for Meli and keep her safe. I presume that Meli doesn't know the truth?"

Isabel glared back. "No! And nor will she. What's done is done and telling her won't change anything." Isabel looked down and held her coffee cup in both hands contemplating her next words.

After a few minutes of silence, she looked up and spoke quietly. "I would not have Sophie's best friend turned out into the street and you've ensured Meli's safety. I owe you that much at least, so yes, you can stay. As for Meli knowing the truth…this is the last conversation I will have with you on that topic. Understood?"

CHAPTER THIRTEEN

MELI WANDERED OUT TOWARDS THE PASTURE LOOKING FOR WHERE Nicole had run to but couldn't see her anywhere. Thinking that she may be around the front, she followed the path around and sure enough she was just ahead, sitting on the rock wall, petulant and angry, tears streaming down her face.

Meli had no clue as to what she should say or do, so she quietly walked up and sat down beside her without saying a word.

Obviously embarrassed, Nicole wiped her arm across her dripping nose and mumbled, "What do you want?"

Meli shrugged. "Just to sit with you."

Nicole squinted, then looked away staring into the distance. "You should have seen all the stranded cars. Citroens, Peugeots, Renaults all broken down and littering the side of the road. Every car was bulging with people and luggage. It was like everyone in Paris just packed everything they owned and left any which way they could. The roads were so congested that we couldn't drive any faster than people could walk. Then when the car we were in finally ran out of gas, we had to do what everyone else was doing, abandon only what we could carry and walk. We walked for days. Sometimes we were offered rides on wagons but mostly we walked. Had that farmer outside of town not given us a ride, I'm sure I would have died from exhaustion." Pounding her fists into the rock, she screamed through her teeth, "It's just not fair. I hate it here and I hate my mother for making me come."

Meli was getting frustrated. "Look, I'm sorry you had to leave your home, and you must miss your dad, but that's not my fault."

"You don't get it at all. It's all her fault. She ruins everything. He was never home because of her and that's because she was always out, at her parties or the cabaret, or with other men. She thinks I don't know but I do. If she hadn't argued with him and done what she was told, we'd be safe, rich and not living with people I don't even know in a barn."

"But once he knows where you are, he'll send for you won't he?"

"You must be stupid. He had his own mistress and I very much doubt he'll send for either of us."

Meli leaned forward and rubbed the back of her neck. Her brows knitted in confusion, and she didn't know what to say. "I'm sorry for you. I know this isn't what you're used to in Paris."

Nicole was petulant. "How would someone who doesn't even have an indoor toilet understand. I suppose there's nothing to do around here either."

"Not a lot. Most of the men have gone to fight, so the women have to take up a lot of the work that the men did. Lots of women have to run small farms with older family members and young boys. We all do what we can because we don't have a choice. I always wanted to go to Paris. Sophie always made it sound so exciting."

"It was, well, until everyone had to carry around gas masks.

She and my mom used to go out every night and come home very late and very drunk. And the parties they held at my parents' apartment were legendary. Everyone who was anyone was there. Writers, artists, jazz singers even Édith Piaf."

"Édith Piaf? You met her?"

"Of course, her and lots of other people. I used to go to parties with my friends and of course there were plenty of boys. You should have seen the dresses I had to leave behind. I only hope that they are still there when we return."

As much as she didn't like to admit it, Nicole was starting to remind her a lot of Sophie, sophisticated, pretty, worldly and probably liked a lot by boys.

"She used to tell me all about the films she saw."

"She may have told you about the movies, but I'll bet she didn't tell you everything. Your sister had a lot of secrets."

"Like what?"

Nicole gave her a condescending smile. "Wouldn't you like to know? And with an air of sophistication added, "Unfortunately, I'm sworn to secrecy."

Meli pursed her lips and pasted a false smile on her face. *You're not remotely like Sophie.* Jumping off the wall she brushed off the dust from her dungarees and looked back. "I have chores to do. Do you want to come along?"

Nicole simply stared back at her with a slight smirk. "I very much doubt it."

As Meli headed back to the cottage trying to calm down, Berthe was just arriving and announced that word of their guests had already spread through the village.

As they walked through the door, Helene, who was sitting alone at the table, glanced up at Meli, obviously questioning how Nicole was.

"She's fine. I'm sure she'll come inside in a bit."

Berthe wasted no time sitting beside Helene and holding her

hands. "I am so sorry for you. It must have been awful, but you're safe now."

Helene lips quivered and she looked as if she was about to cry all over again. "Our suitcases contain the only treasures of value we could grab before escaping Paris. It's all we have left." Overhearing this, Meli only hoped that some of the treasures they rescued involved sugar, flour or real ground coffee.

From the top of the stairs, Isabel yelled down to the kitchen. "Meli, is that you? Can you come and give me a hand upstairs?"

"Oui, Mamina. I'll be right up. Berthe is here as well."

Berthe shifted out of her chair. "Tell you what, we'll all go up."

They found Isabel placing fresh sheets on the bed in the spare room which to-date, had lovingly been called Berthe's. "I think, Meli, that you and Nicole will need to share a room."

Meli's face immediately fell in horror. She had automatically assumed that Nicole would share a room with her mother.

"What about that room beside the attic? I could make my bedroom there."

"Well, I suppose…but are you sure?"

"Yes!" Meli replied a little too enthusiastically. "I can get started right now cleaning it up."

"That's fine, if that's what you want. Berthe, give me a hand and we'll grab some more bedding."

When they had left the room, Helene, who had been just standing in the corner in her own little fog, seemed to momentarily wake up and grabbed Meli's arm.

"Meli, I have something of Sophie's. Nothing of importance, just a small box of her things. Tuck it away somewhere, won't you? I don't want to upset your grandmother any more than I already have."

———

By the time the bedrooms had been organized and tidied, there was little time for anything else but for Meli to complete the rest of her chores and get ready for dinner.

Heading down the path towards the forest to forage for rabbit greens, she was relieved to have some time alone. As worldly and exotic as Nicole was, she was also obviously spoiled.

What would it be like, she wondered, to live in Paris, wear fashionable dresses and attend parties? Obviously, that had been Sophie's world. No wonder she didn't want to come back here to the country. Little wonder as well, why she and Mamina had clashed so often. The farm was worlds away from the glamour and flash of Paris and certainly not a world that Mamina would approve of.

But nor was it how Sophie had been raised. She may have been seduced by the glamour and excitement, and the freedom of a non-judgmental city, but it was clear to Meli she had still carried the Languedoc landscape in her heart. Stopping for a moment, she closed her eyes and inhaled the deep woodsy scents of wild mint, moss and dark earth. How could she not love it here?

By the time she had climbed the back stairs to her room, she was exhausted and grateful for having chosen the room for herself. There was no way she wanted to share a bedroom with Nicole. Besides, being away from the other rooms, there was a quietness here that she appreciated.

Flopping onto her bed, she gazed around her new room taking it all in. The last strains of light faded through the casement window and she rolled over to turn on a small lamp before the light faded altogether. Reaching out to pull the chain, she noticed a small round hole in the floor close to the corner wall.

Curious as to what its purpose could be, she got down on her knees and felt around for an explanation. As she pressed the board around the indent, she could feel that there seemed to be some play, indicating that it was loose for a purpose and that the floorboard itself had been purposely shortened. Suddenly, there was a change in the air, like tiny sparks of static electricity, she could physically feel it, and once again there was a sense that she was being watched. She held her breath.

Turning to the door, she hesitated for a moment. Everyone was either downstairs or had gone to their room so she knew that no one was there, but she couldn't shake the feeling and waited for a full minute, intently listening before she slowly lifted the slat.

The cavity was dark, and she momentarily hesitated before reaching down to feel her way around. Her fingers tingling, she reached further in and excitedly felt something hard and square. Sliding it towards her, she lifted it out with both hands and gently placed a small, ancient wooden box on the floor. Covered in heavy dust, it was obvious that it had been there a good long while, if not lifetimes.

Placing the floorboard back into place, she looked around for a cloth or something to wipe it down. Finding nothing immediately nearby, she grabbed her dirty socks and gently wiped away the dust and grime. She was immediately rewarded with her efforts with a beautifully carved scene on the lid. On the top was an intricate landscape of mountains and the ruins of a citadel at its peak. In the sky, flew a single bird in the shape of a dove.

Curious, she reached for the lid, but before she could open it, the air again felt electric and seemed to shimmer around her. She froze.

From somewhere behind her, came the lightest of whispers. Too faint to hear the words, she looked around, confused as to where the sound was coming from. Then, as suddenly as it appeared, it stopped. A little shaken, she slowly turned back to the box and touched the wood with her fingertips. She knew without opening it that it held ancient secrets and without even knowing how or why, she also knew that it was meant for her.

Placing it on her bed near the light from the lamp, she slowly unfastened the tarnished latch, raised the lid and peered inside.

It contained a folded page of yellow-brown parchment and as she carefully picked it up, she noticed that underneath lay a frayed piece of string, a faded square of material, and a small curved piece of gold.

Bringing the parchment closer to the light, she carefully unfolded it and was immediately taken aback at the beautiful flow of curves and arches of the handwriting. Heart pounding, she began to read.

I am writing these words knowing, trusting, that whoever receives my message, will be in need of its guidance. There is a kind of magic in this knowing, a trust that my words will reach you at a time when they are most needed. So, whether you are from now or lifetimes from now, there are things that never change for those of us who are chosen.

When you are born different from those around you, there is a hollow that cannot be filled by anything mortal. You shift constantly between the two worlds, never committing to one or the other. And even when you are solidly in the material world, you are only a whisper away from the world of dreams as if it were as easy as walking through gauze into a clear day.

I too used to believe that if I could just fit in, I would be like all the others. But how could I be? They are not me and I am not them. They are not you. They have not been charged with guarding the greatest of secrets.

In this small casket you will find a piece of string, a square of velvet, and a broken ring, all from long before your time. Their monetary value is nothing, but my earthly treasures are priceless for the memories they hold. I promised once, to those whom they belonged, to remember them. These small items are my way of honouring that request and to remind those who come after that we existed, that we lived, that we loved.

India

Gently folding the delicate parchment back up, she placed it back into the box then picked up the piece of string, the cloth and the broken ring. In an instant she was flooded with visions, a little girl with big brown eyes, a woman cradling her baby and a young man with love in his eyes.

Shaken, she put them back into the box, closed the lid and sat in silence on her bed.

When you are born different....

CHAPTER FOURTEEN

W OLFGANG K OCH LOOKED AROUND THE SMALL BUT EFFICIENT room he had rented from the very capable Mme St Pierre. The landlady had looked at the size of him and suggested another room due to the larger bed size, but no, this was the room he wanted. His eye for detail took it all in. The single bed next to the wall. The plain little desk, sturdy wooden chair and an old worn lamp was all he needed and wanted to see.

So, this was where M. Schreiber had stayed while in Lave-lanet. Taking out two books from his satchel, he tossed them on the bed for later. He wanted to get a sense of this Victor fellow. Sort out what he was about. He had been briefed of course, but in order to really understand him and how he thought, he had to follow in his footsteps. Talk to people who knew him. Only that way could he follow the trail to his goal. But reading could wait till later.

Closing the door to his room, he made his way to the salon where he hoped to find Mme St Pierre. He was not disappointed.

He guessed her to be in her late fifties. The full-length crisp, white apron wrapped around her ample figure, while the short sleeves from her printed dress peeked out from underneath. Her dark hair, lightly streaked with grey around the temples, was primly pinned back in a stylish chignon. Delicate laugh lines creased around her lips and blue eyes suited her congenial manner.

"Ah, Madame, I was hoping to trouble you for some tea or coffee."

The landlady, who had been tidying up, looked over towards his voice and wiped her hands on her apron. "Why yes, of course. The coffee is a bit of a blend, I hope you don't mind."

"Not at all, Madame. I assume that you are finding it difficult to purchase real coffee?"

"Yes, sir, but of course, everyone is."

"So I understand. Perhaps I can help you with that. Give me a moment, won't you?"

"Of course, I'll wait right here for you, sir."

Returning to his room, he opened the satchel on the bureau and reached inside to pull out a small package. He chuckled to himself at his foresight as he walked back to the salon. With a brief nod and a smile, he placed the small package in the hands of the grateful woman.

"For you, Madame. The very best of coffee, with my compliments. Perhaps you would like to join me?"

With a brief nod and a smile, he placed the small package in the hands of the grateful woman.

Her face lit up as she nodded. "Thank you, sir. Please sit down, Lieutenant Koch and make yourself comfortable. I'll go make it right away. What a treat. Thank you so much."

As her heels click, clicked their way back into the kitchen, Koch wandered around the room, examining a few of her small china figurines before finally sitting down.

A few minutes later she returned with a silver tray, coffee pot, two cups and a few digestive cookies. Placing it on a small side table, she proceeded to pour him some coffee placing his cup and a few cookies in a side dish close to him. After she had served herself, she sat down as well and smiled politely.

"Thank you again, Lieutenant Koch, I'll be sure to save this for your pleasure alone."

Wolfgang sipped and smiled politely. "You must be very busy this time of year."

"We used to be of course, but with the war…" She looked uncomfortable, as if worried to offend him or to suggest that the war was personally his fault.

"It's fine, Madame. I understand."

"Have you been managing this auberge very long?"

Mme St Pierre finished swallowing her tiny bite of cookie before she continued. "My husband and I took it over from his parents about twenty years ago. But since his death, six years ago, I have managed it on my own."

"My condolences, Madame."

"Thank you for saying so, Lieutenant Koch. I can't say it's been easy, but I do what I can."

"You must have seen some interesting characters over the years. In fact, I am reading a book right now by Victor Schreiber. I believe he may have stayed in this area for a while."

"Oh, my goodness, Lieutenant, he stayed here and as a matter of fact, this will amaze you, but he stayed in the very room that you are in now."

"No! Well, this is quite an amazing coincidence! Did you meet him?"

"I did, indeed. He stayed here for several months. A very quiet man, although several of his friends would come for tea and discuss all of his ideas. It's a tragedy what happened."

"Yes, indeed. Did he have many friends in this area?"

"Not a lot, but there were a few regular friends. He and another fellow in town would spend days investigating the local areas, caves and such, and then of course he had some friends near the Montségur area. There was a young woman I believe, who worked in Paris…although I can't remember her name. They used to have tea right in this very room. Lovely girl. Came from a long line of Cathars herself, or so she said. Whether he believed her or not I can't say.

"I only know this because I accidentally overheard them one day. He was quite interested in them you know. That local fellow would know. I can't remember his name either—Paul someone… I think. Mind you, when I think about it, I haven't seen him around in quite a while."

Koch was quite certain that she would continue on all afternoon if he didn't interrupt. "I'd be very interested in speaking to him. By the way, I'll be expecting an assistant tomorrow morning. If you'd be so kind, please show him in when he arrives."

Finishing his coffee before she could start up again, he rose from his seat. "And now you will have to excuse me, Madame. I have work that is in need of my attention."

Leaning forward, while fluttering her hands, the Mme St Pierre gushed out a reply. "Of course, Lieutenant. If there's anything that I can get for you, please don't hesitate to ask."

———

The following morning, as Wolfgang was finishing his breakfast in the dining room, there was a knock at the front door. The landlady, in an obvious attempt to reach the entryway, created quite the racket from the kitchen before the guest knocked again. Flustered that she barely achieved her goal, she wiped her hands on her apron and breathlessly greeted her guest. He could hear their muffled introductions and then a louder, "He's just in here, sir, and expecting you," as she escorted him into the dining room.

Koch looked up towards the door to see a slightly built young man enter the room. His youthful baby-face was framed by wire-rimmed glasses and he appeared to be no more than twenty. In his crisp new uniform and black boots polished to a mirror shine, it was clear he had never seen a day of combat in his life. He was not at all what he expected. He wanted a man but what just walked through the door was a boy.

He could only presume that the young man was some high-ranking officer's nephew and given this job for either punishment or to keep him out of trouble. Looking at him, he had a pretty good idea which one it was. No matter, all he needed was someone to drive him around and do some research. Surely, he could handle that.

Standing straight as a pole, eyes facing dead ahead, the young man cracked his arm out with a prompt, "Heil Hitler. Good morning, Lieutenant Koch. My name is Tomas, Heinrich Richter, and I will be your driver. Your car is parked outside and available whenever you are ready. With your permission, I will wait for you there."

"Very good, Private Richter, but no, I would prefer for you to sit and have a coffee with me first."

"Yes, sir, of course, sir. Thank you, sir."

Koch nodded to the landlady. "Madame St. Pierre, would you kindly get Private Richter a cup of coffee."

"Of course, Lieutenant Koch, right away."

As the landlady scurried to the sideboard for an extra cup and saucer, the young man pulled out a chair and sat down opposite to his superior.

"I just want to say what a privilege it is to be your assistant, sir."

"Oh, really, why is that?"

As the young man fumbled his reply, Wolfgang dismissed the question with a wave of his hand. "Never mind. So, tell me, Tomas, how did you manage to get this position?"

"My uncle, sir. He's a close friend of Reichsführer, Himmler. He felt that I would be useful to you."

"Is that so? In what way?"

"I recently trained as a pilot, sir, but in University I studied medieval history. I wanted to, well, still hope to be, a professor one day."

"How very interesting. And does your studies include French history?"

"Yes, sir, very much so, sir. I am also fluent in French. In preparation, I read both of Victor Schreiber's books on the Cathars and found the subject very riveting."

"Hmmm. You've pleasantly surprised me today, Tomas, and I am rarely pleasantly surprised."

"May I ask, sir, where we'll be travelling to today?"

"Of course, Richter. Nowhere far for the moment. I'll be visiting some local spots today and next week we'll travel to some small little villages a few hours away. I'd like though, to discuss your opinion of these Victor Schreiber books."

"I'd be happy to share what I know, sir, or at least what I've been able to research so far."

"Go ahead then."

"Well, as far as the Cathars go, they believed in two opposing deities. The first was a good God, portrayed in the New Testament and was the creator of spirit, while the second was an evil God, called Rex Mundi, or King of the world as depicted in the Old Testament. He was the creator of matter and the physical world.

"They believed that the good God's power was limited by the evil God's power and vice versa. Most importantly because all visible matter, including the human body, was created by *Rex Mundi*; matter was therefore tainted with sin.

"In his second book, Schreiber talks about how the Cathars believed that humans were actually angels seduced by Satan and forced to spend an eternity trapped in the evil God's material realm, in other words, earth. They also taught that in order for a human to regain angelic status, one had to renounce the material self completely. Until one was prepared to do so, they would be stuck in a cycle of reincarnation and condemned to live on a corrupt Earth forever."

"Interesting, and a very academically sound review, but what about this Grail legend? Why them?"

"Well, sir, they were considered more Christian than the Christians themselves and may have had a direct lineage to the Magdalene, who it is rumoured fled to French soil and settled in the Provence area. In fact, there is a basilica dedicated to the Magdalene in Saint-Maximin-la-Sainte-Baume. They apparently parade around her skull every year.

"As his wife, Mary Magdalene was considered the rightful leader of the church that Jesus had started and continued his teachings along with their daughter Sarah. The Grail was passed down and guarded through the generations by the true believers of this faith.

"In 1202, Robert de Boron wrote a tale called 'La Queste del Saint Graal' and described the Grail as the actual cup used by Christ at the Last Supper in which Joseph of Arimathea later caught his blood during the crucifixion. The Grail then became a symbol of a holy search for God, one who reveals himself only to the pure in heart according to the Christian definition. It also became a symbol for ultimate power."

Koch was impressed. This young man was a regular encyclopedia. "Go on."

"In the tale of Perceval, the 'Tale of the Quest for the Grail', the French author, Chretien de Troyes, wrote that the Holy Grail was hidden in a huge cave known as Montsalvat. There are only two caves with this name. One is in Spain, which I understand Herr Himmler has already inspected, and the second is at Montségur, France. Based on everything I've just stated, it was Schreiber's belief that it's located there."

Koch took a sip of his coffee and took a good long look at the young man in front of him.

"And do you believe this?"

"I believe, sir, that the physical Grail exists and can be found. Whether it has supernatural power is not for me to decide. Only the one who possesses it will know the truth."

Koch nodded his head in agreement. "You'll do very nicely Richter."

CHAPTER FIFTEEN

BERTHE HAD ARRIVED EARLY THE NEXT DAY IN ORDER TO HELP with the soap making, as she had better access to beef suet from the local butcher. Rendered and clean, she was eager to get started, but a single look from Isabel was a clear indication that she needed a chat first. As Nicole sat sullenly at the table, it was also clear that she wanted privacy.

"Give me a hand in the garden for a minute will you, Berthe?"

They had barely reached a few feet away from the cottage when Berthe asked, "What's up?'

Looking around to ensure they were far enough away from the kitchen door, Isabel rolled her eyes and sighed. "Where do I begin?" She continued in a low voice, "Helen's husband left her. So, they are homeless and have no money."

Berthe shrugged. "Does she know where he is?"

"No. And that's not the worst of it. She says he left with his mistress and her daughter. How am I expected to feed two extra mouths? It's not like either of them will be useful or could earn extra money."

"What will you do?"

Isabel shook her head. "It's that Paris craziness Pétain was going on about. This wild need for excitement and parties. To be honest with you, Paris needs the Germans to straighten them out and instil some solid family values."

"So, what did you say to her?"

"That's the problem, Berthe. I have no choice but to help her. Look what she did for Sophie, even though I still blame her part in it. Besides, she knows too much about Meli. I can't take the chance."

"God, Father Pelletier would have a heart attack if he found out and the scandal…"

"What about her daughter?"

"Apparently, she doesn't know, but I somehow doubt that. Berthe, I am so angry at this being dumped on my doorstep, I can't think straight. Her daughter is a spoiled brat, let alone a bad influence for Meli. She does nothing but complain and does nothing to help. And even when she does, it's done so badly that I have to do it over again."

"Okay, listen, here's what we'll do. Since M. Dupont has been away at the front, Mme Ferras has been managing the library in the village, but she's late into her pregnancy and could use the help. They asked me, but it may be better to give it to Nicole. They don't pay much, but it would help you out and keep her busy."

"Berthe, I don't know what I would do without you."

"It's fine, my friend, besides, you would do the same for me. How about Meli and I make the soap while you get some other chores done."

———

Meli measured the lye into the cauldron of cold water then immediately took a step back in order to not breathe in the fumes. Coughing as a tiny bit of the cloud hit the back of her throat, she took a deep breath then stepped forward again in order to break up solidified chunks of lye to dissolve. The old wooden spoon that she used had been eaten away with lye. A small drop of the liquid inadvertently fell on her arm and she quickly grabbed the small bowl of vinegar on hand to wipe it away and relieve the itchy sting.

In the meantime, Berthe had been melting the fat in a large pot on the burner. The fact that she had brought beef suet was a real treat and would ensure a more solid bar that would last longer.

It was a large batch and both ingredients would take time to melt and cool off. "It looks like we'll have some time for the lye and fat to cool down first. How about I go pick some greens for the rabbits? By the time I'm done, we can make the soap."

"That sounds fine but how about I help? We can grab some dried lavender for the soap on the way back."

As they walked towards the pasture, Berthe noticed that Meli seemed to be a little distant—quieter than usual. "So, how are you managing with Nicole? Are you getting along?"

Meli tugged at a few dandelion greens and placed them in her basket. Standing back up she looked at Berthe and pursed her lips. "She's okay, I guess. She's grown up differently than me. I know she misses her dad and is angry at her mother for taking them here. I know I'm definitely not someone she would have been friends with in Paris, so I guess it's not surprising that we're not best friends here."

"Well, I suppose that's true enough."

"There is something that's bothering me though."

"What's that?"

"She said things about Sophie that made me think I didn't know her very well."

Berthe's eyes riveted to Meli's. "What kinds of things?"

"Just about parties and men and stuff."

Berthe took a deep sigh and bent down to grab another handful of greens. Placing them in the basket, she couldn't look Meli in the eye. "Your sister was full of life and she enjoyed it to the fullest. You know that."

"I know, but Nicole made it sound like she had secrets. She even said so."

"Nicole is just an angry young lady and is jealous of you."

"Jealous of me? You're talking craziness. Why would she be jealous of me?"

"Because you are loved. Now, enough chatter and let's get back to that batch of soap. I'll go get the lavender and you run ahead to feed the rabbits. I'll meet you back in the yard. I can't do all the stirring by myself."

When Meli arrived back, Nicole was sitting sullenly watching Berthe. "I've already combined the fat, Meli. How about you take a turn stirring. I want to talk to Nicole about helping out at the library."

Meli watched with interest as they both slowly walked down the lane with presumably Berthe explaining the opportunity. She was curious how Nicole would take this and didn't have long to wait. With a sudden turn on her heel, Nicole screamed out a "NO! And you can't make me!" before running back to the house and slamming the door. Even from the yard they could hear her screaming at her mother.

Turning around, Berthe looked back at Meli, shook her head and raised her hands in surrender. She had tried her best.

———

The household had fallen into an irritable type of rhythm over the next few days. Nicole fought bitterly about helping out with the library until Isabel, disgusted with her whining, snapped, "It's either that or you can clean the barn."

Later that evening, while they sat in uncomfortable silence at the table, Helene, in an attempt at conciliation, patted her daughter's arm, cooing that she may even like it. Nicole gave her a quick look that would wilt fresh flowers and continued her frosty silence. Helene's hand automatically gravitated to her forehead with the intended dramatic effect. Everything was just so difficult for her.

Isabel was having none of this. "Meli will take you into the village next week so Berthe can show you around."

Nicole's response was as snippy as she looked. "Fine."

Meli herself, wasn't too happy with this arrangement. "I could help if they want, after all, I'm the one who wants to be a writer."

Isabel was tired and irritable. "You are needed here."

Meli silently pouted her resentment. It wasn't fair. She was the one who loved books. She was the one who wanted to be a writer. One day someone else would milk the goats, feed the rabbits, weed the garden, and wrap the Banon. No wonder Sophie ran away to Paris. She was the lucky one. Looking at both Nicole and Helene, she wished that they would just go back to Paris.

———

Helene watched Meli as they ate. Sophie would be so proud of her, that much she knew. God, she looked so much like her that it seemed foolish to even pretend otherwise.

She felt bad dumping all her baggage on Isabel, but hadn't she been there for Sophie? Besides, they really had no choice. What a mess she'd made of things. She missed Sophie terribly, even more so now. By God, they had had fun though—dancing, men, clothes, although in hindsight, introducing her to Jacob might have been a mistake.

Even now she didn't completely understand exactly what had happened. She knew Sophie and Isabel had a challenging relationship and looking around she could understand why. Sophie wanted more than goats and cheese outside a tiny Provincial village. Who wouldn't?

It didn't help that Isabel was so serious, so old-fashioned. She remembered the day when Sophie had cut her hair in the latest bobbed fashion—she knew that Isabel would flip—and she did. As she did with the silk stockings, the red lipstick, the secretary job—it was all too much for Isabel.

Thinking of her own daughter though, she softened a little. Hadn't Nicole become her Sophie, and hadn't she become an Isabel? Afraid for her rebellious daughter. She chuckled. What would Sophie have said to that?

Meli had the same 'otherworldly' side to her that Sophie had. 'She's away with the fairies', as her Irish Grandmother would have said. Perhaps it was the landscape around here. It was certainly romantic.

Sophie was lucky she had Isabel to raise Meli. At least she had known where her child was, participated in her upbringing, albeit as her sister, but she was still a part of her life. And frankly, had she not taken the child in, Isabel would be the one regretting that decision now. Meli was the only thing she had left.

Minoux jumped onto the table and butted her head into Helene's hand. As she scratched behind the cat's ears she thought about Sophie and her friendship.

As long as Sophie was around, she felt brave, but without her she just felt lost. She threw herself into parties and being the perfect wife, but she was never quite good enough. She kept making the tiniest of compromises, the smallest of decisions, not realizing that the small things added up until she was forced to face the person she had become.

She had the best of intentions; to do better than her mother had, to keep the peace, to smooth her rough edges and become something better, shinier, and more acceptable to him.

She had become like the figurines in her cabinet, smooth, ornate but delicate and hollow. Do not touch. For display only.

He told her what he wanted her to wear, what he wanted her to say, to do, how to act, when to laugh, when and what to eat. Until she no longer recognized who she was.

There were always women smarter than her, prettier than her, more clever than her, and she wasn't blind as to how they caught her husband's eye. Politics wasn't something that she was especially interested in, not like Sophie who seemed to know everything and followed all the issues, all the players, and the dangers ahead. She was smart.

She was also much stronger than Isabel gave her credit for. Sure, they partied and had fun with men, but didn't everyone?

Sophie, when she was serious, was focused on whatever she felt needed her attention. Helene was never anything but the sidekick in their friendship.

Hans simply wanted someone who could manage the illusion of grandeur and that Helene could do. Dinner parties was something she excelled at. Sophie was the powerhouse that made the party exciting—electric. She was fearless.

After she died, Helene stopped the parties for a while. She attended others but didn't host for at least a year. It didn't seem right. And it wasn't fun without her. She took up with that jazz player because she was vulnerable, at least that's what she told herself. He made her feel pretty in her dull grey world. Made her feel smart, even loved and how she wanted to feel loved.

Sophie was the same way; they both needed to be loved. She thought that Jacob loved her and would one day leave his wife, but even Helene knew that would never happen.

Sophie didn't care that he was Jewish. He certainly didn't care that she wasn't. Until, of course, she got pregnant, then suddenly he was all family man who couldn't possibly marry her. If he left his wife, his family would disown him. He would be disinherited, and his grandmother would have a heart attack and die. Did she want that on her head?

He refused her calls. Refused her tears. Refused the baby. By the time Meli was born, Sophie no longer cared.

Looking around at the rustic kitchen, uneven walls and flagstone floors, she and Nicole were at least in agreement on one thing. She couldn't wait to get out of here and back into her Paris apartment. Hans owed her that much at least. Things would be different then. It would be just her and Nicole and somehow when this war was over, she'd make damn sure that they were in a financially secure position.

CHAPTER SIXTEEN

Ever since the dream, Meli, had felt differently. It wasn't anything that she could name or describe but different like an anticipation of something she couldn't name.

Even the cottage felt different. She felt older, no, more than that. It was as if someone older from another time inhabited her brain, shared her thoughts; their memories trickling through and intertwining with hers, like fine multi-coloured threads.

Sometimes at night while lying in her bed, she would raise her arm above her and swirl her hand around in the dark, sensing the flow of magic around her. There was nothing she could see, but she could feel the energy as it spun around and around. She felt a little childish thinking this, but despite what anyone might say, it felt real.

Her dreams were getting stronger and another voice was inside of her rising to the top and this confused her. *When you are born different...*

She wasn't strong like Sophie had been or Mamina was. Isabel was invincible and always completely in charge. You didn't need to think when Isabel was around. You just had to do what you were told, and everything would get sorted out according to Isabel Durand's grand plan. So why was this happening?

Why did she have to remember who she was? Why was she remembering things from a life that wasn't hers? She knew that she shouldn't talk to Mamina about the dreams, that much was certain. Berthe would listen but would she have answers? The library might have information, but could it explain what was happening?

She had to do something and decided to start with Berthe. After all, her grandmother was a Romani gypsy. Who better to ask?

Now that the house was full, it was difficult finding opportunities to speak to Berthe without arousing suspicion. But an opportunity did arise the following week. Berthe needed help with clearing out an extra room in her home and Meli had agreed to help.

She had arrived after her milking chores and had brought a jar of fresh goat's milk with her and three bars of the cured soap.

"Oh, lovely. That's just what I needed. I used up the last of my milk yesterday. Thanks for helping me today, Meli, I really appreciate it."

"Why do you need the room emptied? Are you expecting company too?"

"No, no, but you never can tell, eh?"

The room was on the second floor and faced the back of the house with a window that looked out towards her back shed and simple vegetable garden. Berthe surveyed the space and decided what needed to go where. The dresser could stay as could the large wooden chest. The old bed frame could stay but the mattress would need a good beating and airing outside. Meli could handle that. Everything she didn't need could get packed away in boxes and put into the attic and that would be that.

"What's in all the boxes?"

"Oh, memories, old clothes mostly, things from my husband

before he died. I wasn't ready to get rid of anything and putting it all here seemed to be the best idea. Years later, it's all still here, so I guess it's time. There are people who could use the pants and shirts and we can unravel the wool from the sweaters. How are things with Nicole? Any better?"

"Hardly. I'll be glad when they go home."

"Well, that may not be for a while."

"Maybe she could stay here?"

"Ha, now why would you wish that on me? I thought we were like family."

"We are and I wouldn't wish her on you. It's just that things are so weird lately. Remember that dream I had?"

"Yes—why has there been more?"

Meli looked down and sighed. "Yes and no. That is, I don't think they are dreams. It feels like I have someone else's memories. Someone that lived a long time ago."

Berthe stopped in the middle of moving a box towards the door and stared at Meli. "Tell you what, I need a bit of a break before we really dive in, so how about we go downstairs and make ourselves a cup of coffee and you can tell me all about it."

Once they got themselves settled, Berthe encouraged Meli to continue.

"So tell me, is the dream the same as last time?"

"No, it's nothing like that at all. It's more like I am watching a movie of myself where I can feel and think but it's not me, it's someone else. Does that make sense?"

"Who is this person and what are they saying?"

"Her name is India and she said she's a believer. When she was a little girl, she found an amulet, a hand-carved dove flying over some ruins at the top of a hill. She has a daughter named Sophia, but it felt like she was my daughter. It was like I was seeing everything through her eyes and when she looked at her stone cottage, it was our stone cottage. She said what she was about to do was for her daughter and generations to follow. She said we must never forget. Then she said *my* name, and that *I* must never forget."

Berthe was silent for a long while as if she was having difficulties weighing her words. She lowered her head and shook it silently. Finally, she spoke.

"Meli, have you ever heard of reincarnation?"

"I know what it means but not much more about it."

"I know you know some of this but let me carry on. I'm sure you've heard of the *bonhommes*, the "good men.""

"Of course. In the twelfth and early thirteenth centuries there was a religious sect in the South of France where we live now, called the Cathars."

"Exactly. They believed in a world that is made up of two opposing forces: good and evil, light and dark. Our world, the world of matter, is the creation of the dark forces where the light has been imprisoned. They believed in many things, that Jesus was a human being who married and had children, that Mary Magdalene was his wife and it was she, not Peter who was head of the church. They did not eat meat, they were pacifists and believed in reincarnation."

"I think Sophie told me some of this when I was little."

"I wouldn't be surprised but let me continue. The Cathar faith was made up of Parfaits, similar to our priests, and believers, much like the congregation in the church."

"The woman in my dream said she was a believer."

"Exactly. In the 13th century, the papacy considered the Cathars, the Parfaits and believers to be a danger to the Catholic Church and slaughtered them all."

"But why?"

"The easy answer is that the Cathar faith required less of the everyday person. There were no massive cathedrals because the parfaits delivered their sermons out in nature or in friends' homes. No money was asked of them to support their church other than providing shelter or food for their Parfaits or priests.

They lived their lives simply and were respectful of their neighbours. And because their faith was more popular in the countryside than the Catholic religion, the church felt it was necessary to eradicate the religion before their numbers grew even more.

"In reincarnation, energy never dies. It's transferred back and forth endlessly, occupying different dwellings or bodies. Once energy escapes an expired body, it's only a matter of time until it re-enters a new one.

"If someone died suddenly or tragically, leaving unfinished business, their spirit will reincarnate and will be reborn into the family circle where they not only felt most loved, but also into situations that allow them to resolve what was left unfinished. You, Meli, come from a very long line of Cathars, as does your Mamina."

"But Mamina is Catholic."

Berthe sighed deeply. "Well, yes, she is now, but it was not always so. There is more to this Meli, but it's not my story to tell. Clearly you are here for a reason and it is important for you to remember why that is. Maybe you should write these dreams down in the book I gave you for your birthday. In the meantime, I'll help you all I can to understand."

"What about Mamina?"

"Leave her to me, Meli. Now, let's get back to clearing out that room."

CHAPTER SEVENTEEN

The following week after breakfast, Meli walked with Nicole down to the village to the library. As usual, Nicole was sullen, Meli frustrated.

"So why can't the man who usually manages the library do this?"

"It's M. Dupont and he's now at a work camp in Germany," Meli patiently repeated.

"So why doesn't the other lady do it then?"

"Because she's pregnant and due any day now."

The library was a small part of the community hall in an old building with uneven shutters and a crumbling façade. Built at the turn of the century, it had been maintained haphazardly since the Great War, bearing scars of weathering and use. Inside, the most attention it received was that its wooden boards had been religiously swept clean of dust, sand and dirt by Mme Ferras. Two large pots of red mums, also planted and maintained by her, framed the door and welcomed them as they stepped inside. Wooden shelves held several hundred books, its collection having grown by donations, estate sales and the church.

Once Sophie had told her about a wonderful bookstore in Paris called, 'Shakespeare & Sons'. She said it was filled with books from floor to ceiling and all the famous writers went there. She had even promised to take her one day. She wondered whether Helene or Nicole had been there, but she didn't dare ask, lest Nicole tell her she had and with Sophie.

Meli loved the smell of books. Especially the old ones. She loved how they felt, the weight of them, the promise of what was to come. Different worlds, different thoughts, poetic words that she wished she had thought of. Getting deliciously lost in a book was her favourite pastime and it irritated her that this was how Nicole would get to spend her time.

She, who had grown up here, who wanted to be a writer, who knew every single section, was left to feed goats and do endless chores. It wasn't fair and she hated Nicole for it. She had probably never even read a book in her life and probably never would. The only thing she cared about was looking pretty, yet another thing that Meli would never be good at.

The war was no longer phony. Berthe said that refugees were starting to trickle in, not like the other larger towns, but people talked of travelers, families with suitcases dusty and dirty from farmer's wagons, walking, endless trains escaping to who knows where.

For the first time in her life she felt fearful about the future. But here, here in the library surrounded by books and words and stories, she felt safe.

She could hear Berthe walk Nicole through the process of lending out a book, something that she could do with her eyes closed. She watched as Nicole huffed and rolled her eyes. The library was small and the process not at all difficult, but you'd think that she was being forced into some great imposition by having to listen.

Berthe was talking patiently through her attitude, but barely.

"Write their name down along with the name of the book, neatly in this ledger. See here?"

Nicole simply gave a look and pouted a "fine."

Berthe who rarely lost her temper was losing it now. "Nicole, attention please! You must mark down the book here and the name there. This is not hard."

"Fine...name here...book there."

"The books are all numbered and should be put back into the proper section. If you're not sure then ask me, or Meli—she certainly knows the library inside out." Looking towards Meli, Berthe smiled, while Nicole scowled in her direction.

"How long do I have to stay here?" She pouted.

"Well, they try and keep it open at least three days a week, so Monday, Wednesday and Friday afternoons. I could walk down here with you after my coffee with Isabel and Meli could come fetch you when you're done—at least until you're sure of the way yourself."

At that moment, a young girl of about ten ran into the library and directly to Berthe.

"Mme Chastain, you need to come quick. Mama is in labour and the midwife is already out with Mme Ferras!"

Berthe immediately recognized the child and although she was a hefty woman, she launched into action.

"Meli, you'll need to stay here and help out Nicole for the day. I'll send Marie here to let Mamina know you'll be late. Don't forget to lock up." And with that, she was gone.

Meli was in her glory and other than helping the occasional old lady look for something romantic to read, she spent the morning in the history section researching anything she could on the Cathars. Not a word was spoken between them other than the sporadic 'Hmmmph' from Nicole who pouted her way through old fashion magazines.

She noticed him the moment he walked through the door. Not because of the German uniform or the giant of an officer who entered before him, but because the air changed just before he entered. It was deeper, more vibrant. *Why would German Officers come to a village library?*

She noticed him as well. Nicole looked up from what she was doing, and in that moment, it was like a storm wave had crashed against a cliff. Nicole was in her full presence and with the way she filled out her dress, her long legs and blonde hair waved into the latest fashion, who could notice anything but Nicole.

Meli shriveled into her desk, fidgeted with her sweaty hands and watched as if in a dream. *What did they want? Would they arrest them?*

The older officer, obviously in charge, spoke directly to Nicole. His uniform and height alone was intimidating, but what really struck fear in her soul was the scar from a deep gash that stretched from his mouth to his ear.

The younger one looked to be around 18 or twenty years of age and wasn't exceptionally handsome, but neither was he ugly. In fact, there was a gentleness about him that was completely opposite from his scarred Commander. His physique was slender, and he did have some height, but it was the small round glasses that gave him the look of a scholar that Meli found attractive.

"Good morning, Mademoiselle. We are here to use your library facilities and would appreciate your help. This is Private Richter who I will leave in your good care while I attend to other things. He will explain what it is that we are looking for."

Turning to the young man, he addressed him next. "Richter, I will return in an hour and expect an update on your research."

The young man clicked his heels and saluted his superior. "Yes, sir."

After his commanding officer left, Nicole wasted no time. With a smile and a toss of her hair, Meli watched as Nicole demonstrated her unspoken appreciation for his uniform. Didn't they have words for girls like that?

Nicole was laughing now at some joke that had been made or

maybe a compliment on beautiful French women, who knows. Obviously, she was amused or just flirting.

Why was he here? What did he want?

"Oh Meli?" She was now calling her over like she was *her* personal assistant. She felt embarrassed by her peasant clogs and her dirty fingernails. Her lack of height made her look years younger than she actually was and her small bosom didn't help. Meli walked over, gave a quick little smile at the German as Nicole continued to act in control.

"Meli, this fine officer is interested in the local history of this area and would like a recommendation on a book of Cathars."

The young man looked into her eyes and for a fleeting second, she thought she saw a glimpse of interest, but that was silly and confusing. Why would she care what the enemy thought and with Nicole there with her hair and long legs, why would he even look at her?

She mumbled something ridiculous, how she was reading the exact same thing, and could feel her cheeks flush with embarrassment. Then, because she knew her cheeks were red, she blushed even more. Mortified, she blurted out the section to the left and retreated to her desk.

She could hear Nicole's little giggle and the smirk in her voice as she said, "Children." She then walked over to the section with him, probably gloating over Meli's shame as she coquettishly turned her head to listen to what he said.

Good Lord, if that was flirting, Meli would never get the hang of it. She wasn't even sure that she wanted to. And if that is how things were done in Paris, she wanted no part of it.

He was asking her questions that Nicole couldn't answer. Of course she couldn't. She wasn't from here and couldn't have cared less about its history or religion or castles and heritage. Not like Meli, who knew all of this, was raised in these hills. She could answer all of his questions but someone like him would never look at someone like her. *Why would that even matter,* she wondered. *He's a German—the enemy.*

She listened to their conversation while she pretended to read a book. She didn't want to, but she couldn't concentrate on anything else. He was a scholar he said, and Commander Koch's assistant. His French was impeccable, a little too perfect maybe, but that wasn't his fault. The old ones in the village spoke French for practical reasons but between themselves only spoke Occitan and tended to trust those who could speak it, much more than those who couldn't.

His manners were faultless. Surely the sign of a well-bred high society family. Nicole would have clued into that in a heartbeat.

Taking several books off the shelf, he chose a small table by the door then nodded his thanks to Nicole who, with a bit of a pout, recognized that her charm wasn't going to be his focus.

For the next hour he made several notes, looking up every now and then and once, catching Meli's eye with a smile. It was silly she knew, but this German boy, this young man made her heart skip a beat. How pathetic was she?

Later, when his commander returned, they quietly discussed his notes in the far corner of the room. His commander seemed pleased. Standing up, he turned to Nicole and simply announced that they would return tomorrow as Private Richter cleared away his notes. The younger officer politely stacked the books he had been looking at and brought them to Meli's desk.

He nodded and mumbled a "thanks," and as he handed them to her, the tips of their fingers briefly touched. And in that moment, in the briefest of connections, something shifted within Meli. It felt oddly enough as if she had made a friend.

———

Meli could barely fall asleep that night just thinking about Private

Richter. Why did the enemy have to be so normal and polite? He certainly didn't feel dangerous. How she wished she could be there tomorrow when he came back. She lay awake for what felt like hours thinking about all the ways she might make this happen until she finally fell into a deep sleep and dreamed.

They arrived three days later on a rainy afternoon. The wheels on their overloaded wagon caked with mud, water dripping from the wagon's wooden sides. She greeted her old friends warmly and hustled them inside from the bad weather. Old Pierre would take care of the horses and everything else could wait until they had been fed and warmed by the fire.

"There were no issues?" she asked Benoit.

"No, none," he replied. "Although I can't say that I would want to make that journey again."

"Well, you won't have to, now that this is your home."

As they entered the cottage, the smell of a hearty stew assaulted their senses making their mouths water and stomachs rumble.

"Here, sit down by the fire and I'll get you both a bowl of stew. You must be starving. Sophia should be back in a moment. She's just locking the chickens away for the night."

As Benoit rubbed his hands near the fire, his wife Marie Ange looked deeply into India's eyes. She was a petite but sturdy woman, with a ruddy complexion and a determined look about her that reminded the sleeping Meli of Berthe for some reason.

"Are you sure that you want to do this, India? We are indebted to your father for his kindness and of course will gladly do what you ask of us. But are you sure?"

India held the woman's hands and smiled a sad, lonely smile.

"Marie-Ange, I have always known that this day would come, and I would entrust my treasure with no one else. It is I that am honored and grateful that you would take on this task for me."

Benoit nodded silently into the fire. "Speaking of your treasure, where is she? I expected a hearty welcome by now."

As if by magic, Sophia burst through the door, three small discs of cheese in her basket. Thoroughly wet, but smiling brightly, she raced to Marie Ange arms and held her tightly. "You're here!"

"Oh, my, look how much you've grown ma petite!"

After satisfying their hunger and Sophia had been sent to bed, the three of them sat by the fire and discussed what was to be done. They kept their voices low so as not to be heard.

"When will you leave?" asked Benoit.

"I think I should leave first thing tomorrow. I'll be joining another small party of believers and then we'll head to the cave at Lombrive."

Marie-Ange tried to sound stoic, but she couldn't hide the desperation in her voice. "India, are you sure there is no other way? We could hide you here, keep you safe."

"Bless you both, but this is no longer about my safety. I cannot stay and keep Sophia or anything else safe. You know yourselves what is at stake."

Benoit shook his head and the pain he felt was clear on his face and the tremor in his voice. "India, we'll take care of Sophia as if she was our own and in time, she too will take over our role. We'll guard the cave and its contents with our life. This I promise."

India, with tears in her eyes, could only nod her gratitude.

Meli awoke suddenly from the dream and pulled the covers closer. She knew she was in her room, but felt disoriented—*was it present day or another century? Was she alone?*

Pulling the chain on the small lamp beside her bed, she rubbed her face and surveyed the room in the soft light. She then pulled out her writing book to do what Berthe had suggested. She would write down everything she had remembered.

Still a little confused, she tried to recall every detail and as she stared off towards her dresser, she remembered the box of Sophie's that Helene had given her to put away. She had forgotten all about it and was suddenly curious as to what it contained.

Taking it to her bed, she climbed back under the covers and opened the box.

Several loose pictures lay inside. Picking them up, she looked at each one individually, curious as to what she found. She smiled. The very first one was of four teenage girls on the beach. Clad in bathing suits, they lifted their legs in unison, each holding the next girl's leg up while the other hand was on the girl in front's shoulder. Meli looked closer realizing that Sophie was the leader, her free arm waving to the photographer, her head tossed back, laughing to the sky. That laugh. Full, throaty, fearless as to who heard her or not and she smiled.

Laying the picture of Sophie aside, she found a small velvet pouch secured at the top with a piece of string. Loosening the strings to see what was inside, she tipped it over into her palm and gave a little gasp.

In her hand lay a long silken cord with an intricate wooden amulet of a hand-carved dove flying over some distant ruins. Exactly the same amulet she saw in her dream and exactly the same design carved into the box.

Placing it over her head, she knew that its purpose was to keep her safe. *But from what?* She was also certain of one more thing. These weren't dreams, they were memories.

CHAPTER EIGHTEEN

THE NEXT MORNING, MELI DUTIFULLY WALKED WITH NICOLE TO Berthe's home in the village. She had brought her bike so that she could then bicycle back in order to do her chores. Nicole was dressed in an old skirt of Sophie's that they had found and a blue sweater that complimented her eyes. Meli felt even more dingy than yesterday in her overalls, but she had chores to do.

Nicole seemed less combative today in her demeanor. "What was he asking about yesterday?"

"He wanted information about the Cathars."

"And who exactly are the Cathars?"

"Around here, we call them les bonnehommes or les bonnefemmes—the good-men and good-women. They lived all over this region in the 1300's. Sophie once told me when I was little that they even lived on our land."

"Why would he want to know about them?"

Meli shrugged. "I don't know, maybe they are looking for the treasure."

"What treasure?"

"A long time ago the Catholic Church hunted them all down. Many of them escaped to Montségur and the night before the stronghold was breeched, four people escaped with the treasure and hid it somewhere and to this day it's never been found. Everyone around here knows this story."

"What kind of treasure?"

"I don't know, maybe gold, silver and jewels I guess, but some people think it was also the Holy Grail."

"Seriously? What happened to them?"

"They were all burned at the stake."

"Hmm, sounds like a fairy tale to me."

Meli placed her palm on the amulet hidden beneath her overall bib. It tingled.

"Hmmm maybe, but some people still believe it."

When they arrived, Berthe was already sitting on a chair by her front door, propped up with her walking stick, smoking her pipe. The worry lines on her already furrowed brow registered that she was anxious about something.

"Ah Meli, I'm so glad that you're here. Can you give Nicole another hand today?"

Meli's face brightened as she readily agreed, perhaps she thought a little too quickly, but hopefully neither Nicole nor Berthe noticed.

"Mme Dupuis had a difficult time yesterday and she'll need some help. Nicole, here's the key. Meli you may want to bicycle back home first and let your grandmother know what's going on. Make sure you tell her that I appreciate her letting you help out."

She couldn't peddle back fast enough.

Meli found both Mamina and Helene in the garden pulling up cabbages and carrots to store for the winter. As she explained the situation, Isabel wiped her cheek with the side of her palm leaving a dirt mark, then took a deep breath. She wasn't happy about the decision but admitted in the end that she and Helene could cover everything needed to be done. Tomorrow though, the garlic bulbs would need to be planted.

Meli readily agreed and raced back to the house. She was about to grab her bike and go straight back when she decided to quickly change from her dungarees into a skirt and sweater, telling herself that it had nothing to do with the young German officer. As she switched into the sweater, the amulet was no longer completely hidden in the bib of her overalls and she debated whether or not to take it off.

She had a feeling that she should keep it safe in her room, but in a rare moment of defiance, she kept it on and peddled as fast as she could back to the village.

Arriving back at the library, she was surprised and admittedly a little excited to see a large black Mercedes parked outside.

Two old veterans warily eyed the car from the comfort of their bench and nodded dourly to Meli. Giving them a quick smile back, she narrowly missed running into three little boys daring each other to touch the fender. Leaning her bike on the side of the building, she smoothed down her skirt and looked around, well aware that behind every lace curtain would be a pair of watchful eyes.

As she entered, she could see Nicole was already in conversation with the young officer and his Commander. Private Richter looked up and smiled, making her heart flutter. His superior Officer seemed to be listening patiently to Nicole but as he turned his head to watch Meli walk towards them, his eyes were suddenly riveted to her necklace. His blue eyes darkened his scar became more pronounced.

"Excuse me, but where did you get that?"

Meli blushed and tugged at her earlobe at having brought attention to herself, then stumbled out a reply. "It's a family heirloom."

"How interesting. And do you know the history of this heirloom?"

"No, not really, it was my sister's."

"And who is your sister?"

"Sophie Durand. She died in a car accident a few years ago."

At the mention of Sophie's name, his posture stiffened, and his eyes narrowed. Then, hesitating for only a moment, he regained his composure and spoke very softly.

"My family was in antiques and that looks like an interesting piece. May I?" As he reached out to touch it, Meli shivered, then cringed and backed away.

Tucking the amulet under her sweater, she stammered. "I'm...I'm sure it's nothing, Monsieur." There was a darkness about this man that made her wary.

His eyes held her gaze, and then suddenly he was smiling like a Cheshire cat. "I'm sure you're right."

Speaking to his assistant, he suggested that they do their research in the library for the day then turned on his heel and walked towards an old table with several chairs placed around. "I think this will do quite nicely, don't you, Private Richter?"

The younger Officer looked a little awkward but readily agreed. Placing his briefcase on the table, he began to take out several books to review. Nicole, who had followed them there, took a look at the cover of the top book and gave a little squeal.

"Oh! Victor Schreiber ...I know him. Well, I don't know him, but I met him at one of my mother's parties. He was a friend of Sophie's, I think. She said he was an author."

The Commander looked at Nicole, held his index finger to his lips, and then looked back to Richter. "I suddenly realize that I need to go back to headquarters to take care of some urgent business, but I think it would be very helpful if my assistant could stay here in this charming village to continue the research perhaps in the spring. Wouldn't you agree, Richter?"

"Yes, sir. Whatever you need me to do, sir."

Rubbing his hands together, he spoke to them both, but

looked directly at Nicole. "Would either of you young ladies know of a room that he could rent?"

Nicole didn't even hesitate. "I do." And then turned to Meli as if to establish her upper hand. "Berthe has an empty room, doesn't she, Meli?"

Lieutenant Wolfgang Koch smiled and stroked the scar on his face. "This will work out very nicely for all of us, I'm sure."

CHAPTER NINETEEN

ISABEL WAS IN THE KITCHEN SCRUBBING FRESHLY DUG POTATOES IN the sink while Helene and Berthe sat at the table chopping carrots and shelling peas for their dinner. From the snippets that she heard as she walked in, they were discussing the Kowalski family. But the conversation abruptly stopped when both girls came through the door.

"What's happening with the Kowalskis?" Meli asked.

Berthe turned to look at Helene and lowered her eyes. "Nothing *as yet*."

"Are they in trouble?"

"We don't know," Isabel replied still peeling away.

"But why? Why would they even care about them?"

Isabel whipped around and snapped, "Good Lord, Meli, because they're Jewish." And in that moment, her eyes caught sight of the amulet. Her face turned pale, contorted and in a thin raspy voice she pointed towards Meli. "Where did you get that?"

Meli's hand immediately grasped the necklace. "It was in a box of Sophie's things that Helene brought. I liked it so I put it on." She looked over to Helene for support.

Helene, anxious to appease Isabel, added. "I'm sorry, I gave it to Meli to tuck away somewhere safe. I didn't want to upset you. I actually had no idea what was inside."

Isabel's eyes flickered to Helene in disbelief. *You didn't know what was inside…and you gave it to Meli?*

Turning back to her granddaughter, she held out her hand. "Take it off, Meli, take it off now and give it to me."

Shocked and hurt at how angry Mamina appeared, she just stood there, hot salty tears threatening to flow any second. "Why?"

"You have no idea what that is."

Pulling the cord off around her head, she could feel her face redden in frustration as she placed it in the palm of her grand-mother's hand.

Isabel, appeased that it was in her possession, was transfixed as she gently stroked the intricate carving. To no one in particular she whispered, "I thought that it was lost forever."

Nicole cleared her throat and was anxious to change the subject.

"Berthe, a very respectable young German officer is looking for a room to rent to continue his studies in the spring and we suggested that you may be interested in renting out your room."

Berthe's eyes widened in amazement. "To a German? Are you crazy? Why would you do that?"

Nicole was flustered but undeterred and carried on. "He came into the library today, well yesterday really, but he came back today with his Superior Officer, who I have to admit is a scary-looking man, but the younger one, the one who needs a room seemed very nice. Didn't he Meli? His Superior, Lieutenant somebody, anyway, his family deals in antiques and seemed inter-ested in Meli's amulet—said it could be quite old. Oh! And mama, do you remember M. Schreiber, that writer friend of Sophie's? He's reading his books."

At the mention of the name Schreiber, both Berthe and

Isabel visibly paled. It was Isabel who spoke. "What exactly are these two German officers researching?"

"Just local history. Why?"

"They're researching the Cathars," added Meli.

Isabel hands were shaking as she placed the amulet in her apron pocket. "No reason…. Meli, take over peeling the potatoes. I need some fresh air."

Turning to Berthe, she eyed the doorway for her to follow.

Once outside, Berthe put her hand on Isabel's shoulder. "It's time, Isabel. This is no coincidence and you and I both know who he is."

Isabel shook her head in frustration. "She's still a child, Berthe. Give me a few minutes. I'm fine. I just need to think."

"Why were you so upset with Meli?"

"Because I… Because I thought Sophie was wearing it when she died."

CHAPTER TWENTY

THE WINTER CAME AND WENT, AND LIFE WENT ON, LESS efficiently, less comfortably, but it went on nonetheless. They had lived out the winter on cabbage, carrots and rabbit stew. The preserves that they had put by in the fall were almost gone and would need to be replenished.

The young German officer had returned with his Commander to Germany instead to remaining in their village which relieved both Berthe and Isabel.

As more Parisians left the city for the provinces, where there was more food and fewer Germans, supplies grew even more scarce and food prices escalated. People came up on the train from Beziers and got off at the Saint-Sauveur station, trading soap and oil for eggs, butter and potatoes. The Parisians talked very little of the political situation—told them nothing. They knew everyone in the Zone Libre were communists.

Isabel said that the shortage of food was the only thing they could count on. After food it was gas, clothes, shoes, all hard to find. It became necessary to either do without or create something from nothing. Everyone shared resourceful tricks that they used or remembered from the Great War and applied them again.

From the boxes of clothes that Berthe had gone through, Nicole and Helene made do with old coats and boots that Nicole had to stuff with newspapers in the toes in order to fit. She wasn't happy about it, but when the snow fell, she conceded that they kept her feet warm. Berthe braved the weather when she could and brought news from the village, which one of the old ones got sick, who needed help, who died, who recovered.

Anti-Semitic decrees were now being posted in town warning about Jews and soon after a "*Statut des Juifs*" ("Jewish Statute"), was passed that excluded Jews from public life, and forced their dismissal from positions in the civil service and the military. Soon after they were barred from occupations in industry, commerce, medicine, law, and teaching.

Meli had grown an inch and she had finally started to fill out. Throughout the winter, her 'dreams' seemed to fade away to normal. She had already exhausted the library's section on Catharism and had started reading Parcival for good measure. She had even managed to get Mamina to listen to the BBC Londres a few times.

Helene found her greater purpose in unravelling old sweaters and learning to knit under Berthe's watchful eye. Nicole was ever so slightly less obnoxious (at least in Meli's opinion) and even Mamina appeared to soften.

The relationship between Helene and Nicole seemed to be less volatile as well. There were less fights and if there were, it was due to Nicole being unhappy, being bored, being angry or just wanting butter.

But what was most exciting for Meli, was that she had started to write a story. Well, at least had the inspiration to start a story.

Now that she was sixteen, she was privy to more adult gossip and with an all-female household there was plenty to go around.

They couldn't very well shoo her away when Nicole was considered old enough to listen and listen, she did.

One rainy afternoon they sat at the table and after Isabel had wiped clean the old crockery mugs and poured the wartime brew into their cups, they settled in for Berthe's latest news from her cousin's daughter, Francis' daughter, (this was the only way she ever described her.) The bottom line though, was that she was forever getting herself into trouble. To Meli, the twists and turns in the story were almost as good as a movie script. Because Helene and Nicole had never heard of Francis or Celine, Berthe started from the beginning.

"It's just that it was such a bad business from the start." Berthe sat in silence for a moment as she gathered her thoughts.

"His name was David, a rogue through and through if you ask me and wise enough to know not to toy with the affections of a young girl."

She then turned to both Nicole and Meli and raised her eyebrows. "But he was also a man with all the natural needs and wants of young men his age if you catch my drift."

"He was travelling the country as I recall— 'finding himself' as he called it and I suppose to be fair, was quite taken with Francis. She was quite the beauty at sixteen. One thing led to another and she found herself pregnant. It should come to no surprise that he didn't bother to stick around.

"She was lucky then that another young man pining after her was more than willing to save her reputation and marry her. There was talk of course but no one could prove anything. Soon enough little Cecile was born and in truth there was no prouder father than Pierre. He loved her from the moment he laid eyes on her. She was the light of his life and there was nothing that he wouldn't do for his little girl.

"All was well for about eight years. Francis settled into married life until the summer of '32 when he, 'the rogue', returned and manipulated his way back into her heart.

"I don't know what she was thinking back then. Perhaps she was bored, who knows? They say no one forgets their first love and I can only think that that's what made her want to be with him, but the facts are that she started seeing him on the sly. He knew that Cecile was his daughter and wanted to see her, which she apparently allowed him to do on several occasions. Of course, these situations never remain a secret for long and soon after, tongues were wagging. That's when Pierre got wind of it.

"From what we could piece together, Pierre had gone home early and had found the two of them together. Cecile was at her grandmother's house at the time, thank goodness. The two men fought, and Pierre threatened him with a knife. During this time David, the rogue who started all this in the first place, was fatally wounded and Pierre, still in a rage threw Francis into the car.

"Witnesses told the police later that they had seen him driving erratically before they went over the bridge, drowning them both. Whether they were fighting, or he did this on purpose we will never know."

Berthe then leaned forward. "But this is not the end of the story. Here's the latest! Little Cecile is now sixteen years old and has just run away with a man twice her age! He left his wife and children for her. Can you imagine?!"

Isabel tut-tutted her opinion and wasted no time at all weighing in on Pétain's code of ethics. More discipline was needed when Celine was a child.

All Meli heard was the plot for a story.

In the meantime, spring was just a promise away.

CHAPTER TWENTY-ONE

WOLFGANG BUTTONED UP HIS COAT AND QUICKLY WALKED TO the intersection of Boulevard Raspail and rue de Sèvres, adjacent to the Métro station, in the area of the 6th arrondissement.

He was to meet Himmler for dinner at the Lutetia Hotel, named for the pre-Roman town that existed there before Paris and one of the best-known hotels on the Left Bank. Built in 1910 in the Art Nouveau style, it had been requisitioned by the counterespionage and used to house, feed, and entertain the officers in command of the occupation.

The Lutetia was known as the place where the anonymous could be found alongside the famous. A place of intellect; a place of experiment, gifted for creating and developing ideas.

Tonight, he would give him a review as to what he had accomplished to date and what his next steps would be. Hopefully, he would be pleased.

Crisp-collared waiters glided elegantly around with champagne on their trays to a crowded room of uniformed officers and their pretty French guests.

Himmler was already seated, so he was escorted to the table by the maître d'.

Facing his superior, he extended his right arm in the air, clicked his heels and snapped, "Heil Hitler."

Himmler acknowledged his gesture of obedience and nodded for him to take the seat that was now being pulled out for him. The maître d' gave them both a menu and added, "Gentlemen, your waiter will be with you in a minute."

Almost magically, the waiter arrived a few moments later. Standing beside the table, he gave a small bow in the older man's direction. "Would you gentlemen care for a drink?"

Barely acknowledging the man's presence, Himmler took off his glasses and wiped them clean with a handkerchief, before asking the waiter to bring a bottle of his best Merlot.

"Certainly, sir. I'll be back with your wine and take your food order."

While they both consulted their menu, his superior looked over to Wolfgang.

"Well, Koch. I hope that you have some good news for me?"

"I believe that you will find it very interesting, sir."

"Good, good. I am looking forward to our conversation in more detail after dinner. How is the young man working out? What's his name again?"

With a deadpan face, Koch replied, "Tomas Richter, sir."

"Ah, yes. I promised that you would keep him out of trouble. I hope that that continues to be the case?"

"Certainly, sir. His ahh…intellectual talents are certainly being put to good use."

"Good. As I understand it, he's quite the academic."

The waiter promptly returned with a crisp white towel over his arm and a bottle of Merlot. Bowing before showing the label to Himmler, he poured a small amount into his wine glass.

Wolfgang was impressed as Himmler went through the ritual of swirling his glass, then raising it to eyesight level to appreciate the appearance of the wine, then bringing it to his nose to enjoy its aroma. Finally, he drank a small sip to taste its flavour. "Ahh, blood-red, my favourite colour."

Once he nodded his approval, the waiter poured the ruby liquid into Wolfgang's glass and stepped back.

"Are you ready to order, gentlemen?"

"What do you recommend this evening? The veal or the duck?"

"The duck, sir, seems to be the most popular and receiving excellent reviews."

"That will do."

Turning his head to the Lieutenant, he asked. "And you, sir?"

"I will have the duck as well."

After the waiter had left, Himmler picked up his wine glass for a toast, then nodded to Koch. "To the successful conclusion of our quest."

As he fussed with his napkin, he carried on. "The French cuisine here is superb but I find that the French themselves are eating far too well in the more, shall we say, luxurious restaurants. I am of the opinion that this excellent cuisine should be reserved exclusively for us. Their restaurants are full of black-market traffickers filling their pockets from overcharging Germans. It's ridiculous! Except for the collaborators and black marketeers, everyone else in Paris is poor."

The waiter briefly returned with a small basket of bread and as Koch passed the basket to him, Himmler continued. "So, what have you learned, Koch? Anything useful?"

"Actually, sir, we have learned quite a bit and I am confident that what you seek is within our grasp."

Himmler leaned forward and widened his eyes. "Really?"

"Yes, and the young officer you sent me was instrumental. It would seem that the acquaintance of M. Schreiber that was such a fly in your ointment so to say, has a younger sister who happened to be wearing a very interesting amulet that I strongly suspect dates back to the Cathars. I further suspect that this family has a very long lineage dating back to Montségur and the treasure."

"Do you think they know where it is?"

"I suspect more than that, sir. I suspect they may be the actual guardians."

"And how do you propose to find out where it is and secure it for the Reich?"

"I still need to firm up my plans but have a feeling that Tomas may be able to play a very key role in our quest."

Himmler leaned back and rubbed his chin. "Well done, Koch. We still need to manage this in a timely manner though. The war is going well, so I see no reason why we can't begin early spring."

"Glad to hear it, sir. I heard there are thousands of French joining the Forces Françaises Libres. Is this creating a problem for the Reich?"

Himmler lit a cigarette and chuckled. "Not at all. We've sent droves of Germans to enlist in the Legion. As a matter of fact, around 80% of the French Foreign Legion is German officers, all Nazis who act as spies, collecting lists of Jewish or Freemason Legionnaires. They've started to figure it out, but so far, we've weeded out about 2,000 undesirables, so it's been worth it.

"We're stepping up our Obligatory Work Service programs. We've demanded that France provide 250 thousand volunteers and if that doesn't work, we'll impose forced recruitment of both men and women. As for the undesirables, we've rounded up thousands of non-French Jews already in Paris. So many in fact, that I'll need to implement a more final solution. But I digress.

"You're confident, Koch, that you're on the right trail?"

"Yes, absolutely, sir."

"Excellent. On that note, I have a number of pressing things to take care of. I'll look forward to your reports, Lieutenant."

CHAPTER TWENTY-TWO

GASTON, A GRIZZLED OLD FARMER, HELPED BERTHE ONTO HIS wagon where they did not say a word for the first half hour.

Finally breaking the silence, he asked her if it was true that she spoke some English. When she replied, "Oui, yes a little." He nodded a "Bon" lit a Gitanes and quickly surveyed the country-side. "We're going to take the back roads for a while.

"This is your first time so don't be afraid, but I would rather not be stopped by the Germans. If we are stopped for any reason, you must simply say that you are a mid-wife checking on my pregnant daughter-in-law. You understand?"

"Yes, but isn't that the truth?"

He hesitated a moment, took a long drag from his cigarette, looked in the other direction and replied, "Bien sûr, of course."

Terrified that they would come across the boche, Berthe constantly scanned the fields and roads as they drove on. The morning wore on and the view of the countryside lulled her into a false sense of security. Eventually she even found some small pleasure in seeing small herds of cows and sheep and felt relieved. In such a landscape, the Germans had surely missed this area. She felt serene and untouched by the ugliness of war.

"Are we safe now?"

Gaston whipped around with a scowl and growled out a reply. "Are we safe? We will never be safe as long as France is occupied. France has suffered one of the greatest defeats in her history. Vichy is crowded beyond capacity full of well-to-do refugees from occupied France, immaculately accoutered French officers and political aspirants. They crowd the cafes, hotels and boulevards enjoying the calm and the pleasures to be had there."

It was then that they saw a German convoy rise up before them over a distant hill.

Sitting up a little straighter, Gaston shifted in his seat and looked towards Berthe's uncovered head. Get your scarf on and cover up. Look straight ahead and do not look at anyone in the eye.

Ahead, a German military convoy stopped on the road and facing them was a tall, brutal looking SS officer, with shiny boots and an eye patch over his left eye. Holding up his arm, he bellowed, "Halt!"

They halted and in the eerily quiet landscape, no one said a word. Berthe's heart pounded as each of the soldiers stood there looking them over. Then after what seemed to be an eternity, a soldier came up the hill from around a curve in the road and said something to the SS Giant. He looked straight at Berthe and she shivered.

After a full minute, he saluted and then waved them by. As they came around the curve, they understood what had taken place. A staff car had run off the road and was being towed back on by a cable which was stretched across the road.

Gaston lit another cigarette and for that brief moment, Berthe could see the tremor in his hand. Looking down at her own shaking hands, she clasped them together and took a deep breath.

Their destination was a secluded farmhouse tucked into the surrounding hills where Gaston's daughter-in-law was in full labour and in considerable pain. Fortunately, Gaston's wife Carole had recognized the signs of a breech and had sent her husband to fetch Berthe. But that wasn't the entire reason she was there. The situation had simply moved up their timeline.

———

Berthe was greeted by Carole at the door and followed her into a back bedroom where a panting, terrified young woman lay exhausted on the bed. Berthe worked with Carole as her assistant and finally in the wee hours of the morning a healthy baby boy was born, but not without significant tearing to the mother. It had been a long night.

Sitting at the kitchen table, Berthe savoured a cup of tea as Gaston walked in and sat down at the table beside his wife.

"How's Solange?" She smiled at him tenderly, stroked a curl from his forehead and nodded that she was fine.

"And the baby?"

"He's doing just fine. You're a grandfather now, Gaston."

Kissing the top of her head, he smiled. "Any visitors today?" For a brief moment she quickly looked in Berthe's direction before shaking her head no.

Gaston finished his, tea then stood up looking at Berthe. "I'll head to the barn to tend to the goats, then I'll take you back home. Everything is ready so it's best we travel now."

Before he left, he stopped at the door and lit up a cigarette. "It's not too late to say no."

Berthe looked up and nodded an affirmation that she understood, but her demeanor was resolute. She couldn't sit back and do nothing. *Everyone's life would be on the line.*

Once they arrived back at Berthe's home, Gaston pulled the cart forward so that the back end faced the side of her house and the forested area. The clouds covered the moon, making it almost impossible for anyone to see a young man's figure slide out from the false bottom on the cart and slip into her back door.

Gaston kept his head down and quietly whispered to Berthe. "You'll be contacted in a few days. Just keep him hidden and all will be well."

A minute later he was gone. The only sign that he had been there was the clop, clop, clop of his horse's hooves as he headed back home. Berthe looked on as he headed off—as a mid-wife it wasn't at all unusual for her to be summoned in the middle of the night. Tonight would be no different except for one thing.

Inside, Berthe directed her guest to the upstairs room that had been cleared and turned on a small lamp.

Dressed in old dungarees and a stained shirt, he looked like any other young Frenchman. She noted that he was of medium height and build which would make it much easier to find clothes to fit him. His dark brown hair needed a wash and although he appeared calm, he couldn't hide the fear in his eyes.

"Welcome to my home. You will be safe here."

The young man turned to look at her in surprise and in a strong Bristol accent he whispered. "You speak English?"

Berthe smiled. "Only a little. What is your name?"

"Jim, but me mum and sister Shirley calls me Jimmie. I don't mind either way, though. Thank you for your kindness, Ma'am."

"You are welcome, but I think, Jim, you will not be here that long. They will have you back home in no time. For now though, this is where you will stay. It's not much, but it's dry."

She nodded to the window's shutters that were closed. "It faces to the back but keep them shut. You understand?" He smiled and nodded yes.

Let me show you where to hide in case anyone comes. Leading him down to the kitchen, she opened a door that led to a small storage area. They both looked around the room where one wall had old wooden shelves with a sack of flour. Herbs, onions and garlic were hanging from the wooden ceiling along with balls of cheese in cheese cloth. A large bin had been placed against the far wall where the shelving made a natural barrier. Lifting the lid exposed an empty cavity where there was just enough space for a medium-sized adult to crouch.

"Now you sleep."

Shutting her bedroom room door behind her, Berthe felt anxious but also a little excited. She was doing something to help, but this was not a secret she could share with anyone.

CHAPTER TWENTY-THREE

MAURICE CHEVALIER CROONED AWAY IN THE BACKGROUND TO 'ÇA sent si bon la France' while the household of women quietly knitted socks by the warmth of a fire.

Frustrated with her lack of talent for knitting, Helene released a loud grumble and began to unravel her last two rows. She was seriously considering just giving up on her attempt on a scarf. She was never really good at this stuff and frankly when the war ended, she wouldn't care less if she ever saw a pair of knitting needles again.

Isabel's and Meli's nightly ritual of knitting away in the sitting room, fireplace blazing while listening to Radio Paris and the occasional BBC Londres, seemed to be an easy way for her and Nicole to help out. However, she didn't have the skills and Nicole lacked the inclination. The most her daughter would contribute was unravelling some old sweaters and vests that Isabel had found in the cupboards.

Nicole, who was sitting in the corner chair, simply rolled her eyes at her mother's audible frustration. "I don't know why you even bother." As if in reaction to her anger, she crossed her eyebrows, then clutched her chest and coughed.

Panicked, Helene sat up straight and watched in fear as her daughter finally stopped hacking and relaxed.

"You should sit closer to the fire." Looking over to Isabel for support, she also suggested that an extra blanket might help, but Nicole just complained even more.

"I'm already too hot as it is."

Flustered, Helene said to no one in particular. "She's always been delicate." She was worried though about a cough that Nicole had recently developed and dutifully picked up the scarf. Nicole getting sick was the last thing she needed. Who knew what doctors were like around here? Did they even have one?

Despite what her husband Hans had said, Nicole had always been a delicate child. So sensitive to colds that the first sign of a sneeze, she had routinely called the doctor just to ease her mind that it was nothing serious. Hans would shake his head and tell her she was over-reacting, but she didn't care—she called anyway. All this walking back and forth to the village was ridiculous, especially in this weather. It was fine for someone like Meli who had been raised in this area, but certainly not for her daughter.

As the radio announcer rattled off the latest news, she looked over at Meli who gave her a quick smile.

"Need any help?"

"No, thank you, I've got it now." She looked so much like her mother. However, did Isabel think that she could keep it a secret? If she could see it, then surely everyone in the village knew.

Nicole coughed again, raspy and deep from her chest. Helene again looked at her daughter, her eyebrows creased together in worry. She was far too thin. It was clear that she needed more nourishment, but Isabel was stingy with the portions. Surely, she could give Nicole a little extra before the cough turned even worse.

"I don't think Nicole should be going anywhere this week until her cough clears up. Wouldn't you agree, Isabel?"

Isabel stopped knitting and rested her hands mid-stitch, before slowly looking up at Nicole. Nodding in agreement, she said, "You may be right. Perhaps Helene, you could help Meli with her chores so that she could go instead?"

Helene gave a small jolt. She hadn't thought of that. Taking a quick look at her dry, cracking hands and her short uneven fingernails, she only hoped that it had nothing to do with animals.

Just then the announcer began to broadcast his daily news report and Isabel turned to Meli. "Turn that up."

"That was Maurice Chevalier with his latest song, 'Ça sent si bon la France'—It feels so good France'. M. Chevalier has recently appeared in a successful revue in the Casino de Paris, *Bonjour Paris*, so you can see that nothing has changed under the occupation. Paris is still Paris.

"And now for the news. Here is the latest on the STO Obligatory Work Service. Throughout German occupied Europe, young men have been called up to participate in the war effort. The German powers require France to provide volunteers before the end of July. Both men and women are called to participate with a target of 250 thousand. Ages include men from 18 -50 and single women from 21-35. This has now become French Law to all French citizens where concerned and includes 'Zone Libre.'

"A reminder to all that that travail, famille, patrie, work, family, fatherland is what we all should be striving for to ensure that our great nation stays strong.

"And now I'd like to play for you a great friend of Maurice Chevalier and our own little songbird who is taking Paris by storm, Édith Piaf."

Helene looked over to Nicole who connected with their eyes. "Thank God, you are only 18."

Nicole simply shrugged and shushed the cat away from the

unravelling wool. "I told you we could have stayed in Paris. Even the announcer says that everything is back to normal."

"But that's not what I'm hearing in the streets, Nicole," replied her mother. "You know yourself food was scarce even before we left. Had it not been for Isabel helping us, it would have been worse."

Meli seemed to perk up with that statement and she looked questioningly over towards Mamina, who simply kept her head down and carried on knitting.

Nicole began to cough again and after several moments, Isabel snapped out a decision. "Right, so Meli, you go to the library tomorrow, Helene can take over your chores and Nicole, we'll find you something quiet to do indoors. Perhaps Meli, you could also stop off at Berthe's and get some of that cough syrup she makes."

CHAPTER TWENTY-FOUR

Tomas Heinrich Richter had been born into a wealthy family from Baden-Baden in southwestern Germany's Black Forest, near the border with France. As an only child and sole heir to the family fortune, it was not surprising that some of that wealth was prudently used to ensure that he did not see active duty. Not that he minded. He considered himself to be more an academic and the occasional poet rather than a killer. It was books he loved, the smell of them, the history of them, the protection of them, the knowledge they shared, the secrets they imparted.

He was, therefore, delighted to oblige Herr Koch by researching whatever it was he wanted. Especially if it involved two pretty French girls.

He and his family had spent many summers in France when he was younger and had always loved the endless colours of the provincial skies. He had heard of the Cathars before and knew something of their beliefs, but after reading Victor Schreiber's books he was completely fascinated by the religious sect and the secrets they purportedly protected. Like Schreiber, he felt that he understood these Cathars and their pacifist beliefs.

It was obvious that Koch didn't like him and thought even less of him for his privileged background. His reputation for cruelty preceded him, so he was well aware how dangerous he was, but he was here to do his duty, not bring shame on his family. That was exactly what he would do.

Taking a draw from his cigarette, he looked around at what appeared to be a deserted village street. But he knew better. Behind every lace curtain would be an old crone, dressed all in black, casually smoking a pipe, watching his every move. What would they see? A tall and slender young man of twenty or just a German, the enemy smoking a cigarette in the street.

He thought of the girls inside. What did they see? He had never been a lady's man like his friend Rolph at University. While Rolph was handsome and funny, he was shy, awkward and unsure of the female sex. He never knew what they wanted from him. In school, it had been far easier to let Rolph take the lead and entertain while he preferred to slink off to read a book. Pushing back his glasses, he looked up at the door, threw away his cigarette stub and walked into the library.

As he stepped inside, he almost bumped into the younger of the two girls. Dressed in a skirt and blouse, she struggled with an armload of books, bracing them with her chin to keep them from slipping. Her eyes widened with panic until he smiled and turned his head sideways to read off the titles on their spines. "Babar the Elephant, Babar the King, Gone with the Wind, a dictionary, and several books on Cathars and reincarnation. Impressive reading, Mademoiselle. Are these your personal choices?"

She smiled back at him, blushing so much that he offered to take the pile from her and placed them on a nearby table.

Nodding her head, she thanked him, then added, "I'll be right back," before taking the children's books over to two little girls who sat swinging their legs at a far table.

Their eyes were big as they watched him, leading him to believe that perhaps he was the first German officer that they had ever seen. Nodding his cap to Meli, he walked over to their table and pulled out two pieces of chocolate and handed them each a piece. There's nothing like chocolate, he thought, to put a smile on a child's face. Leaving them giggling, he turned back to Meli.

"I'm back if you don't mind, to use your library services. I remember where the books are, but I see that maybe you've beat me to some of them.

"I didn't have the opportunity to properly introduce myself before to you. My name is Private Tomas Richter, and I am sorry miss, but I have forgotten yours."

In a jumble of words, she replied, "It's Meli, sir, well, Melisende really, but everyone calls me Meli. You can call me whichever one you want."

"Meli it is then. May I sit over there? I'll try not to disturb you. Last time I was here there was another girl as well. She's not here today?"

Meli's face looked crestfallen, but she politely replied that Nicole was sick and wouldn't be there.

He spent most of his morning sitting facing Meli as she helped out the girls and the occasional villager who came in for something to read. He found himself thinking about her. She was pretty in her own way and obviously smart. He especially liked that she appeared to be quiet like he was. Nicole was pretty and more his age, but she was like a shiny city girl and certainly not someone who liked history. There was a quietness about this girl that drew her near to him and he wondered what she thought of him. Was he the enemy who had marched into their country and took what they wanted?

Sliding out from the table, he walked over to the front to where Meli sat absorbed in a book of her own. With a little cough, he caught her attention and she blushed again. "Sorry, sir, I was lost in my own research."

He smiled and liked that she smiled back. "And may I ask, Meli, what you are researching?"

"I'm reading about reincarnation."

"Really? How interesting. Do you know that the Cathars that I am researching believed in reincarnation? It's actually a very interesting subject."

"Do you think so?"

"Absolutely. The Cathars called themselves the friends of God and claimed to be the living inheritors of the true Christian heritage that had continued in secret. Like the original Christians, the Cathars were vegetarians and believed in reincarnation. They believed that one would be repeatedly reincarnated until one commits to the self-denial of the material world. Because of this belief, the Cathars saw women as equal and very capable of being spiritual leaders. I have to say, I agree with them.

"The Cathars were respected for their goodness, even by their opponents. The Catholic Bernard of Clairveaux said: 'If you interrogate them, no one could be more Christian. What they speak they prove by deeds. As for the morals of the heretics, they cheat no one, they oppress no one, they strike no one.' Despite this, the infamous Inquisition was set up by the Catholic Church specifically to eradicate them all, which it did with ferocious enthusiasm, burning alive men, women and children."

"And do you think that there are still Cathars in this day?"

"I think, Miss, that if there were, they would be wise to keep it a secret."

"Why?"

"I think that I would like to believe that the Cathar spirit lives on and the belief that people could live in peace. But right now that doesn't seem to be the case and what I've just told you could get me into serious trouble. So Meli of 'Montferrier', I must swear you to secrecy. You hold the safety of my future in your hands. For now, though, I wonder if you have any books on the caves around here? For instance, Lombrive?"

At the mention of Lombrive, Meli's face dropped and she felt a shiver go through her spine. Lombrive was where the India in her dream had headed to.

"We do, but may I ask why Lombrive?"

Tomas smiled. "You are a curious girl, aren't you? Because some historians believe that the Lombrive Cave was the last refuge of the Cathars after the fall of their strongholds. It is rumoured that the very last members of this religion were killed in 1328 inside the 'Cathedral', the gigantic chamber inside the cave."

"But why are you searching for them?"

Tomas pursed his lips and looked her directly in the eyes. "To be honest with you, Meli, I don't know why I am telling you this, but I don't know why. Because I am being told to, I guess. Because I want to survive the war and continue my studies, to see my family again, to have things return to normal. I am sure you understand."

Meli nodded in agreement.

He looked down at his feet and looked back at her. "There's something about you, Meli, that makes me want to be your friend. Is that possible, even though I am a German?"

Meli simply blushed, smiled, and then nodded her head. "I'd like that."

"Maybe one day we could go to Lombrive together? It would be an adventure, no?"

Meli was too ashamed to say that she wouldn't be allowed to, so the best she could answer was, "Sure, I'd like that." *But why Lombrive? Was it a coincidence that India was there? That he wanted to go there?*

At the end of the day as she locked up, she tried to calm down, but the excitement of Tomas' invitation was too much to keep in. So much so, that she almost forgot to stop in at Berthe's for the syrup.

As she arrived at the doorstep, she usually gave a quick knock and walked in, but for some unusual reason her door was locked. She could see Berthe take a quick peek out through the curtains first, then answered the door. She seemed a little on edge, but still invited Meli in and quickly got the syrup from the back room. "I'm sure your Mamina will want you straight home so I'll let you get on your way."

A little confused at Berthe's reaction to her visit, she was so excited with Tomas that she savoured the walk home, reliving every moment of the day, forgetting all about Berthe.

CHAPTER TWENTY-FIVE

THAT NIGHT, SHE TUMBLED RATHER THAN FELL, INTO A DEEP sleep. Reaching out with long slender fingers, it pulled her down and held her close, down into the abyss of dreams… Too weak to resist, she let herself plummet into the past.

Meli, when you are born different, you see the world through a different light from those around you. You shift constantly between the two worlds, never committing to one or the other, and are only a whisper away from the world of dreams as easy as walking through gauze into a clear day.

She could feel the chill in her bones and numbing cold of chilblained hands. She could hear the crunching sound of stiff, frost-bitten grasslands under her feet. She was her. They were one and the same and in that intertwining of threads, her story became Meli's.

After weeks of walking and crisscrossing the mountains on foot, they finally arrived at the 'lair of the giant', the entrance to the cave of Lombrive. A lush green carpet of foliage folded around the rocks and enveloped the opening like a thick protective blanket. The interior was deep and welcoming, large enough for hundreds more, should they too make their way here.

Lighting torches to guide their way, they began the slow and careful walk to the cathedral, the large cavern, deep into the cave's system. The moist slippery rocks formed tunnels adorned with curious stalagmites and long galleries as they went deeper and deeper into the cave. No one spoke, as if the passage itself was a sacred journey.

At long last they reached the cathedral, an immense chamber where they would wait out their days in safety or until Fournier found them.

Others had arrived before them and a small group of adults and children huddled together near a fire, cooking something fragrant and spicy in a large black cauldron, while others set up similar stations at the far end of the chamber. The yellow light of their torches flickered and danced along the rocky walls, creating long jagged shadows of people as they wandered around. How many years had this cave provided shelter she wondered?

The cavern held secrets in its womb and the echoes of the ghosts of others who had sheltered there were only a whisper away. A little girl of around ten years old stared at her as she walked by and she thought of Sophia. Would she ever see her daughter again?

A group of men entered the cavern with bundles of wood strapped to their backs, while a few others carried bushels of cabbage and turnips. Looking around in the semi-darkness, she wondered for a moment if she should have brought her daughter, but she knew that Fournier would be hunting her. Leaving her was the only way to keep her safe. The only way to lead him away from her home and the cave of secrets.

CHAPTER TWENTY-SIX

A BUNDLED UP, RUDDY-CHEEKED BERTHE, BURST THROUGH THE door earlier than usual, with white puffs of cold air escaping from around her scarf as she tried to catch her breath. Waving her hands at Isabel, she anxiously looked around to see if they were alone. Isabel, who had been warming her hands next to the woodstove, looked back with confusion. "Sit down, sit down, and catch your breath. What's wrong?"

Sitting down in a chair, she unraveled her scarf and she struggled to get the words out.

"Isabel…it's the Kowalskis…they've been taken away…all of them."

"Calm yourself, Berthe, you'll give yourself a heart attack. Here, let me help you with your things. I can put your mitts by the stove to get warm and I'll make us something warm to drink. As she helped Berthe off with her coat, she said, "They've been taken away where?"

Berthe creased her eyebrows and stared hard at her friend. "Isabel, do you not listen to the radio? They've been taken to one of the concentration camps."

"You mean those work camps? Phh. I hear they are eating better than we are. Besides, Pétain said that this is simply a way to regain our French identity."

Berthe looked at her friend, then pursed her lips. Her frustration was visible on her face. "Isabel, are you still listening to Radio Paris? I told you, this is all propaganda!"

"Shhh, be quiet or someone will hear you!"

"Someone like who, Isabel? You? I told you, if you want the truth, start listening to the BBC Londres."

"You know as well as I do it's illegal to listen to them. You'll get yourself in trouble by doing that. Where's your sense, Berthe? What if someone finds out?"

"Isabel, these work camps are nothing more than extermination camps."

Isabel shook her head and turned to face the window. "I don't want to hear this, it's not true. Pétain would never agree to this."

"It is true and pretending otherwise will not keep Meli safe. Pretending that your background is a myth will not keep her safe. You make me so angry Isabel! It is already happening in front of you and all you want to do is pretend that it will all just go away. I know you my friend and I know you feel the stirrings as much as I do."

"You're wrong, Berthe. I know nothing of the sort. Pétain says keep our head down and that's exactly what I will do. Sophie is dead because of that myth and I won't lose Meli because of it."

A few moments later, Meli slowly came downstairs looking concerned and gave them both a quizzical look. Without saying so, it was clear that she had heard their cross words.

"Everything okay?"

Isabel answered. "Everything's fine. The coffee is on the stove."

The frustration of the one and the anger of the other hung over the kitchen table like a heavy cloud as they drank their coffee in silence. It wasn't long before Nicole and Helene dragged themselves downstairs and while Nicole plopped herself down and complained of a headache, Helene poured themselves two cups of the dark liquid.

Berthe did not stay long, but then lately she had not been around as much. She brought more cough syrup for Nicole and welcomed some eggs in return. Isabel blamed the weather, but something niggled away that there was more to this than the cold. Berthe had lost weight, as they all had, and she wasn't her jovial self. She gave Isabel a hug when she left, but there was clearly a wound that needed healing between them.

Later that evening, as a soft moon illuminated the landscape, Isabel sat alone at the kitchen table and stared out the window as heavy snowflakes fell on the already silent diamond-crusted countryside. She couldn't sleep and deep down she knew Berthe was right. Lurking in the corner of her mind was the clinging fear that everything could once again stop. She had already lived through a time when there was no gas, heating, light or hot water, no soap, no shoes, no food. Now, once again, they had to cope with only what they had. A lack of fuel meant they had to return to long hours of farm labour done by hand. A lack of coal meant a reliance on the fireplace and her old wood cooker for a stove.

And it wasn't just her. The burden of everyday life fell on every woman's shoulders, concentrating what little energy they had in holding on, getting through *les années noires,* these black years. Their priority was simply survival.

Over the last few months, the growing demand by the Germans for French produce was causing acute shortages. Along with bread, sugar, butter and coffee, more and more essential goods like cheese, eggs, fruit, meat, chocolate, fresh fish and vegetables were added to the rationed list. Last week, four of Isabel's goats had been taken away by the authorities, leaving only two and only because they had been hidden away along with the five hens. Lord knows what they would do if they were found out.

She, along with everyone else, had been assigned *un bon de décharge*, a ration book of vouchers to be exchanged against the rationed commodity, and set according to the item's availability. It was no secret that France's needs were consistently set below those of Germany.

Isabel sighed. As much as she never thought it possible, it was normal now to see German trucks filled with German troops and German officers, administrators and officials. Why here? Why should they bother with us? Is Paris not enough for them?

Posters had begun to appear in the village, popping up overnight as if by magic, of a snowy-haired Pétain, brandishing a kind smile as the father and saviour of the French nation; reminding everyone of *Travail, Famille, Patrie*, stressing the value of hard work, motherhood, and service to the nation.

But there were other posters displayed as well. Others that demonized France's perceived enemies: the Jews, freemasons, as well as the British and the Americans. Perceived as thick as thieves with the 'verminous Jew' in undermining France, cartoon drawings exaggerated them as hook-nosed profiteers. Up until now, she had been lulled into thinking that their village was safe, but this was no longer true. Berthe's visit this morning had shattered that illusion and she needed to think about what all this meant.

She thought about the Kowalskis being loaded into a truck with others. How the last time she had been there, the youngest girl with her little body framed between a lace curtain, had pressed her face to the window, intently watching her as she walked towards the house. How the little boy, who poked at the ground with a stick, ran up to help carry the small pail of milk for them. The baby in the oldest girl's lap and the mother silently weeping as she scraped potatoes for their dinner. There had been a time in their past where their own ancestors had been persecuted—hunted down like dogs. She hoped that they would be okay.

She couldn't help but feel that things were slipping out of her control. That as hard as she tried, the thread that she held on to so tightly was about to unravel and there was nothing that she could do about it. She had sought solace and peace in the church and maybe for a time that worked, but things were changing, and she didn't know what to do.

Helene had been right about changing Meli's birth certificate. Had she not, Meli would have been in real danger, but she was safe, now wasn't she? Isabel sighed at her own stupidity. The truth was that Meli would never be safe, just as Sophie had never been, just as she had never been safe. It had only ever been a matter of time.

She rubbed the tops of her hands and looked up at the ceiling beams, the dark oaken bones that had been in place since the cottage's existence. She marveled at how they had withstood the test of time, providing a safe, strong foundation for the cottage generation after generation.

She knew that she would have to tell Meli the truth. That no amount of Sunday masses and Hail Marys and crosses would keep her safe. She had known from the beginning, in fact all three of them had, she, Sophie and Berthe. What else would a child who bore the mark be expected to do, but fulfill a role she had sworn to take on lifetimes ago?

Before she disclosed everything though, there were things to be done. Things were unravelling too fast.

Wrapping her shawl even tighter around herself, she stood up and took one last look outside before heading back to bed. For a brief moment, through the heavily falling snow, she thought she saw a woman standing against a far tree staring back. But when she looked again, she was gone.

———

The following morning, Nicole was far too sick to even get out of bed. Helene, frantic with worry, wrung her hands and screamed for Isabel. Racing up the stairs, both Meli and her grandmother found Helene standing in the corner crying. Placing her hand on Nicole's forehead, Isabel confirmed what she could already see. Her face was flushed, and she was sweating excessively. Shivering, she moaned as her heavy eye lids attempted to focus on Isabel's face. Nicole was clearly in immediate need of a doctor and antibiotics.

Isabel acted swiftly. "Meli, I need you to run into town and see if Henri Bouchard can take you in his car to fetch the doctor. Now." Meli, understood the urgency in her grandmother's voice and without a hesitation, ran to get dressed.

Turning to Helene, Isabel explained. "Dr. Magnan lives in the next town. It's the only way to get him here in this weather. I will run downstairs and get some cloths. We'll need to make cold compresses and you'll need to keep applying those to her fore-head to keep the fever down. Do you understand me?"

Helene's eyes widened in fear as she rattled on. "But what if she dies? What if there's no penicillin? What will I do? Why did we leave Paris?"

Isabel bellowed sharply. "Helene! Pull yourself together. Help me bring up a more comfortable chair from the living-room. Then we're going to move that dresser closer for the basin of water to sit on. It's going to be a long day, now let's go."

As they headed downstairs, Meli, who was already out the door, didn't hear her Mamina yell after her. "And stay away from the boche!"

———

By the time she arrived in the village, Meli was cold, wet and exhausted from trudging through the snow and by the time she had reached the post-office, Henri Bouchard had already left. Not sure what to do, she began to walk towards Berthe's, when she saw the familiar figures of Tomas and his Commanding Officer walking towards her.

It was Lieutenant Koch who addressed her. "Hello Meli, I was hoping to run into you. I'm sure you remember Private Richter. We were hoping to have access to your library today."

"I'm so sorry, I could get someone to open it for you, Lieutenant, but I have to find someone to take me to the doctor's. Nicole is very sick and may need medicine."

"Nicole is the young blonde girl that was at the library," he replied. "Is that correct?"

Meli nodded. "Yes, sir."

"Perhaps then, Mademoiselle, we could be of some assistance. Allow me to make my car available. It would be our pleasure to drive you to the doctor and then safely back home again, wouldn't it, Private Richter?"

"Yes, sir, absolutely, sir."

For a moment she hesitated, but Nicole's fevered face flashed before her and she knew that she needed to make a quick decision. Meli blushed. "Thank you. That's very kind of you."

"Then we had better get started."

Although there was something about Lieutenant Koch that didn't sit well with Meli, he seemed polite enough. The scar on his face was frightening, but again, he was clearly trying to help and with Tomas there, she felt at little more at ease. The Mercedes was luxurious and warm inside, and Meli felt a little overwhelmed in something so expensive. She gave Tomas the directions as she sat in the back seat with the Lieutenant.

"So Meli, Private Richter tells me that you are keen on history."

Meli brushed her fringe out of her eyes. "Yes, sir."

"Odd for a young lady like you. You might be interested then in an excavation I am organizing for the spring. It will be at the fortress of Montségur. Have you heard of it? What am I saying, but of course you have."

I know some of the history from books. My older sister went there.

Koch's face went cold. "Did she?"

"Yes. She told me once when I was little, but that's also where she died, so it's a bit sad for me." It did not escape Meli's notice how Tomas' eye flickered back to Koch, in the rearview mirror.

They drove carefully over the snowy roads but finally arrived at the doctor's home, a sturdy farmhouse just outside of town. Meli climbed out of the car and was met at the door by the doctor's wife with a surprised look on her face.

"Meli Durand isn't it? What are you doing?" She didn't say the words but did a quick look towards the car and wondered what she was doing with Germans.

Meli gave a quick smile and said, "It's okay. M. Bouchard wasn't around, and they offered to give me a ride. Our family friends are with us and her daughter is really sick and needs to see Dr. Magnan."

"He's out seeing someone right now but should be back soon. When he does, I'll send him over to your Grandmother's place right away. Does she have a fever?"

"Yes, really bad."

"Your grandmother will know what to do." Eyeing the Mercedes, she said, "Go back home right away and Dr. Magnan will be there as soon as possible."

Climbing back into the Mercedes, Meli reported that the doctor would be coming as soon as he could. "If you could drop me off at the village, I can make my way back home from there."

Koch, however, wouldn't have it. He insisted on taking Meli back home himself to ensure that everything was alright.

CHAPTER TWENTY-SEVEN

Isabel looked up and went to the window as she heard the sound of tires on crunching snow on their lane. *Thank God the doctor has arrived.* Peeking through the curtains though, she did not expect to see a large black Mercedes-Benz.

Heart pounding, she watched as it stopped outside her door. She couldn't explain the fear that held her spellbound as a young man got out of the driver's seat and walked around to the passenger door. *What was going on?* As an older man got out and stood up to his full height, goosebumps crawled all over her skin. She didn't recognize his face, but her senses were at full alert. What she didn't expect, was for Meli to come sliding out after him.

Helene turned from wiping Nicole's brow and with a look of desperation whispered to Isabel. "Is it the doctor?"

"No, not yet. Stay here and watch Nicole. I'll see what's going on."

As she reached the bottom of the steps, Meli and her two guests were already coming through the door. While the two men waited at the entrance, Meli rushed forward. "Mamina, it's okay, the doctor is coming. M. Bouchard wasn't around, and Lieu-tenant Koch was kind enough to drive me instead. Dr. Magnan was with someone so he insisted that he drive me home."

Isabel looked at both men in her doorway. The older and larger man was dressed in a warm winter coat with a cashmere grey scarf tucked in at the neck. His cap revealed seniority but what startled her more was the arch of a scar that started from the edge of his mouth to the tip of his ear.

Trying not to stare, she was wary, but knew better than to be rude. "Thank you. Lieutenant Koch, is it? Your kindness is appreciated."

"It was our pleasure, Madame. May I properly introduce myself? My name is Lieutenant Wolfgang Koch, and this is my personal assistant Private Tomas Richter. We have been using your library facilities for research and Meli has been very helpful."

Isabel flinched at his last statement, but extended her hand, nonetheless. It did not pass her notice that the young assistant who stood slightly behind his boss, looked only at Meli and smiled.

"I understand that you have a sick young lady in your home. I wonder if you would permit me to have a look. I have some medical training and can perhaps ascertain the seriousness of her illness. If I can put your mind at ease I will do so."

Isabel had a pretty good idea herself as to what Nicole had. "As much as I appreciate your offer, sir, I wouldn't want you to catch anything contagious."

"Please, Madame, let that be my concern. I am happy to help. Private Richter stay down here. Perhaps Meli could provide you with something warm to drink."

Isabel nodded in agreement. The less bodies upstairs the better. "Meli, please listen for Dr. Magnan as well." Taking their coats, she then turned back to the man who gave her chills and said, "Follow me."

As they climbed the stairs, Helene, who obviously had heard their voices, was anxiously waiting by the bedroom door. Although confused at the German officer coming up the stairs, she was beyond caring.

Her lip quivering, her eyes tearing up, she looked to the Lieutenant first. "Are you a doctor?" She then looked to Isabel who led the way with a pleading look. "She's worse. I think she's hallucinating."

Koch hurried into the room and took a quick look at Nicole, who struggled to breathe as she moaned and turned her head from side-to-side. Covered in sweat, her sheets were soaked, her cheeks flushed and her lips a bluish-tinge. Gently taking her arm, he placed two fingers on her pulse and turned to Helene and Isabel. "Her pulse is racing."

Helene immediately grabbed Isabel's arm but kept watching her daughter in fear that if she stopped looking, she would lose her. "What does that mean?"

Isabel opened her mouth to speak, but it was Koch that answered. "It means, Madame, that she is very sick." Helene collapsed in the chair and began to sob unconsolably.

Turning to Isabel, his face was serious. "Get a large basin and get Tomas to fill it with snow, lots of snow. It's critical that we get her temperature down now. Both you and her mother, he nodded in Helene's direction, will need to keep cold cloths under her armpits, her head and her groin area. One on each side and keep this up. I will stay with her and her mother while you get this done."

Isabel looked over to Nicole, nodded to this giant of an enemy, and then purposefully headed down the stairs.

———

Once she had left, Koch turned back to Helene, bent down and took her hand in his. "You must be strong, Madame. Your daughter needs you right now. Can you do that?"

Helene could only keep staring at Nicole, but after a moment she slowly turned and looked up at his face. He knew that she had registered his scar as most people did, but she didn't flinch.

She spoke softly. "Can you help her? I'll do anything, anything you want, just please don't let her die."

At that moment, Isabelle entered the room with a large basin of snow, followed by Dr. Magnan who nodded politely to Koch but then focused only on Nicole. "The snow is a smart idea."

Quickly placing his two fingers on her inner wrist to take her pulse, he then opened his worn black bag and pulled out a glass thermometer, giving it a quick shake before he placed it in her mouth. After a minute he took it out and read the results, pursing his lips as he did. During the examination, Koch backed off towards the door so as to not interfere or be in the way in such a small room. But he also knew he had an opportunity that he was absolutely going to take advantage of. The doctor pulled down the sheets and then placed his stethoscope on the girl's chest and was clearly alarmed with what he heard.

Turning to both Isabel and Helene, he instructed them to immediately apply the cold compresses. Looking directly at Helene, he looked at her gravely and shook his head. "I'm sorry, Madame, but its pneumonia. She needs penicillin and with the war on…he looked towards Koch, it's difficult for me to get my hands on some.

Wolfgang immediately stepped forward and looked directly at Helene. "If you will allow me, it would be my privilege to provide you with whatever you need. Doctor, I will leave immediately and be back with the medication within a few hours. Will that be soon enough?"

"She'll need it as soon as you can. In the meantime, Helene, I will suggest you feed her some warm broth if she'll take it and we'll try and keep the temperature down. I'll stay until he gets back, but until she gets the penicillin it's in God's hands."

Isabel nodded. "Now that you're here, Doctor, I'll see the Lieutenant downstairs and get some fresh sheets." Dr. Magnan took a deep sigh and nodded.

When they reached the kitchen, Tomas immediately stood up at full attention. "Sir." Meli put down her coffee cup and looked up at Isabel. "How is she?"

"She's very ill with pneumonia and for now, Meli it would be best if you stayed away from her room. Lieutenant Koch, thank you so much for your generosity. Meli will see you to the door while I see to the clean sheets."

Koch gave a small nod. "We'll return as soon as we can with the medications." He then leaned in towards Meli and said quietly, "I see you're not wearing your amulet today. I hope it hasn't been lost."

Momentarily surprised, she reached for the amulet and was then reminded of how upset Mamina was. Blushing heavily, she stumbled out a few words. "No, no not at all."

"Oh good, it's such a lovely piece, I'd hate for you to lose it."

As Meli closed the door behind them, she quickly caught the eye of Tomas who gave her a quick smile back. She was confused. Tomas was a German soldier and part of what was going on in her country to good people like the Kowalskis. But he *felt* different. He felt kind-hearted, someone that she could have been friends with if there wasn't a war. It was Koch with that gash across his face that felt dangerous and although he seemed polite enough there was something about him that she couldn't shake.

CHAPTER TWENTY-EIGHT

ABOUT AN HOUR AFTER THEY HAD LEFT, BERTHE ARRIVED FULL OF questions. More than a few villagers had seen Meli get into their car and it wasn't long afterwards that the gossip found its way to Berthe's ears. Knowing there must be a good explanation, Berthe headed up to the farm, checking first to ensure that the only car parked was the doctor's.

She found Isabel in the kitchen quietly sipping her coffee-like brew with an exhausted long face. "Is everything alright?"

Isabel proceeded to pour her friend a cup of coffee and gave her a shortened version of the events. "Meli brought Nazis here?"

Isabel sighed and shrugged her shoulders. "I know, but what else could she have done? I don't know if it was bravery or naiveté that made her get in their car, but the truth is that Nicole won't survive the night without that medication. I never thought I would say this, but I wish they would hurry up."

"It's that bad?"

Isabel nodded, tapped her fingers and kept watching out the window. "Unfortunately, yes. I know she's a spoiled brat with a useless overdramatic mother, but I wouldn't wish this on anybody."

"Where's Meli now?"

"Out tending to the goats and rabbits in the barn. Best to get it done while they are gone."

"And the doctor?"

"Upstairs with Helene. I understand she's worried, but she has been sobbing away all day. It got so bad that I had to give her two shots of sherry just to calm her down. I came down here for a break. I'm sorry to leave her with him but if she doesn't calm down, I'll kill her myself. She's no use to Nicole this way and it means we have to babysit her as well."

"Can't blame her I guess."

"I suppose."

Isabel took a long sip of her coffee and looked at Berthe. "You haven't been around very much."

"Oh, I've been busy helping out here and there."

"I hope you're not involved with anything that could get you into trouble. I heard that there are some resistance fighters—the maquisards, causing trouble."

"What makes you say that? And do you seriously see me as a Maquisard Isabel?"

"Isabel chuckled. "No, but they say there are people hiding escapees and even allied soldiers."

"Don't be silly, Isabel. I'm not that brave and if that's local gossip it's not true."

"No, it's not local gossip. But I know you. If anyone would take people in, you would. I guess I wondered after all these years why you would clean out that back room. I worry about you."

"Now you're being silly. Clothing is hard to come by and it's time I put George's sweaters and coats to good use."

"Hmmm, if you say so. I hope you're not still angry with me?"

Berthe gave a crooked smirk and shook her head. "I'm not

angry, Isabel. I'm frustrated with you, and you know why. But you're still my friend."

Isabel looked down at her reddened hands, calloused and dry from the cold, then rubbed away a small mark of dirt on her thumb "It's just that I'm worried. I have to keep her safe. You know I do."

Berthe patted Isabel's hand. "I understand that, but our families have been friends for generations. It was my ancestors who protected what needed to be protected on this land in trust for yours. We share not only friendship and family we share secrets and we each have our duties. Do you really think that Meli would have been born with the mark if she wasn't capable of bearing the weight of what needs to be done? From the moment you saw her as a baby you knew your destiny was to not only protect her, but to prepare her as well. In this one aspect you have failed...so far."

Isabel was too tired to argue with her and could only nod her head in agreement. "I know you're right. I mean I *know* you're right. I just keep thinking later, I'll tell her later, but later never comes. She's still a child."

Berthe creased her forehead and took Isabel's both hands in hers. "Promise me this, Isabel Durand. That should anything happen to me, you will tell Meli the truth."

Isabel tried to pull her hands away and laugh off Berthe's comment as something silly, but Berth held on tightly. "Promise me, Isabel. Promise me now."

Uncomfortable with the conversation, Isabel finally agreed. "I promise."

In that moment, Meli walked in from the cold and announced that they were back. "I saw the car driving up the laneway. They should be here in a minute."

Berthe finished off her coffee and suggested that she should get going, in fact she seemed anxious to, but Isabel wanted her to stay. Koch made her feel uneasy.

The Lieutenant and his assistant were already at the door and while Isabel let them in Berthe noticed how Meli had quickly run upstairs to change out of her dungarees. She had already seen the young bookish officer around the village. *Not interested in boys, eh?*

Koch was speaking with Isabel and handed her a small package which she proceeded to rush upstairs. "Please excuse me for a moment while I get this to the doctor. Please make yourselves comfortable in the kitchen." Koch however followed her. "If you don't mind, Madame, I'll speak with the doctor as well to ensure that this will be enough or to see if she needs to be rushed to a medical ward."

The younger officer entered the kitchen carrying a large tin of what appeared to be coffee. Catching Berthe's eyes as they widened, he smiled and placed the tin on the counter. "Excuse me, I had a taste earlier of what *cannot* be called coffee. It's a small gift."

Not sure what to make of this, she simply replied. "I'm sure it will be appreciated."

Walking over to the table, he held out his hand. "Permit me to introduce myself, Madame. My name is Private Tomas Heinrich Richter, but my friends call me Tomas."

Berthe responded cautiously. "Berthe Chastain. I am a family friend."

"May I perhaps sit with you, Mme Chastain?"

"Yes, of course."

As he pulled out the chair and sat down, he spoke softly and quickly looked up towards the ceiling. "How is the young lady doing?"

Berthe gestured with a pursed mouth and waved her hand horizontally to indicate Nicole's health could go either way. He sighed deeply then nodded to indicate that he understood but said nothing more.

Just then, Meli entered the kitchen, scrubbed and changed

into clean pants and a warm blue sweater that set off her eyes and newly brushed hair. She blushed as she entered and noticed that the young man smiled back, obviously appreciating the effort she had made. Turning towards the counter she immediately noticed the tin of coffee.

"Is that real coffee? Oh my goodness, can I make some?"

It was the young man who blushed this time. "Yes, of course. It's for you."

Meli, who was blushing furiously by now, seemed glad of a chore to keep herself busy. Soon after, Koch and Isabelle came downstairs and to Isabelle's surprise the aroma of real coffee assaulted her as she entered the kitchen.

"Is that what I think it is? Coffee?"

Meli, in a voice that was a little too excited, answered, "Yes, Tomas brought it for us."

Cutting her short, Isabel said, "Thank you, Tomas. That is most kind of you. In fact, we must thank you both. The doctor says that the medicine that Lieutenant Koch has brought will save Nicole's life. I'll take a cup upstairs to Helene. I'm sure she will appreciate it."

Koch nodded, approving of her gratitude. "Perhaps I can take the cup upstairs for you, Madame. It's been a long day for you, I'm sure. Please sit and let me do this small favour."

Berthe watched as his manners and intent seemed impeccable but underneath this façade, deep in his black soul, there was a smouldering fire of deceit and evil. This man wanted something, that much was certain, and she had a good idea as to what that would be. She thought back to the reading she had given to Meli. *All the players were in place and Isabel was running out of time with the truth.*

When he returned to enjoy his own cup, he seemed to be watching Berthe intently or at least that's how she felt.

"You live in the village, do you not, Madame?"

"I do, yes,"

Koch took out a package of Gitanes from his pocket and proceeded to light a cigarette. "If I am correct, I understand that you may have a room to let, that is, if it isn't already taken."

Berthe could feel all the blood drain from her face and she stuttered her reply. "Um, of course. It still needs a good cleaning though and the space may be too humble for your needs. But please let me know when you will need it."

"It won't be for me. It will be for Private Richter, but I'm sure you'll hear from me soon enough, Madame. Now, unfortunately, we must go." Turning to Isabel, he took her hand. "May I have your permission, Madame, to come back in a few days to check on the young patient upstairs?"

Isabel smiled politely. "Of course, Lieutenant. We're honored by your concern."

Turning to Tomas, Koch's smile faded as he barked that he was ready to go.

———

As the car drove down the lane, Wolfgang stared blankly out the window. The snow-laden trees reminded him of the countryside around where he grew up. Bregenzerwald, deep in the western Austrian forests, boasted as many cows as it did people who thrived in the valley and high mountain pastures. Like here, the farms were small, no more than twelve cows per farm and from their milk came the most delicious of Alpine cheeses. In winter, after he and his brothers completed their chores, they glided over the slopes and ridges and gently rolling hills on their cross-country skis. For the briefest of moments, he missed his homeland, but quickly reminded himself that there was business to be done.

Thinking back to the day's events, he eyed Tomas in the rearview mirror from his viewpoint in the back seat. It had not escaped his notice of the little crush between the young lady and his young officer. In fact, he wanted to encourage it, just as he would use Helene to his own advantage.

Lost in thought, he rubbed off the tiny flakes of skin from his dry lips, while he pieced together what he already knew. There was no question in his mind that these people were exactly who he was looking for, and it would have made sense for Victor to trust them with his last manuscript. If it indeed gave away the hiding place of the Grail, where else would he have hidden it, but a tiny out-of-the-way cottage. And if, as the older daughter had confided to Victor, that she was the Grail's keeper, he was exactly where he needed to be. The amulet that Meli had worn that day proved it. What confused him though, was the amount of crucifixes in the cottage. As far as he could tell, there was at least one in every room. That didn't make sense.

The first question was, where was the manuscript being hidden and how could be obtain it? He had already caused the death of the older daughter, so Meli or her grandmother wouldn't be a problem.

The second question was who knew enough to tell him everything to save the other? The old bat or the naïve little girl. The other option was this Berthe person. He knew fear when he saw it and she was clearly hiding something. He wondered briefly whether she could be running a safe house and made a mental reminder to himself for someone (perhaps the ever-helpful mailman or even his wife perhaps?) to keep a watch over her house. He also had the excavation at Montségur to organize for the spring and it was important for his own neck to provide Himmler with regular positive updated accounts. The manuscript, the grail, the books. One thing at a time. The manuscript would lead to the grail, and the books would hopefully be with the grail. Unless…

What he needed was someone to be his eyes and ears, inside the house and out. He thought of the tearful Helene and congratulated himself on connecting with such a desperate woman. Yes, she could be very handy, and she did say *anything*. He rubbed his chin and noted the stubble. Grateful women could be so pathetic.

It had started to snow again and as Tomas slowly made his way to their hotel in Lavelanet, Wolfgang stared out the car window and plotted what needed to be done. He wasn't a fan of Himmler's belief in the occult and he certainly wasn't convinced that a grail actually existed. Books he could accept, but a cup from the time of Jesus? That was stretching his imagination and besides, no one even knew what it looked like. How was he supposed to find something that no one had ever seen? There was always the possibility, of course, that as long as he brought something Himmler would accept as authentic, but he'd only use that as a last resort. The books were another matter.

He wondered at the sense of having killed Victor Schreiber, but that wasn't his call to make. And it certainly wasn't his fault that Sophie Durand had happened to be in the car with him. She would have been useful now. A little leverage using the mother and sister as bait would have been handy.

Turning to Tomas, he looked at the bookish officer and thought about his privileged background. Mommy and daddy keeping him out of trouble. There was nothing hardened about the boy at all. He was too polite, too studious, too milquetoast and it wouldn't surprise him at all if, when all this was over, he was headed for a career as a teacher. Mediocre, that's what he was. A mediocre little milk sop with a crush on a mediocre little girl, as studious as he was.

For now, he'd use the little wimp where he was best needed and, if he was lucky, he wouldn't need to teach him what it meant to be a soldier. If not, well maybe mommy and daddy might get back a broken little boy. Something that wouldn't be his fault of course. Wolfgang was getting very tired of being nice.

CHAPTER TWENTY-NINE

At long last Meli made her way to bed where, under the warm comfort of blankets and quilts, she fell into a deep but confusing sleep. As she slipped into the darkness of dreams and visions, strains of music teased her into following the melodic voices of men, women and children singing the gentle hymn of the Cathars, 'Lo boièr'—The cattle herder.

Lulled into the song's magic, she found herself deep in a dark cave, the flickering yellowed lights of rushes wedged into the rocky crevasses and the sound of a familiar voice. One that she now recognized as well as her own.

I did not see Sophia again after I reached Lombrive. Fournier, I knew would hunt me but as much as it was my intention to go elsewhere for shelter, I left it too late and underestimated Fournier's intent to wipe us all out. Did he know I was there? I suspect so, but he didn't find me, at least not the woman he was looking for. Would he find what he sought? I prayed that he would not, and at least with that I have succeeded for now.

The day they stormed the cave came upon us as a surprise. Hidden deep within, we were temporarily lulled into a sense of safety, going about our daily routine. It was never going to be a long-term solution and even though we knew our days were numbered, for now we felt safe.

The clanking of steel, the war cries and howls of an army of rabid men intent on blood, thundered into the cave and was an ominous warning of what was soon to come. Mothers urged their children to climb up into cavities and hide, while others held each other close knowing that this day would be their last.

In preparation for me leaving what should have been the day before, my hair had already been cut short and my skirt exchanged for leggings in order to hide my femaleness. In order to hide who I was. We knew they would be looking for the woman who bore the mark. As I said before, I knew this day would come and I was prepared.

When they finally winded through the caverns and stalagmites and low chambers they entered the cathedral where the slaughter began. Men, women and children all dead, all slain. I too lay in a puddle of my own blood. I will not relive this moment with you in your dreams, but you must hear my words, Meli. Your life depends on it.

Long before your time, a seer prophesied that seven hundred years will pass before the laurel will be green once more. That seven hundred years is upon us. This is our opportunity for the underground rivers of knowledge to water and nurture the seeds of a new renaissance of mankind. On March 16, 1944, on the anniversary of the fall of Montségur, we will reach that seven hundred years.

Now is your time to awaken as to who you truly are. There is no more time for doubt or indecision. You will not be alone in your task. Pay attention to the signs, listen to the whispers of the shadows of those who watch. The amulet is your armour, wear it and guard it with your life.

Stand tall, there are secrets yet to be revealed.

CHAPTER THIRTY

Two days later, Wolfgang and Tomas pulled up front of the cottage in the large Mercedes and made their way to the front door. Isabel and Meli were out tending to chores, so it was left up to Helene to answer the door.

Expecting the doctor to be checking in, she was surprised and a little taken aback to see the Lieutenant with his assistant behind him holding a large hamper of meats and vegetables. Automatically smoothing her hair down, she smiled politely and ushered them in out of the cold.

"Lieutenant Koch, what a pleasant surprise. And what do we have here?"

"Madame, may I say you are looking much better than the last time we met. I take it then that the young lady is doing much better as well?"

"More than better, Lieutenant."

"Please call me Wolf, but not the kind with big teeth." Laughing at his little joke, he instructed Tomas to present the basket for her viewing.

"We have brought a few items that I am sure will help your daughter recover."

Helene looked longingly at the basket containing what was obviously wrapped meats, potatoes and a fresh chicken and hesitated for a moment but Koch was too quick.

"Please, Madame, for your daughter's sake, you must accept my small gift."

"Thank you, of course…for Nicole's sake. I'll put it in the kitchen."

"Tomas will be only too glad to do this for you. And where are the other ladies today?"

"Meli is off doing chores, and I believe that Isabel is off to the Banon cave."

Koch's eyes snapped to Helene's. "There is a cheese cave on this property?"

A little flustered by his reaction, Helene stood back, but then directed him towards the front sitting room. "Yes, Isabel's family has been making Banon for generations. It cures in the cave. I've never been there myself, but the cheese is delicious."

Wolfgang lowered his head as he walked through the doorframe into the small sitting room where a fire small fire burned away.

"If you'll excuse me, I'll check on Nicole, then make you a coffee, if that's what you prefer."

"Please allow Richter to make the coffee for you, Madame. I assure you he's very adept at this and won't mind at all. Then after you check on your daughter, perhaps you and I could have a chat…just us two."

"If you're sure."

"Of course." Walking back to the kitchen, Koch instructed Tomas to brew the coffee and bring out the plate of sugar cookies into the sitting room when it was done. "Oh, and Tomas, I don't want to be disturbed while it's just us here. Understood?"

Tomas nodded and replied crisply. "Yes, sir."

By the time, he returned to the sitting room, Helene had also returned and by the look of it had brushed her hair and removed her apron. He was pleased with the gesture and smiled warmly as he rubbed his large hands by the fire.

"How is your daughter?"

"She's sleeping comfortably, thank you. Lieutenant Koch…"

Koch playfully wagged his finger. "Ah, ah, ah…"

Helene clasped her one hand into the other and rubbed her fingers across the top of her hand. "Wolfgang…Wolf… I can't thank you enough for your kindness. I don't know how I can possibly repay you."

At that moment, Tomas entered the room with the small plate of cookies and two coffees. Nodding to Koch, he disappeared back to the kitchen. Koch passed the cookies to Helene and continued where they left off.

"Think nothing of it, Madame, or may I call you Helene?"

"Yes, of course."

"Koch leaned forward, close enough to slowly stroke the top of her knee. I imagine it can be very boring for someone like you who's used to the bright lights of Paris."

"Yes, it is. No one else seems to understand that." She looked slightly uncomfortable but didn't slink away.

"Perhaps you would be interested in joining me for dinner one evening. At the Ritz perhaps?"

"That would be lovely, Lieutenant Wolf, but you tease me. There is no Ritz around here and you can appreciate in a small village the need to be discreet."

"I understand completely, Helene, and let me assure you that when I said the Ritz, I meant Paris. I can vouch for your safe journey there and safe return here, but perhaps you are tired of living here in the country?"

Something in Helene changed. Recognizing an opportunity when she heard it, she was keen to see it through. "It's true, both

Nicole and I miss Paris, but we are without funds and I don't believe that my husband will be returning."

"Then I think you and I could come to a mutually beneficial arrangement that would suit you and your daughter financially... long term. Your own apartment, food, wine and monthly stipend should suit wouldn't you say?"

"What is it that you want, Lieutenant?"

"Ah, a woman able to get straight to the facts. What do I want? Information, for starters. I understand that you were an acquaintance of Victor Schreiber, the author?"

"I met him several times certainly, but he was better friends with Sophie, who unfortunately was with him that day in his car."

Koch cleared his throat. "Yes, such a tragedy. And you had been friends with Sophie for many years?"

Helene's voice sounded distant. "Yes, she was my best friend."

"Her friendship with Schreiber seems odd but he was writing about the Cathars, so I suppose they had that in common," Koch said.

Helene knitted her brows in confusion. "Yes, as far as I know, Sophie's family ancestors go back to the middle ages in this area. This farm alone has been in the family for generations."

"That's very helpful. And her family? Isabel? Her sister Meli?"

At the mention of Meli, Helene looked down at her hands and wouldn't look him in the eyes. "Sophie didn't get on very well with her mother. Isabel expected her to stay on the farm, get married and have babies."

"I see."

"You know what I find interesting, Helene, is how alike Meli seems to look like her sister Sophie. Don't you think so?"

Helene looked at him confused. "You met Sophie?"

Koch smiled back. "Briefly. Obviously, it was a few years ago now, but long enough to see a resemblance."

"Meli's parents were killed in an accident and she was adopted by Isabel as a baby."

"Is that a fact? I presume there is all proper documentation for this...adoption."

"I'm...sure there must be."

Koch knew a lie when he heard one.

"Helene, I can see that you and I are going to have a lot of fun together, so here's what I propose. There's something that I am looking for that I suspect your friend Sophie may have hidden here. It's a manuscript that Schreiber wrote, and I want it. Find it for me and you have my word that I will ensure that both you and your daughter will be living in far more suitable..." he looked around, "accommodations. I suggest in a few weeks we could make this arrangement when your daughter is in better health?"

"Yes, that would be wonderful"

"To your daughter's health then and to the return of the manuscript."

The stomping of boots from the kitchen alerted the two that someone had returned from their chores.

————

Isabel, who had come from the back facing the forest, had not seen the car, so was surprised to see the young German officer sitting alone at her kitchen table and the smell of coffee coming from the moka pot on the stove. Looking from Tomas to the basket of foodstuff, she wasn't sure what to say.

"Good day?"

Tomas jumped up with an awkward look and immediately apologized. "I'm sorry, Madame, Lieutenant Koch felt that it would help Nicole. He's with Madame Moser in the sitting room where it's warmer."

"And you?"

"I'm fine sitting in here, Madame. I took the liberty of making coffee. I hope you don't mind."

"Not at all."

"There are sugar cookies in the basket."

"Are there?"

"Courtesy of Commander Koch."

"Who is in the sitting room with Helene?"

"Yes, madam."

"Then I suppose I should join them. You won't mind waiting here, will you? I'm sure Meli will be along any minute."

At the mention of Meli's name, his eyes brightened as he looked out towards the window. It didn't take much for Isabel to recognize young love. *Thank God they are leaving.*

As she entered her sitting room, the energy in the room felt stifled, as if she had caused a conversation to end mid-sentence.

Nodding, she smiled and acknowledged their guest. "Lieutenant Koch, how lovely to see you again. I see from the kitchen we must thank you again for such a generous gift. With the prices as they are, this basket must have cost you a small fortune."

"My pleasure, Madame, and as I mentioned to Helene, it's for Nicole's health."

"Of course, of course."

As Isabel sat in the chair by the fire, Koch spoke to her directly. "I understand, Madame, that you make cheese."

"Yes, we had a small herd of goats, and my family has been making Banon for generations."

"Then we have something in common. The area of Austria where I come from is famous for its Alpine cheese. My grandparents were cheesemakers and I have fond memories of helping them as a boy. We used to joke that there were more cows than people there. I understand that you have a cave where it ripens."

Isabel looked once at Helene, wondering what she had shared, then stared straight ahead as she pursed her lips and said, "Yes, but it's just a small little cavern really. Hardly comparable to the local caves for Rochford or Camembert."

Koch smiled back at her, his scar causing his face to distort into something ugly and fearful, despite the soft words that followed. "I'm sure, Madame, you are being modest. Perhaps you would be so kind as to show it to me one day. To remind me of home."

Isabel's face blanched. She was running out of time.

———

As Tomas drove the Mercedes back to Lavelanet, he took a quick look at his Commander in the back and wondered who this man really was. Driving in silence, he let his mind wander over the day's events.

Tomas was under no illusions as to what his Commander's game was. His reputation for being a cold-hearted bastard to get what he wanted preceded him and it was clear that Tomas was far less than what Wolfgang Koch considered a soldier. He clearly disliked Tomas, his privileged upbringing and his parent's interference, but that had had nothing to do with him. When they learned that he had wanted to train as a pilot, their own concerns were in motion and so here he found himself, assistant to Lieutenant Wolfgang Koch. He was, however, doing what he loved and what he was far better suited to than his superior. Koch was an engineer and an out-of-the box thinker but poring through books was not his strength.

After reading all of Victor Schreiber's books, he could see that the author/archeologist was enamoured with the idea of the Cathar beliefs. In fact, he shared the pacifist beliefs with him, but found himself in the same unfortunate situation. Victor Schreiber had followed the Grail and had linked the Cathars to the holy vessel along with several books on Alchemy and magic. Schreiber was under contract by the Reich to write a last novel disclosing the whereabouts of the Cathar treasure, but in the end was unwilling to hand it over. It was very likely, Tomas surmised, that he had a change of heart. The fact that he had supposedly begged Himmler to be allowed to quietly retire in the Languedoc in isolation spoke volumes.

Tomas' thoughts then turned to Meli, of whom he felt strangely protective. He couldn't explain why or how, but he felt connected to her for some reason. She was smart and obviously shy like he was. He liked that in her. She seemed genuine, not like Nicole.

The other evening over coffee she had explained that Helene and Nicole had left Paris to come live with her Grandmother and her and how Helene had been her sister's best friend in Paris. Even he had to admit that her sister's connection with Schreiber was unusual but so what if her ancestors had been Cathars. Wasn't everyone in this region connected to them in some way?

Meli was all of sixteen and Isabel an older woman trying her best to keep themselves in food and warmth. Did he really believe they were hiding something? It was, of course, possible that Sophie had hidden the manuscript for Schreiber, but it was also possible that Meli and her grandmother would never have been aware of this. Tomas thought that if he could somehow search the house before Koch took matters in his own hands, then Koch would be able to forget them and direct his focus elsewhere.

He was already organizing an archeological dig at Montségur for the spring, but he needed the manuscript to finalize exactly where the dig should be focused. Find the manuscript.

He could always ask Meli, but he worried about compromising their friendship. What if she knew where it was and was purposely hiding it? Should he confide in her? Let her know what Koch was up to? What she was up against? It would be safer to just give him the manuscript.

Tomas tried to sort his thoughts out logically. Meli was reading books on the Cathars and reincarnation. That indicated that she wasn't informed but knew enough to be curious. What sparked that interest?

It could be simply that she liked history. But what about the amulet? She said it was her sister's. So, it's logical that she would wear it.

What worried him most, was that Koch was taking an unusual interest in the family, which meant that he knew something that Tomas didn't.

CHAPTER THIRTY-ONE

That night after a rare dinner of chicken and rutabagas, Isabel and Meli washed up while Helene went into the sitting room where Nicole had been bundled up with a quilt by the fire. She was gaunt and had lost considerable weight which made her look even thinner, but other than being exhausted all the time, she appeared to be on the mend.

She thought about the offer Koch had made and saw no other way out. If Paris was back to normal, then obviously it was better that they return financially stable now, rather than missing out on this opportunity. And if she found the manuscript, she reasoned, his focus wouldn't be on Meli.

Meli came into the living-room, plopped down on a chair and looked over to Nicole who was quietly reading 'Gone with the Wind'. She smiled warmly to Helene as the radio played songs quietly in the background. Picking up her knitting she began to work away on some socks that she had started the night before.

"Where's your grandmother?"

"Mamina's bringing some chicken pieces to Berthe. She'll be back soon."

"But the chicken is for Nicole! She needs it to keep up her strength."

Much to Meli's surprise, Nicole raised her head and crossed her eyebrows. "For God's sake, Mother. We've been eating their food for months and how many times did Berthe bring me her cough medicine."

Helene looked chastised but commented under her breath. "For all the good it did."

Wanting to quickly change the subject, she spoke to Meli. "You know, Sophie used to be quite the reader. As I recall she had a few books that maybe Nicole could read while she is recovering."

"There's a drawerful upstairs in the attic. I could get them for you if you like."

But Nicole was having none of it. "I've only just started this one and by the thickness of it, it'll be summer by the time I'm done. Just let me finish this one."

Meli, relieved to not share, leaned forward to turn up the radio. "I think the news should be coming on soon."

Helene looked back at Meli and thought, *"The attic, of course!"*

————

It was dusk when Isabel left, so by the time she arrived in the village it was rapidly getting dark. Few people were outside, but those that she did pass gave her a funny look. She knew that the word had gotten around about Germans being at her home, so she wasn't surprised. She understood their attitude, but what was she supposed to do, tell him to leave?

Clutching her basket a little tighter, she did have to admit that she felt somewhat guilty about the food. If she was truly patriotic, she would have refused to eat the chicken and told Meli to not eat it either, but it smelled so good. Patting her well-wrapped parcel, she walked on to Berthe's front door and as usual, knocked lightly, opened the door and walked right in.

What she didn't expect was the flurry of movement from the back room and a flustered Berthe bustling to herd her into the kitchen.

"Isabel, what a surprise! What are you doing here?"

"I brought you some cooked chicken courtesy of the boche. I also need to talk to you about something."

Berthe looked at the basket and raised an eyebrow. "Hmmm, I'm not so sure that I'd rather starve."

"I thought so too, but I figure that it was probably a French chicken and should rightfully be eaten by French citizens."

"Well, since you put it like that. What's going on up there? There's been a few unkind comments started by you-know-who."

"Rose Bouchard?"

"Who else."

"Well, let her talk away. There's not much I can do if the giant wants to show up. I don't trust him though, and I certainly don't trust Helene. She'd sell her soul for some pretty clothes. Anyway, that's not why I'm here." Isabel squinted her eyes and turned her head to the side, "You're alone, right?"

Berthe looked fidgety and answered a little too quickly. "Of course, of course. Let's go sit in the kitchen and I'll make something hot to drink. I won't insult you by calling it coffee though."

"Look in the basket, my friend. Yet another little gift that I wanted to share."

"Oh, real coffee! Well, there's a nice surprise. Give me a minute, I'll put the chicken into the back room and then get the moka pot on the stove."

Isabel reached over, grabbed the plate of chicken and began to walk towards the back room. "I'll do it. You get started on the coffee."

Berthe almost fell over intercepting her friend from leaving the room.

Isabel, stopped, then stared hard at her friend. "Okay, what's going on? And this time I want the truth."

Berthe gave her a quick look, then shook her head. "It's best you don't know, Isabel. Come back and sit down…please."

Silently turning around, Isabel went back to the table and pulled out a chair for herself.

In a whisper she confronted Berthe who sat facing her at the table. "You're hiding someone aren't you?" Berthe simply looked down.

"Don't tell me anymore. I don't want to know."

"That would be best. He'll be gone in a day or two anyway."

"They will kill you if they find out."

"I know, I know, but I couldn't sit by and not do anything. You should be careful too. What is it that you wanted to talk about?"

"Meli."

"What about Meli? You're not worried about that young officer, are you? He'll be gone soon enough."

"I want to tell her the truth."

Berthe took in a deep breath and widened her eyes. "The whole truth?"

"Yes."

"For this, my friend, we will make real coffee and celebrate. Why the change of heart?"

"Because I know what Koch wants and so do you."

Berthe nodded in agreement as she placed the moka pot on the stove. "I agree it's time, Isabel, and we both know you've done your best but we also both know that this is what Sophie would have wanted."

Isabel nodded in agreement and waited a few minutes before she added. "I want you with me when I tell her. It's only right that you are there."

"Of course, my friend. Of course, I'll be there. Just tell me when."

"It will be soon, Berthe. It will be soon."

Later that evening, Isabel walked home under a cloudless sky of stars with the moon to light her way. Just making the decision took a weight off of her that made her feel lighter. This time as she walked, she felt an enormous embrace of love surrounding her as if she had made someone very happy. It wasn't hard to figure who that might be.

"You're welcome Sophie" she whispered to the night sky as she headed back home.

CHAPTER THIRTY-TWO

THE NEXT DAY AS ISABEL AND MELI WERE OUT DOING CHORES, Helene waited for Nicole to fall asleep.

If there were books in the attic, that was where she was going to start. The narrow stairs were difficult to navigate, and as she climbed the well-worn risers, she wondered what Sophie would have made of all this. What had her friend got involved in? She theorized that if she could find the manuscript, wouldn't that be protecting Meli even further? Surely it was a win/win solution. She and Nicole would return to their more luxurious life and leave all this behind.

Gripping the walls for support, she reached the small landing and faced an ancient wooden door to the right. The door groaned against the intrusion as she grasped the handle and gave it a good push. Opening it wide enough for her to slide herself inside, she adjusted herself to the light and gave a little gasp. A smoky form in front of the dimly lit far window stared back at her. But when she looked again, it was gone. *Did she really just see something?* A little shaken by the experience, she waited a full minute before even moving a muscle. When she was satisfied that it was just her imagination, she took a deep breath, then committed herself to the search.

Taking a look around at the dust laden boxes and crates, she wondered at the possibility of the task. There were so many things, and everything was covered in dust. It was also freezing, and she scolded herself for not bringing her coat. Huddled over, she wrapped her arms around herself and rubbed them to keep warm while looking around for something clean to throw over her shoulders. Little puffs of chilled air escaped when she breathed, and she was near tears at the enormity of finding anything in that cluttered space.

Opening a nearby chest, she shuddered at the sight of a mouse's nest snuggled into what might have once been a blanket, but she wasn't about to touch it to find out. Disgusted, she turned and searched elsewhere trying to remember what Meli had said. She'd seen books in the attic in the past somewhere…but where? Worried that this was taking so long, she began to fret. She hated being here and was so cold that she couldn't stay here much longer.

It was then that she spotted the dresser and it all came back. Making her way over, she opened the top drawer and found it empty. The second drawer, however, had some weight to it. She had at least found the books. An old folded sheet covered half of the drawer and when she pulled it aside, she gave a little squeal of joy. *Thank God!* There, at the very end, tucked away underneath was a manuscript tied up with rough string. Picking it up with both hands she looked at the front cover and saw what she needed, Victor Schreiber's name scrawled across the front. *She found it.* Why he wanted it, she couldn't care less, but this was her and Nicole's ticket back home. In style. She could already taste the croissants and butter.

Putting the manuscript down for the moment, she closed the drawer, cradled the precious package in her arms then smiled. No one would even know it was missing. She was willing to bet that Isabel probably didn't even know it was there in the first place, so what harm could there be?

Before she left, she looked around to ensure everything was back in order, then closed the door. She would never know that it was Sophie who watched from the window and smiled back.

CHAPTER THIRTY-THREE

TWO DAYS LATER THE POSTMAN, HENRI BOUCHARD KNOCKED AT the kitchen door bright and early. Inviting him in, Isabel offered him the usual cup of coffee, but was careful to pull out the blended version in order to not add to any wagging tongues. As Isabel pulled out a cup from the cupboard and poured him some of the brew, he looked around at the table, nodding to Helene and Meli. "Berthe is not with you today?"

Isabel looked a little surprised but said, "No."

Crossing his eyebrows, he looked at her as she placed his cup on the table in front of him.

"No, I haven't seen her a couple of days. Why? Is she alright?"

"I don't know, maybe, maybe not. No one has seen her."

Meli looked worried and said to Isabel, "Maybe she's fallen and hurt herself again. Has anybody checked inside her house?"

Henri looked at Isabel and looked down at his coffee. "The Milice were there last night. No one saw her leave with them so I thought I would ask if you had seen her."

Isabel's eyes widened in fear as she put both hands on her mouth. "No."

Meli, looked confused and concerned. "But why would the Milice be there?"

"Henri looked embarrassed but shrugged his shoulders. Apparently, she was suspected of running a safe house. I thought you should know."

Isabel's face was drained of colour and in a low voice she asked, "Have you heard where they have taken her?"

"As I have said, Isabel, I only know what they suspect and that they went to her house last night. Do not be surprised if they come here as well."

———

Within the hour, Koch's Mercedes pulled up to the cottage and as Tomas held the door open for him, Koch, with a curl in his lip, ordered Tomas to stay in the car and wait for him there.

Isabel ushered him in and invited him into the sitting room. "Can I offer you something to drink, Lieutenant?"

"No, nothing. In fact, I am here, unfortunately, on official business. May I ask, Madame, whether you have seen your friend, Mme Chastain around lately?"

"No, Lieutenant Koch, we were just discussing the other day that we haven't seen her around lately."

"Why do you ask?"

"Oh, come now, Mme Durand, I'm sure the word has already reached your ears that your friend was running a safe house for the local Maquis."

"Lieutenant, I assure you that I know nothing of the sort. Berthe is an old woman like me and hardly agile enough to be doing something like that. I'm sure someone has made a mistake."

"Oh, there was no mistake. The trouble is that she's gone missing and due to our association, I thought I would do you the kindness of looking around your house, rather than the Milice, who I understand can tend to be rather messy with other people's things. You understand?"

"Yes, Lieutenant, I understand completely. I am more than happy to show you around my home and outbuildings to your satisfaction. My friend is not here, and I do not know where she is."

Leading him from room to room, Koch looked in cupboards and under beds, but found nothing. As they were coming down the stairs, Helene was waiting at the bottom for him and by widening her eyes, let him know that she wanted a private conversation. The gesture did not escape Isabel's attention.

Turning to Isabel, he said, "Perhaps I will take you up on a little refreshment, Madame."

Helene piped up, "If you'd like to join me in the sitting room, Lieutenant, I'll keep you company until your coffee is prepared."

"Of course, it would be my pleasure."

After Isabel had left the room, Helene, whispered excitedly, "I found the manuscript!"

Koch was both impressed and pleased. "Well done, Madame. And you're certain it's Victor Schreiber's?"

"Yes, it has his name on the front. I can get it now if you like."

"No, I'll continue my chat with Isabel and perhaps you could hand it to Tomas out in the car. As long as you're discreet, no one needs to know anything."

"Yes, of course. And Nicole and I?"

"Of course, my dear, I haven't forgotten. I think, though, it might be better for you to sit tight for a little while. I promise to honour our agreement."

Isabel soon returned with two cups of coffee and as Helene excused herself, she watched her as she left.

Koch was no longer interested in looking anywhere else. He had a book to read, or at least Richter did. He more importantly had an archeological dig to organize, but he certainly wasn't going to let Isabel off the hook so easily. Having Berthe arrested was just the first step in ensuring that she understood just how dangerous he could be.

Drinking down the last of his coffee, his words were clear and cold. "It is my duty to inform you, Madame, that should Madame Chastain be found anywhere on your property you will be considered complicit, charged with treason and shot. Do I make myself clear?"

"Perfectly clear, Lieutenant," she replied.

Koch gave her a good long look. Visibly upset, there was a slight tremor in her hand as she placed her own cup back down on the table. "I appreciate you taking the time to inform me of your concerns, Lieutenant Koch. Please let me reassure you that I have not seen Berthe in the past two days."

Wanting to inform Himmler right away at his success, he stood to leave, when a thought crossed his mind. "I believe you mentioned that you had a Banon cave did you not? Perhaps you would be so kind as to take me there."

"Yes, Lieutenant, we do, and I would be delighted to show it to you, but unfortunately it's not possible with the snow this deep. Generally, we don't go there at all in the winter. You can see for yourself from the kitchen window that the path going up to the cave is unused."

Koch nodded and accepted her answer. He had too much to do to bother with all this anyway.

Reaching out to shake her hand, he walked to the door. "Unfortunately, Madame, neither Tomas nor I will be around for the next while to enjoy your company. But I am sure that our paths will cross again. Until then, be well."

As he walked around to the car, Tomas got out to hold open his door giving a little nod in regards to his questioning look. As he slid into his seat, he smiled at the package beside him.

Looking up at the second story of the cottage, Helene's hopeful face was looking out. Giving a little wave, he acknowledged her then barked at his assistant. "Get me out of here. We have work to do."

CHAPTER THIRTY-FOUR

OVER THE FOLLOWING TWO MONTHS, KOCH WAS BUSY WITH THE engineering details of the excavation and Tomas was consumed in the hunt for the grail through Schreiber's eyes.

Based on his research into Parsival, Schreiber believed that the Holy Grail was hidden under the Cathar fortress of Montségur, which boasted a number of caverns. There were only two sites, though, that he had considered as potential locations for the Grail. One was a large cave known as Montsalvat, and the other was surrounded in myth. Based on boyhood tales from some of the elderly villagers, the more mysterious cave could be found only by first finding a large rock with an iron ring embedded into it. The problem, though, was that although several people had sworn to have seen it, when they returned to show others or to investigate further, it was nowhere to be found.

Tomas knew that prior to his 'accident', Schreiber had been sent to ensure that the cache remained undiscovered by anyone else. This had been done, with Schreiber confirming to Himmler himself, that it was still in situ.

Tomas was piecing too many things together now and

although Schreiber's (and Sophie's) death was considered a tragic accident, he wasn't convinced. He knew that Koch was involved and considering his reputation for cruelty, he shuddered to think of what their last moments would have been like.

The fact that it was Meli's sister who died along with him and that Koch was certain that Meli and her grandmother knew more than they were saying, was concerning. Especially after the arrest attempt on Berthe. They had the manuscript. *Did that mean both Meli and her grandmother knew it was there? What else were they hiding?*

To Tomas, grounded in research and facts, it all seemed so unbelievable. He had, of course, heard the rumours about Himmler—dark ones and his strange beliefs in the occult. But he was Hitler's right-hand man, and no one would dare question his choices.

It was a well-known fact that Himmler was an active practitioner and believer in black magic, who studied and followed several ritualistic traditions, including necromancy and ancient Germanic paganism. There were numerous accounts of his attempts to contact the dead, a practice, it was said he carried out at the sinister Wewelsburg Castle. Located in north-east Germany, Himmler had originally used the castle to establish the SS Leadership academy but as his obsessions grew, the use of the castle became more evil servicing top ranking Nazi officers only. He had no doubts that Koch himself had participated in some of the rituals.

At the heart of Himmler's beliefs was the conviction that the Aryan race, from which true Germans were said to be descended, was superior to all others. To his displeasure, not one person had ever uncovered any temples or artifacts to prove his ancient civilization existed. Hence the need to find the Grail. He fervently believed that finding the Holy Cup would give him super-human powers and help Germany win the war. So confident was he that they were on the right trail, that after Koch's latest report, he had an empty plinth prepared at Wewelsburg for its arrival.

Tomas' hands were tied. He was now not only working with Koch, but with the Ahnenerbe, the Ancestral Heritage, whose main function was the acquisition of said artifacts. With no consideration for anything other than the acquisition of their prize, they seized and collected documents, paintings, sculpture, pottery and any other items considered 'Germanic' in order to 'return' them to Nazi Germany.

Using men gleaned from camps, they laboured daily under Koch's instructions in an attempt to access the cave that Schreiber had identified. Tomas continued his research using Schreiber notes and books as guidance and was required daily to join Koch in his daily overview at what was being accomplished.

Spring had not yet arrived, which made access to some of the rocky outcrops below the fortress challenging, but Koch was undeterred. After several weeks of non-stop labour, creating a safe framework of steel poles for scaffolding and wooden walkways, they were able to access the Montsalvat cave.

Once they had gained access, Koch refused to allow anyone else near or inside the cave. Instead, the workers were sent to scour every inch of the Pog to find the mysterious boulder. Once found, a skeleton crew was instructed to guard the location. Koch wasn't taking any chances.

Tomas and Koch arrived the following morning, just as the sun had crested the horizon sending bright streaks of light through the distant foggy valleys and misty hills. As Tomas climbed the ladder to the scaffold's walkway he looked back to the crisp beauty of the morning. A white mist covered the landscape of peaks and valleys leaving only the hint of grey outlines and subtle shadows that watched their every move. Turning back, he firmly grasped the scaffolding and followed Koch upwards into the mist.

As they entered the cave, Koch pointed towards several lanterns to the side.

"Get those lit and we'll start our search."

As Tomas struggled with striking a match with his numb fingers, Koch continued his demands. "Search everywhere. Every nook, every cranny. There's no question that we're at the right location and I'll be damned if I'm not going to find it."

With the first two lanterns lit, they were better able to see around them. Looking around, they could see that the cavern wasn't large, nor deep, but the walls were riddled with chiseled out enclaves which held the promise of their imminent discovery. Whether it was the Grail or anything else, Tomas shivered with the excitement and possibility of what they might uncover.

As the lanterns flickered their yellow light against the walls, they explored every enclave, every crevice and cranny for the rest of the morning but found nothing. The cave was eerily devoid of any signs of human contact. Koch, impatient with their lack of progress, stomped out to walk off his frustration while Tomas, grateful for a break, sat down on a small boulder, lit himself a cigarette and slowly looked around. *Who were these people?*

Koch returned in a stormy mood. "This place is a waste of time! Pick up those lanterns. They've found the other location and it damn well better be there."

———

In the fading light, both men arrived at the location some distance directly below where the ruins of the fortress stood towering over their heads. A small group of men were already there consisting of two labourers who sat on the ground, two guards standing over them, each holding a heavy pickaxe and a third guard who stood off to the side. Holding a lantern high above him, Koch surveyed the boulder where clearly a rusted ancient iron ring had been embedded in the rock. Tomas stood off to the side looking on. Koch looked over to the head guard and nodded. This was it.

"Where's the cave?"

Pointing in the direction towards a small bush, the lead guard added, "We've found a small entrance, sir, over here, but it will need to be enlarged before anyone can access it. I've been awaiting your orders before moving forward, sir."

Koch took a look and barked the orders to get started. "I want this accessed by tonight."

Then turning to Tomas, he snarled. "You, Richter, can stay here to monitor their progress. When it's been opened, come and get me. I'll be in the car. No one, but no one, is to enter without me present. Is that clear?"

"Yes, sir. Of course, sir."

As the two guards positioned the lanterns in order for them to see, the labourers worked over the next few hours clearing away debris and boulders from the entrance. Tomas quickly realizing that the only way he would stay warm was if he helped, rolled or carried the larger boulders off to the side. By the early hours they finally unearthed the opening to a tunnel. Tomas, exhausted and hungry, sent one of the guards to inform the Lieutenant, while he found a place to sit and light up a cigarette. He calculated that that way he could squeeze in a good half-hour rest.

By the time Koch returned, there were thin ribbons of red and orange streaks in the distance. Hearing the sound of footsteps on loose gravel, Tomas squashed his cigarette butt on the ground and stood brushing himself off.

Koch was in no mood to wait. As the lead guard handed him a lantern, he walked over to the entrance, then looked back at Tomas.

"Grab a pickaxe and a lantern, then follow me."

Koch led the way, leading with his lantern as he squeezed his large frame through the opening. Tomas followed and in the dim light gave a little gasp. Before them lay a small corridor framed by two columns and a collapsed archway in between. Barely visible was a tunnel behind.

Tomas glanced over to Koch who simply stood there, staring ahead, lantern held high like a statue. The smile on his face, altered by the deep scar that sliced through his cheek and the flickering light, momentarily contorted his face into a dark grimace. Tomas shuddered, but not from the cold. This place was sacred.

Slowly stepping their way around and over the crumbled rubble of the arch, Koch again held up the light to see what lay ahead. The tunnel before them seemed to continue for a short distance, but the ceiling was low. He again led the way but was forced to hunch his shoulders over and bend his head in order to carry on. After following the tunnel to the end, he was forced to stop. It didn't make sense. The tunnel led nowhere.

Tomas, despite the chilly conditions, began to sweat. Koch, clearly frustrated, gave the wall an angry kick and was surprised as a small portion gave way and crumbled to his feet.

Without looking back, he yelled. "Get that pickaxe you brought. *Now!*"

With the first blow, the false wall fell away, crumbling into a mixture of boulders and dust before his feet. Jumping back, to escape a falling rock, he couldn't help but smile at his discovery. In minutes, the two had created an opening big enough for them to crawl through and into a modest cavern. Neither of them could speak as they marveled at the faint blue paint and the occasional star that had survived centuries of decay covering the cave's ceiling. This place held magic.

Tomas looked around as if he was in a dream, the silence inside calling to his soul. It was if he had been here before but couldn't remember why or when. Even Koch was in awe.

Before them stood a small altar. A simple table-like structure hewn out of a solid oaken beam with the shreds of what once might have been covered with a white cloth. Centuries of dust and debris covered the top.

Slowly walking towards the altar, Koch looked at the surface. Clearly sometime in the past few years, there had been a square box-like shape that had been removed from the cave. The impression in the dust, the painted cavern, the columns and false cave wall, left no doubt as to what it might have been.

Looking further around the cavern, he discerned a small opening behind the altar where evidently there had been a secondary access. And in that moment, he thought back to Sophie and then to Isabelle's reaction to her Banon.

There was now only one place left to look and Koch had no doubts what was being hidden at a certain cheese cave.

CHAPTER THIRTY-FIVE

THE FOLLOWING MORNING, KOCH ORDERED TOMAS TO arrange for two train tickets to Paris for Helene and Nicole, and then to ensure that they were on the train. When this was completed, he was to return back to Montségur, where they would continue the hunt elsewhere. Barking out his orders, he turned on his heel and left him to follow them to the letter.

Later, over a hearty breakfast, he mentally reviewed the details of his plan. His reasons for honouring his agreement was two-fold. One, Helene was insurance should his plan go badly. He deduced that she may know more than she already disclosed. And as for the daughter, she would be a useful tool in persuading her mother to remember any of those details. If not, then pretty young ladies were always useful.

It was critical for his plan that Meli and her grandmother were isolated as much as possible. Sopping up some egg yolk with his toast, he toyed with the idea of having Tomas pull the trigger. *That would make a man out of him.* As for Berthe, the Milice had ensured him that she had been on her way to Drancy by last Friday. Run by the French police, those detained at Drancy would eventually be deported to the extermination camps in the East. It was now Tuesday. 'Fait accompli.'

———

Tomas shifted his glasses back up his nose as he exited the car and looked around. The sky was clear with the sunshine slowly melting chunks of snow, creating a lacy effect at the top. At the bottom, small rivulets of melting snow ran down the sloping edges until it pooled into shallow little ice-edged puddles.

Looking up at the windows of the cottage he half expected to see Meli looking out, or at least hoped that she would, but the cottage was silent. He presumed that the arrangements were in appreciation for Helene finding the manuscript, but he worried as to what was to come. He prayed that Koch would find what he was looking for while he was gone.

It was Helene who answered the door and with a hopeful smile, looked behind him for any signs of the Lieutenant. Wiping her hands on her apron, she looked back at him, but the smile was pasted on.

"Private Richter, please come in. To what do we owe this visit? Isabel and Meli are both out taking care of chores."

Stepping inside, he took off his cap and tucked it under his arm. With a small nod he explained. "I'm here, Madame, on behalf of Lieutenant Koch and have been instructed to give you these." From an inside pocket of his trench coat he pulled out the train tickets and a thick envelope. Helene's eyes widened as she took both items from him.

"The train, Madame, leaves this afternoon. I have also been instructed to ensure that you are both on it and arrive there safely. The envelope contains enough money to cover your immediate needs and once you reach Paris an envoy will meet you and take you to your apartment. My understanding is that all arrangements have been taken care of."

"So, we are to leave now?"

"Yes, Madame."

Helene could not believe her luck and in her excitement directed him to sit while she collected Nicole.

Running into the sitting room, where Nicole sat fumbling with knitting needles, she took them out of her hands, causing her daughter to crossly shout out. "Why did you do that? You've ruined it."

Helene could barely speak. "Go get dressed. We're leaving now. Hurry!"

Nicole, still angry from the ruined stitches, simply pouted. "Going where?"

"Back to Paris silly. Back to where we belong. Back to your friends. To food and parties. To our own apartment."

"But how?"

"Don't worry about how. Look, I have the tickets and look at this." Showing her the envelope of money, Nicole perked up.

"Quickly. Go upstairs and put on something warm. I don't want you to catch a chill on the train. Don't take anything with you. We'll buy whatever we need when we get back home."

"I wouldn't want to keep anything anyway."

"Tomas is here to take us to the train, so be quick. I'll leave Isabel a note. Hurry now, I don't want her to be here when we leave. Go!"

Within a few minutes they had gathered up their meagre belongings and had thrown everything into one of the beleaguered suitcases that had brought them there.

Tomas nodded to Nicole at the door as he took the suitcase from Helene's grasp. Still gaunt and pale, she was obviously better and able to travel. Helene, anxious to get going, forgot all about the note as she hurried her daughter to the car.

Closing their car doors, Tomas took one last look around and hoped Meli and Isabel were alright. Then getting into the car, he started it and drove slowly down the lane.

———

Isabel tromped through the snow as she came down the forest path from the cave. Much of the snow had melted and soon enough she would be able to take the goats up to the higher pastures to let them graze. Their milk was always better when they were able to feed off the land. She had been barely able to keep them alive as it was, over the winter. In her basket was a few rounds of her Banon—a welcome addition to their diet.

As she made her way towards the cottage, she was surprised to see the Mercedes pulling away and heading down the lane towards the main road. Her eyesight wasn't that sharp so she couldn't see who was in the backseat, only that there appeared to be two people. In a moment of panic, she trudged through the snow as fast as she could. *What if they've taken Meli!*

Grabbing the kitchen door, she yelled out for her but was met with silence. There was no one there. *Where was Helene and Nicole?* Isabel scoured the house looking for both Nicole and her mother, but it wasn't until she saw the empty bedrooms and their second-hand clothes tossed on the floor, that she figured out who had left in the car. Going back downstairs, she looked out the window towards the barn where hopefully Meli still worked away. Knowing she wouldn't feel settled until she saw that her grand-daughter was safe, she hurried to throw on her coat, but in that moment Meli walked through the door.

The intensity of her fear was all too much. Isabel rushed at her with open arms and embraced her in tight hug, unable to let go. Breaking down in tears, she cried. "I thought you were gone. I thought I had lost you."

Confused at her Grandmother's display of affection, Meli hugged her back. "What's wrong? What's happened, Mamina?"

Noting the silence, she looked towards the ceiling expecting noise from upstairs. "Where's Nicole and Helene?"

Isabel released her and dabbed at her eyes with an old handkerchief tucked into her pocket. "We need to talk Meli. We need to talk now. There is something of importance that I have hidden from you for too many years. Sit down at the table and I'll make both of us some coffee." She smiled. "The real kind."

As Meli took off her coat and boots, she watched her grandmother at the counter. "Where's Nicole and Helene?"

"I don't know, but I suspect they've gone back to Paris."

"Did M. Moser send for them?"

As Isabel placed two full cups on the table, she took a deep sigh and raised her eyebrows. "I highly doubt it, but it is partly why we need to talk."

Meli took a small sip and looked perplexed. "Okay."

"The truth is I don't know where to begin, Meli." Looking out the window to the far hills, she warmed her hands. "I've made so many mistakes over the years. There's so much to say."

Looking back at her Granddaughter, she stared at her for a minute. *My granddaughter, looking all of sixteen and yet embraces a spirit that's as ancient as these hills.*

"I've done you a disservice, Meli. Berthe tried to warn me many times, but I refused to listen. I kept thinking of you as a little girl. No, that's not right. I wanted you to stay a little girl, keep you safe. Through you, I would do a better job of parenting. Through you, I would still have Sophie."

Meli was clearly unsure as to where this was leading. "Sophie?"

"Forgive me, Meli, but there's no there's no other way to say this, but Sophie was your mother, not your sister." Isabel waited in silence for Meli's reaction. When Meli slowly nodded, she continued.

"Your father is a very wealthy married man. He is also Jewish so there was absolutely no way that he would have ever left his family to marry Sophie."

Meli leaned forward, her brows knitted with questions. "Did he know about me? Or even want to know about me?"

"To be honest with you, Meli, he knew about you but showed no interest after he found out she was pregnant.

"So, I'm half Jewish?"

"No. Your father is Jewish, but the religion follows through the mother's line, so no you are not Jewish. But you can understand why it's been important for your own safety to ensure that this remains a secret."

"Did Sophie want me?"

"Yes. Very much so. Meli, there is so much more to say and tell you, but I think it's best that we do this slowly. Sophie loved you very, very much but she was unmarried and there were other circumstances. Keeping you here was the best way for Sophie to both love you and keep you safe. I'm telling you this now because it looks like Helene and Nicole have left with those German officers and I am terrified as to what she might tell them."

"What secret does Helene know that she might tell?"

"Enough to get us all arrested or killed. She arranged a false identity card for you. It would implicate her as well, but that's not why Sophie and I needed to protect you."

Isabel then stood up and went to the counter, opening a cupboard door. Reaching inside, she pulled down an old biscuit tin, then returned to the table facing Meli. Opening the tin, she reached inside and pulled out the amulet. Placing it in her hand, she said, "I need you to wear this. Keep it hidden at all times, but never take it off. Promise me."

Meli nodded. "I promise."

"Look, it's been a long day, Meli, and what you've just learned is a bit of a shock."

"Yes and no. On one hand I always wondered why people said we look so much alike and I loved her like she was my mother. But I guess it must have been embarrassing for you to have an unwed daughter who got pregnant or for her to explain who I was. Did Nicole know?"

"I don't think so, but I can't say for sure. What I can say for

215

certain was that Sophie adored you and worked hard to pay for anything you needed. You mustn't ever think that you weren't loved because that wouldn't be true. There were other circumstances that took precedence in keeping you safe, but I don't want to get into that tonight. For tonight, it's enough that you are safe and warm and loved."

Meli gave a small smile and rose from her seat. Reaching out to Isabel she gave her a long, hard hug. "Thank you Mamina, for sharing this with me.' Then reaching for the amulet she held it in her hand. "Thank you for everything."

CHAPTER THIRTY-SIX

Two days later, Koch had Private Richter drive him back to the farm. It did not pass him by that his young assistant looked nervous when he heard their destination. Nor did he miss the budding friendship with Meli. He found it fitting that skinny little bookworm should find a shy awkward sixteen-year-old to be attractive. Well, they would see where that led to by the end of the day.

The extra day of examining both chambers led him to only one conclusion. Whatever had been there had been taken to another location and he meant to find it. Himmler was already anxiously awaiting the news of a successful discovery and he must be able to give it to him. Immediately.

Thinking back to his own role in Schreiber and Sophie's death, he reminded himself that failure was not an option. He was noted for his successful missions and this one would be no different. There was no more time left.

As the car turned into the lane, he congratulated himself for purposely timing their arrival for early in the morning, ensuring that they both would still be there. The last thing he wanted was to have to get either one of them from the village. The less eyes the better. As they pulled up towards the back of the house, he was pleased to see diffused light through the kitchen curtains along with the shadow of someone walking around. Perfect.

The slamming of the car doors caused a curious face to look out, as he knew it would. It was Isabel. *Like a fly in my web.* Koch's eyes held hers with freezing contempt as he walked to the door.

Isabel, dressed in a cotton dress and heavy sweater, opened the door, her face blanched with concern.

"Lieutenant Koch, what brings you here at this hour?"

Instead of answering, he pushed her aside and stepped into the kitchen. "I'm afraid, Madame, that we are once again here on official business. Where is your granddaughter?"

Isabel paled, "What do you want with Meli? I don't know what Helene has told you, but it's a lie."

Koch, smirked, causing his scar to grotesquely stretch across his cheek. *Well, Helene, holding out on me eh? No matter, I'll deal with you later. For now, this is just added leverage and will make today go so much easier.* "Get her now."

He could hear the quiver in her voice as she slowly climbed halfway up the stairs calling for Meli. *Good, he wanted her afraid.*

Turning to Tomas, he stared directly at him watching with interest at his obvious discomfort. "Don't fret, Richter, all will be revealed and if you're a very good boy, I may even let you play." Colour drained from his face as Meli silently followed her Grandmother into the kitchen. She looked terrified.

Koch remained standing, towering over Isabel. "Sit down and we'll have a chat, shall we?"

Isabel's hands shook as she sat down, then moved her chair over as close as possible to Meli's. Taking her granddaughter's hand in hers she looked once at Meli, gave a quick smile, then focused on Koch. "How can we help you, Lieutenant?"

Meli, obviously concerned, kept glancing at Tomas as if expecting some kind of answer. Koch smiled. *Perfect. He now knew exactly what he needed to do, and which one was expendable. Poor Tomas, but these things happen.*

Looking directly at Isabel, he spoke slowly and clearly, his eyes cold and his face devoid of any feeling. Everyone needed to understand that he meant business, including that little pup of a soldier. "Your daughter Sophie died in a car accident three years ago with Victor Schreiber. The weather was rainy and the roads near Montségur were very slippery that day. The flames from the crash were quite spectacular." He then paused for effect.

"It was just before 3:00 as I recall. I remember this precisely, because at 4:00 I had a particularly lovely Chardonnay at my hotel. Do I have your attention now, Madame?"

Isabel slowly nodded her head once, without losing eye contact with her daughter's killer. As Meli's face drained with comprehension, she grasped her grandmother's hand even tighter.

"Good. You see I need you to know this because it explains so much. Why, for instance, Schreiber befriended Sophie in the first place and why Schreiber's manuscript was found in your attic. I must say that your friend Helene was very helpful in that regard."

Pulling out a chair, he sat down and proceeded to pull out a cigarette, while Tomas, who stood behind him, fumbled to pull out a lighter before it reached his mouth.

Koch leaned forward and slammed his meaty hand on the table. "You know what I want, am I correct?"

Isabel's face was ashen. She nodded while tears streamed down her cheeks. It wasn't hard for her to figure out what their fate would be. Meli, however, was unusually quiet and as she stared back at him, her eyes smouldered with hate. *How very interesting. There's a strength there that I haven't seen before.*

Taking a long drag of the cigarette, he continued. "Richter, while the ladies here get their coats and boots on, I'll need you to get the pickaxe and shovel from the trunk. I have a feeling that we'll be needing them. We'll meet you outside." Stretching his hand towards the door, he gestured for them to get started. "Ladies? Madame Durand, I think it's high time that we visit this cave of yours."

———

After a long, awkward slog through the snow, they arrived at the cave entrance. Grabbing Isabel's arm, Koch roughly pushed her forward to unlock the gated entryway. As he did so, Tomas looked quickly back at Meli who was clearly terrified. He didn't blame her. He was as well. *Koch is capable of anything. How far would he take this?*

The gate groaned as its rusty hinges reluctantly gave way and one by one, they entered the narrow passageway. Isabel pulled an old lantern off of a makeshift metal hook and lit it with some matches that she produced from her pocket. Single file they walked the short distance to the cavern. Isabel first, Tomas next, Meli and then Koch at the rear.

As they entered the room, Tomas took a quick look around. Light from the lantern flickered on the cave walls and the noticeably depleted shelves where rounds of cheese would have once been placed to ripen. A few large barrels of eau-de-vie were stacked towards the back, while an ancient wooden table stood towards the side. A plastic pail, discoloured from use, sat on top alongside two large earthenware crocks.

Leaning the shovel and pickaxe against the wall, he turned to see Koch grabbing the lantern from Isabel's hands. Raising it up high, he slowly walked around, lighting up the dark areas as he passed by. Both Isabel and Meli backed up towards the wall as all three watched him. No one said a word. After he had completed several circuits, he slowly turned to Isabel and calmly asked. "Where is it?"

Isabel's voice was small and terrified. "I don't know what you are talking about."

Striding over to the barrels, he rolled one after the other on to the cave floor. As each one crashed to the ground, the brandy poured out, soaking the floorboards in an alcoholic odour. "My patience is wearing thin. Where. Is. It?"

Isabel begged him to stop, but this just enraged him more. A patch of the back wall was now clear and grabbing the pickaxe he began to swing. Tomas half expected that the wall would crumble away as the other caves had, but the axe met with solid rock.

After several wasted attempts, he threw the axe to the side.

Turning back to the women, he struck in a flash. In a single move, he grabbed Meli by the collar and with a vicious yank dragged her over to where an upturned barrel continued to dribble the strong liquor. Throwing her to the ground, he reached for his Luger.

Tomas didn't think twice about the consequences. He only knew he had to do something, and fast. Drawing his gun, he pointed it at his commander. Hands shaking, he faced Koch. "Let her go."

Koch jutted his chin and laughed. "You think you're going to kill me little pup? You don't have the guts."

Tomas gripped the weapon harder to steady his hand. Adrenalin pumping, he screamed at his superior officer. "I said, let her go."

Koch stared at his assistant for a full minute, then with a sneer, pushed Meli over to where Isabel huddled in the corner.

Tomas momentarily relaxed as he saw Meli safe, but it was already too late. No match for the giant of a man, it took only seconds for Koch to disarm him and then backhand him with the butt of the gun. As he slipped into unconsciousness, he saw stars, heard Meli cry out, then everything went black.

———

In two strides the enraged Koch grabbed Meli and forced her on her knees. Placing the gun to her forehead he pulled the trigger back. "Where is it?"

Tears streaked down her face as Isabel pleaded, "Please just let her go. She knows nothing about any of this."

"I will count to three. One…."

Head bent, Meli's eyes looked up towards her grandmother and was suddenly and strangely not afraid. The voice from her dreams was in her head…remember who you are…remember who you are…and in that moment she knew.

"Two…"

Isabel, shaking hysterically screamed. "Don't kill her! I'll tell you anything you want to know, just don't kill her…" But it was Meli who pointed with a confident finger to the back of the cave to an untouched dark corner.

"Well, well, out of the mouths of babes." Kicking Meli towards her grandmother, he pointed his gun at the centre of Isabel's forehead. "Don't move even a muscle and you had better hope she's right."

Putting his gun back in its holster, he swung his arm up to wipe his forehead, then took hold of the last barrel and pulled it aside. As the barrel thumped and rolled on to the floorboards, he retrieved the lantern and placed it near the darkened corner. Lifting the pickaxe he had used earlier he gave a heavy swing and was rewarded with a small hole. Encouraged, he picked up his pace, all the while checking to ensure that Meli and Isabel remained where he could see them. The more he hit the wall, the more the false surface fell in pieces and chunks until he could see inside.

Lifting the lantern, his pulse raced at what he saw. The false wall opened into a similar cavern created at Montségur, only this room had been maintained. The blue ceiling with silver stars was as beautiful as if it had been painted yesterday. A deep rectangular block of white carved marble formed an altar where a small carved wooden box was placed in the centre and to the left was an ancient bookcase where six large ancient tomes were chained to a crossbar. The room was large enough for him to stand, but in order to gain entry, he would have to pick away at the wall. No matter, he could afford to take his time now that he had found it.

Turning around, he looked at both Isabel and Meli. "Well, well, well. You're in quite a predicament, now aren't you? The real question is who goes first? Lifting his arm, he pointed the Luger first to one, and then the other. Should it be the Grand-mama or should it be the granddaughter? Decisions, decisions, decisions."

Slowly moving his gun to face Meli, he smiled. "It would be such a shame to kill you without Tomas watching." He pouted his lower lip. "In fact, I was hoping that he would have the guts to pull the trigger himself, but it appears that he doesn't have the stomach for it. Of course, there's always alternatives and I do like to play. I can only assume you're a virgin, are you not Meli? So, with that to look forward to..." He pointed the gun back at Isabel, then slowly back at Meli, "I'm afraid it's you, young lady, and Grandma gets to watch."

As they heard the click, Isabel stared hard at Koch, her hands still holding Meli's, when suddenly a dark blur sprung from the murky shadows swinging an axe at Koch's head and in that moment, a gun was fired.

Everything next happened in slow motion. The axe, catching him by the side of his head, knocked him off balance. His eyes widened, and as he slowly raised his hand to his head, his eyes rolled back into white as he slumped and then pitched forward. A flow of blood trailed beneath him as his body thumped to the floor. The gun, however, had found its mark.

Berthe rushed over to find Isabel gasping for breath as blood poured from a hole in her chest. The wound was bad. Meli's hands were covered in blood as she desperately applied pressure, to no avail. Tears rolled down as she begged and pleaded. "Please stay Mamina...Don't go...please don't go."

Berthe slowly sat down beside Isabel cradling her head in her arms. "There, there my friend."

As Isabel struggled to stay conscious, she winced, gasping as she attempted to speak. "Tell...Meli...the truth."

"Don't speak, Isabel. Just try to hold on."

With her last bit of energy, Isabel tried once more. "The whole truth.... I'm so sorry Meli. I love you..." and then with a sudden whoosh, she passed.

Neither Meli nor Berthe spoke for several minutes until Meli finally looked up and stared at Berthe. "How is this even possible? I...thought you were in a camp...dead. Yet here you are. I... I don't know what to do."

Berthe looked down at Isabel and took in a deep breath. "There's so much to say."

From over towards Tomas came a moan. As he slowly put his hand to his head and tried to stand up, Berthe launched into an order. "Stay right there, young man. Let me check you out first."

"What...what happened?"

"We'll discuss that later, but first, let me have a look at you." Only after she was convinced that it wasn't anything more serious than a nasty bump on his head, did she move back to Meli, who had wrapped her arms around herself and began to cry in a tiny voice. "It's all right...it's all right..." Tomas slowly stood up, wavered a little, then crept over to sit beside her.

Nodding towards the hole in the wall of the cave, he shook his head in disbelief. "It's real. It's really real. Then looking back at Berthe, he questioned, "Who the hell are you people?"

Berthe looked over towards the wall, gave a deep sigh, and dropped her hands. "All in good time, Tomas. All in good time."

Tomas jerked his head in the direction of Koch's still body. "Is he dead?"

Berthe glanced back and nodded. "I believe so. I can't imagine he wouldn't be."

Tomas, blowing out his cheeks, was obviously nervous. "This is bad. Really bad. They'll come looking for someone like him."

Berthe stood up. "It's not safe for us to involve anyone else and I don't want to leave Isabel here. I suggest, Tomas, that we find that old sled in the barn and carry Isabel back to the house with that. Meli and I will tidy her up and she'll be buried here on the farm. Tomorrow you'll need to dig two graves. We have no choice. We could bury him somewhere in the woods. After that I don't know."

Running her fingers behind her neck, she spoke gently to Meli. "There are things long overdue that need to be said, explained and perhaps that's how we can best honour your grandmother by doing that tonight."

Later, as the three of them sat in silence at the kitchen table, Tomas with his head bandaged, Meli with her red eyes and Berthe with her heart breaking at the death of her friend, she began the only way she knew how, from the beginning.

CHAPTER THIRTY-SEVEN

BERTHE SAT FOR A MOMENT, HER HEAD SLIGHTLY TO THE SIDE, staring off into nowhere and wondered to herself where to begin. Turning to Meli, she asked, "Did Isabel tell you anything?"

Meli nodded slowly but kept her head down. "She said that Sophie was my mother but I'm not sure how I feel about that."

Patting her hand, Berthe nodded in agreement. "I can imagine that it's a lot to take in, but there were a number of reasons why that decision was made. It's true that one of them was to protect Sophie's reputation, after all she wasn't married, but the other was to protect you."

"She told me that my father was Jewish." Tomas visibly flinched, realizing the danger she was still in.

"Yes, he was a rich married man but there was something more," Berthe said softly.

"Meli, the dreams you've been having are not just dreams. I know that you are aware that you come from a long line of Cathars, but your lineage is so much more than that. The woman in your dreams, India Le Tardif, was your ancestor and the Guardian of the Cathar treasure. My family ancestors have been your ancestor's guardians since that time. Isabel and my friend-ship was no coincidence.

"We talked a little bit about reincarnation before, and you already know that they strongly believed in this philosophy. You Meli, are the reincarnation of India Le Tardif. The reason we know this and have known it from the moment you were born, is because of your birthmark. The one that is on the back of your shoulder blade. It meant that Sophie had to protect you and your grandmother had to keep you safe. I won't lie to you and pretend that I agreed with her not sharing this with you. We had many fights about this, and I was adamant that she should have told you all these things long before. It's just that when Sophie died, she couldn't bear to lose you as well."

Tomas shook his head. "So, Sophie was the Keeper of the Grail?"

"No, Tomas. It was Isabel. When Sophie realized that the Nazis were hunting the Grail artifacts, she wanted to keep you both safe and took whatever steps she could to ensure that. We think that's why she was with Schreiber, to misdirect the search, let him think that it was her to ensure the Nazi's wouldn't take the Grail. I don't think she counted on him being so sympathetic to the Cathar cause. I can only assume that's why he trusted her enough to give her the manuscript to keep safe. As you say, Meli, she must have hidden it in the attic."

Meli rubbed her temples. "What about the cave?"

"The cave has been in the family for generations, in fact, the farm dates back to India Le Tardif and her father, whose mother was India Serras, all keepers of the Grail treasure since 1244 and the fall of Montségur. There is an old saying that goes back generations to this time. In 700 years, the Laurel will be green once more."

It was Tomas who asked the question. "I've read that, but what does it mean?"

"The Laurel refers to the tree of life, the growth of knowledge. As the underground river secretly winds its way under our mountains, caves and caverns, so too does the flow of sacred knowledge seep its way into the roots of the land above. As the water of knowledge nourishes the laurel of truth, so too do we nourish our parched souls. Our sacred knowledge did not die, it simply awaited the time for it to feed the seeds of truth and light. That time, Meli, is now."

"There was a moment in the cave when I suddenly knew that everything was going to be okay. I felt like India was there with me, guiding me through, but when Mamina died… I just felt lost. I still feel lost. Berthe, what am I supposed to do?"

"I don't know. I can't answer that for you. But you may find answers in those dreams of yours. I do know that my time will one day end and another will have to take my place. It would appear, Tomas, that that task will one day be yours."

"But why me?"

"I didn't choose, Tomas, you did. For whatever reason you two are connected and one day my role will be yours. For now, I can answer your questions and guide, but the next decisions will be yours and yours alone."

Tomas rubbed the back of his neck and pondered their next moves. "We need to cover up Koch's death somehow or make it look like he's still alive. They'll come looking for him and he answers directly to Himmler."

Berthe nodded and looked at them both. "It will be the same for Isabel. We can't let anyone know that you and Koch were here, or what happened in the cave."

Meli nodded. "We also need to milk the goats and feed those poor chickens. They must be starving."

Berthe clapped her hands to orchestrate what needed to be done. "Right. Tomas, come with me. You and I will do the goats, Meli can take care of the chickens and get started on a light soup. We'll need some nourishment for what's in store for tomorrow. We'll need a good night's sleep tonight and sort out what we need to do in the morning. Tomas, you may want to park that Mercedes further around the back where it's not as visible. Meli, if ever there was a time to dream, tonight would be it."

————

Later, as Meli climbed the narrow stairway to her room, she tried to make sense of what had happened that day. Mamina's death, along with the mountain of information that had become her life, was too much to process, too much to think about. All she wanted to do was to crawl into a little hole and stay there until she awoke from this bad dream. Berthe had already taken her blood-stained clothes, but a rusty smear on her floorboard was a sharp reminder that it had been real.

Too exhausted and numb to feel anything more, she climbed under the covers and tightly held her amulet, her one connection to Mamina tonight.

As she drifted off to sleep, there was a subtle scent of lavender in the room. In her sleepy state, she sighed and imagined it gently swirling around her head in colours of turquoise, lilac and emerald greens, the scent intensifying as it spun her deeper and deeper. Comforting and warm, it pulled her into the abyss of colours until suddenly she was on solid ground.

She found herself standing on a mountain top. Looking down, she wore a long dark indigo shift; her hair, long and loose fell down her back. A gentle breeze played with the loose ends of her hair and the hem of her robe, while a heavy mist clung to the craggy rocks below, hiding secrets of what lay beyond. It was impossible to tell what time of day it was, morning or dusk, it could have been either. The air was neither warm nor cool. There was a magical quality to the landscape's tone and flavour, its colours subdued, ethereal, fragile, heart-achingly beautiful.

Suddenly, a solitary dove launched from the mists below, soaring higher and higher into the sky. She watched as the tiny bird began to spiral on a mountain thermal, tilting its wings this way and that in order to catch the elusive current. Her body longed to be at one with the bird, to free herself, to soar as the bird soared, and for a moment she was there with it, observing herself below. She was free. Free of boundaries, of expectations, gloriously free of fear. But in the next moment she was back on the mountain top, bound to her earthly body.

The solitary dove, the symbol of the Cathar faith, the symbol of peace, continued to play as she watched. Such a gentle, unassuming little bird, she thought, yet so much is expected of it.

In the next instant, it vanished, as did her dream.

————

The following morning a thick fog clung to the hills and forest. The dull, dank day matched their heavy hearts as the three gathered in the kitchen. Berthe was already busy brewing coffee and scrambling some eggs as Tomas sat at the table, deep in thought.

Meli, still in a daze, was the last to join them and as she pulled a chair out for herself, she gave a quick look to Tomas who looked as lost as she felt. Wedges of cheese were already on the table, but she didn't feel hungry.

Berthe poured the coffee, then brought them both a mug to the table, then returned with three plates of eggs and her own cup. As if reading her mind, she looked over at Meli. "I know you're feeling lost, Meli, but you need to eat to keep up your strength. Unfortunately, today is not going to be any easier. We'll need to bury Mamina. Maybe up on the hill that overlooks the cottage?"

Meli nodded in agreement. "She always liked that view. In the summer, we could mark it in some way. Make it special."

Berthe smiled. "I agree, Meli. Maybe we could plant lavender plants all around. What do you think?"

Something about lavender tweaked at her memory, but she couldn't think what. "She always loved lavender."

Berthe took a sip of coffee and turned to Tomas, who had already cleared his plate.

"We're going to have to rely on you to help with that. The ground is quite rocky, but it can be done."

"Whatever you need, Madame."

Meli took in a deep breath, then exhaled. "What do we tell the people in town? What about Father Pelletier? Everyone will be asking questions. What do we say? Is it even safe for you to be here Berthe?"

Tomas added his concerns. "What about Koch and the search? He alerted Himmler that he was close, so something needs to be reported. This won't just go away. If they find out the truth, I'll be court-martialed and shot."

Berthe looked at them both then clapped her hands. "Okay. First things first. We need to bury Isabel. We can't involve anyone else because of the bullet wound, so for now if anyone asks, she's feeling under the weather or busy with chores. Eventually we can tell everyone that she had a sudden heart attack and it was her wish to be buried here.

"In terms of me, you're right. It's not safe. But thanks to Tomas here, who was the one who alerted me in the first place, I'm still here and will remain out of sight."

Meli swiveled to look at Tomas. "What?"

Embarrassed, he looked up once to Meli, then back again to Berthe. "It was nothing."

Berthe stared back. "It was enough, Tomas." Then squinting her eyes in thought she asked, "You said that you had excavated at Montségur did you not?"

Taking a sip of his coffee, he nodded and replied, "Yes."

"And that you found two empty caves, correct?"

"Yes. That's when he knew it had to be here, because of Sophie and the fact that the manuscript was in your attic."

"Is the cave still accessible?"

"Yes, I believe so."

Berthe was silent for a minute, as a plan played out in her head. "And has anyone else had access to it?"

"No. They were on orders to restrict anyone from going inside."

"Okay. What if we give them what they've asked for and an alternative reason for Koch's death?"

Both Tomas and Meli leaned forward and spoke in unison. "Give them the Grail?"

Berthe leaned back and smiled. "Or something like it. There's something that neither of you know. In the cave, there are two small wooden caskets that contain identical cups. There is a story that has been passed down through many, many generations that only one is real. The other is a deadly decoy. Unfortunately, I have no idea which one is real.

"However, if we could somehow plant the false one in the cave, Tomas, you could find it or say that Koch found it. You could say that you and he had returned and after finding the grail he fell somehow. The gash to his head could easily be from the rocks. You could say he wanted to do it alone and you found him like that. It could look like an accident. Then he could take all the success for find the grail and you could take it to Himmler on his behalf. Say that the books were not found with the cup and with Koch gone…."

Tomas knitted his brows, trying to work out the logistics of the plan and if it could even work. "I think it's the only plan we have, other than saying he disappeared with the Grail and books on his own. But Himmler would leave no stone unturned tracking him down. When they didn't find him, they would come here. But how will we know which of the Grails is the real one?"

Meli sat up straight and placed her hand on the table. There was confidence in her voice. "If I am who you say I am, I will know."

Berthe nodded in agreement. "The 16th of March is in two days. We have no choice. BBC Londres says Germany is losing the war. They may be too busy elsewhere to spend time investigating Koch's death."

Tomas asked, "What about the manuscript?"

Meli was firm. "Give them that as well."

"Why would we do that? Himmler will just send someone else to find them."

It was Berthe who replied. "Probably. But Meli's right. All they'll find is an empty cave and Koch is the one who figured it out. No one else will."

———

As Tomas toiled away on the hill, Berthe and Meli tenderly washed and fixed Mamina's hair before dressing her in her best Sunday dress. Berthe talked to her the entire time as if she were simply sleeping. Meli was grateful and it made their task much easier. After they were done, Berthe suggested that they wrap her in a sheet, but Meli wouldn't have it. "No, she needs to be in her quilt. It's cold outside and I want her to stay warm."

A short time later, the three of them stood on the hill where Mamina had been gently placed in the ground. Neither Berthe nor Meli could bear to watch Tomas shovel dirt in her grave so they turned, arm in arm facing the cottage until he was finished.

With a lump in her throat, Meli choked out her goodbye. "Thank you, Mamina, for everything you've given me. I know I didn't appreciate things as much as I should have, but I promise you I do now. I'm going to make you proud."

Berthe struggled to compose herself, managing only a whisper. "I'll miss you my dear friend."

After they had finished, they joined Tomas in surrounding her grave with a circle of loose boulders that were scattered around. As Meli placed the last one and stood for a final few moments in silence, a small little mourning dove who had been watching them from a nearby bush, flew down and landed on her grave. Giving each of them a quick look, the bird spread its wings and took flight.

Holding Meli closer, Berthe pointed upwards as they watched the dove soar into the sky. "That's a message from Isabel." Meli looked back at her with a quizzical look wondering why the dove seemed so familiar.

Berthe smiled. "Our little bird has flown."

CHAPTER THIRTY-EIGHT

LATER THAT AFTERNOON THEY ENTERED THE CAVE. AN OLD blanket, along with some heavy rope, had been brought in order to wrap Koch's body into it. Everyone was anxious with the gruesome task ahead.

Meli led the way up the path, followed by Tomas and finally Berthe trudging her way up with a cane and the occasional help from Tomas. Reaching the entrance, Meli unlocked the iron gate, lit the lantern and handed it to Tomas. Holding the lantern high, they slowly proceeded forward not relishing what they would see. No one said a word.

As they entered the cavern, the smell of copper and urine assaulted their nostrils and as Tomas lifted the lantern higher, Koch's body lay where he had fallen the day before. His head in a pool of red-black blood. Tomas and Berthe immediately walked over to the body and lay the blanket out beside him, but Meli stopped them. "Can we get the Grail first before we do that? I'd rather my mind be clear before…that has to be done."

Berthe and Tomas exchanged looks as Berthe replied. "Of course, Meli, that makes much more sense."

The women quickly turned to the gash in the back wall as Tomas grabbed the axe in preparation to widen the gap, but Berthe stopped him. "There's no need, Tomas."

Walking up to the barrel that partially blocked the way, she put her hand around the back and felt around for the insert that she knew would be there. Hearing the click she stood back as a small seamlessly hidden door swung out from the wall.

Berthe turned, smiled and gestured towards Meli. "You first." Ducking her head and carrying the lantern before her, Meli entered the small chamber and gasped. Tomas and Berthe followed.

Above them, the cave had been painted in a deep blue with silver stars that gave the impression of the night sky. Before them lay a 3-foot chunk of marble polished to a fine finish that served as a small altar that held two carved wooden boxes. Both ornately carved. All three stood in silence and in awe. There was no question that this was sacred space.

Tomas and Berthe held back as Meli took two steps forward and reverently knelt down in front of the altar and lowered her head. The air was thick, and she felt light-headed. Soft subtle whispers filled the cavern as small sparks of light seemed to flash from out of nowhere. And in that moment, she remembered her dream. The whispers, the colours, the dove....*the little bird has flown.*"

Meli looked down at the carved boxes and slowly unlatched the clasp on each and opened the lids. Inside, both contained a plain carved alabaster cup, impossible to tell apart. Closing the lids back up, she reached for the amulet that hung from her neck and examined the intricate artwork on the top of the caskets. *The little bird has flown...*

Comparing the two she quickly saw what she had been looking for. For although both carvings contained birds, only one had the carving of a dove. The other was an eagle—the same symbol used by the Third Reich. It was clear which one she needed to take. Picking up the box with the eagle carving, she then stood and faced the books. These would stay here untouched and unharmed.

Nodding to them both that it was time to leave, she hunched herself forward to enter the main cavern, while Berthe followed with the lantern, Tomas in the rear.

It took only a second for a black shadow to grab her by the throat and roughly thrust her against the cave wall. Dropping the box, she tore wildly at his hands as she struggled to breath.

By the time Berthe and Tomas were back in the main cavern, Koch had released the tension on his grip, enough to allow her feet to reach the floor. In the dim lantern light, she opened her eyes to a grotesque blood-spattered smile and a gun pointed at her head.

"Both of you so much as move a finger and she's dead," he snarled. "You understand me? And you, Richter, you pathetic little traitor. I'll have you shot in front of a firing squad before the week is out."

Pointing his chin towards the far wall, he hissed, "Now both of you over there. Pushing the gun nozzle into Meli's head even harder, she scrunched up her face and winced at the pain. "*Now!*"

Facing him, both Tomas and Berthe backed up to the cave wall where he could clearly see them. Berthe pleaded to the enraged man. "Please just let her go. It's me you want."

Instead, he pushed the gun even further into Meli, causing her to cry out. "You must think I'm stupid, old woman."

Tomas opened his mouth to speak, but Koch was venomously angry. With spittle spraying from his mouth, he screamed. "Shut up! Traitor. Just shut up. One word from either of you and she's dead, understand?" There was no hiding the fear in their eyes as they both nodded.

"Good. Now that I have your attention, here's what we're going to do." In an eerily calm voice, Koch looked to Berthe. "Are there or are there not books in that room?"

Berthe nodded a yes.

"How many?"

Berthe looked confused but answered quickly. "Around six heavy volumes."

With the gun still to Meli's head, he grabbed her shoulder and dragged her over to where the rope lay on the floor and kicked it over to Tomas.

"Take this rope and tie the old lady up to the side post of one of those shelves. Tight. And no fast moves."

Tomas and Berthe walked slowly to the nearest shelf and got Berthe to sit on the floor. Wincing as her arms were pulled back, she watched Meli the entire time.

Once it was accomplished, Tomas waited for his next orders. "Go back in there and take out three books. I don't give a damn which ones. I just want three."

"Yes, sir."

"When you are done, I want you to slowly come back here and pick up the wooden box. The three of us will be taking a little trip." Turning to Berthe, he smiled. "You, Madame, will not be joining us."

Leaving Berthe in the darkness of the cave, Koch directed Tomas forward while he held the gun to Meli's head. Taking one last look in Berthe's direction, he pointed his pistol and shot.

———

The sun was setting fast as Tomas drove to Montségur, with Koch holding the gun to Meli's chest as insurance.

He snarled. Blood had caked over his head wound from the day before and had probably saved his life, but he was still weak and had a splitting headache.

"You must be wondering why we're travelling back to Montségur, Richter?

He could see the flick of Tomas' eye's as he quickly looked back at Meli. "No, sir."

"Hmmm really? And what about you, young lady? Aren't you just the teeniest bit curious?"

Meli managed the tiniest of shaking her head. "No matter, I'll tell you anyway."

"You see, it's the perfect scenario and exactly what Himmler expects. The success of the mission will be attributed to me, with no one the wiser that there are more books. Books that Himmler would pay dearly for I might add.

"Neither of you, unfortunately, will be there at the grand moment of discovery, but these things happen. Sadly, it will be a tragedy that no one expected, but after all, the cliffs are rather steep. I think an accidental fall from the fortress itself would be a rather poetic end, don't you?

"I find the timing interesting. In a mere five hours it will be March 16[th,] a significant date as I recall. What an appropriate time for the Keeper of the Grail to die, right Tomas?"

By the time, they arrived at the base of the Pog, it was completely dark. Grabbing Meli by the collar, Koch yanked her out of the car and instructed Tomas to open the trunk. "Put those books and the Grail box in that backpack and put it on. Then pick up the two flashlights and hand me one."

His instructions were simple. Tomas would lead, lighting their way, while he followed in the rear with the gun pointed at Meli's back. Cutting her wrists loose he pushed her forward with the gun barrel between her shoulders. "One wrong move and she's dead."

The climb up the rocky path was slow and difficult, requiring frequent stops. Koch's headache was worse the more he exerted himself, but he steeled himself against the pain. Their deaths needed to look accidental and needed to be done tonight. The tragedy of it all would add to the mystique, but revenge was his personal focus.

After finally arriving at the fortress, Koch instructed Tomas to drop the backpack down on the ground. The moon shone down, bathing the ruins in a subtle light.

———

Meli looked around at the fortress and felt more than just a connection to where she stood, she felt its powerful magic. Pockets of snow still lay on the ground and the air was still with anticipation. This was where her ancestors had died. Where she too would likely die before dawn's light peeked over the horizon. So be it.

Entering through a deep archway, Koch was now directing them over to the right, where the ruins of an ancient staircase rambled up the side of the fortress wall. Again, he directed Tomas to go first, requiring him to use both his hands to navigate up the slippery snow-covered steps. Shivering from the cold, Meli climbed next, tightly holding on to the wall to prevent herself from falling.

Despite their predicament, the vista from the top was magical and ghostly. As the moonlight highlighted the distant trees and rocky outcrops, Meli suddenly felt calm, as if she were home. This place felt familiar. It felt like her dream. She knew no matter what happened that all would be okay. Turning to look at Tomas she smiled, but Tomas was looking at Koch.

———

Koch rubbed his head, his eyes squeezed into slits as the throb, throb, throbbing wouldn't stop. Dark shadows flew by. *Why would birds be flying at night?* Flying towards him, blinding him. He could feel their wings shifting the air around his head as they swirled and surrounded him. Pointing the gun to a large winged shadow, he shot once to make sure that they stayed away.

The gun cleared his head somewhat, and he focused all of his frustration and anger at the two people who stood at the edge of the ruins. He could see Richter, scared little boy holding Meli's hand. Pointing his gun at the boy, he pretended that he was about to shoot, then laughed hysterically as his eyes went large and wide. His head continued to pound. Boom, boom, boom.

Looking below, he registered that a small push off the edge wouldn't be enough. No, they would need to be flung. Meli could be shot, but Richter must look like an accident or kept alive for court martial. What to do, what to do?

Pointing the gun at Meli, he winced as a sudden flash of light blocked his vision. He felt dizzy and stumbled forward and in that exact moment a young man's boot connected with his gut and he lost balance. Struggling for his weapon, he desperately tried to blink away his blurred vision, but an unseen pair of hands, (*or was it several?*) pitched him forward with an inhuman force that caused him to fall in a long wide arch. In the next moment everything for Lieutenant Wolfgang Koch went dark.

———

Too shocked to move, both Meli and Tomas watched in horror as Koch's body launched into the air, as if a freight train had hit him. As he plummeted hundreds of feet below, he bounced off several rocky outcrops until finally there was silence. This time, there would be no question of him surviving.

They stayed there for a few minutes more, sitting on the rampart, watching the moon, listening to the owls, with Tomas' arm around the shaking Meli, until a shard of light indicated a new day was about to unfold. March 16th, 1944, the 700th anniversary of the massacre of Montségur had arrived.

CHAPTER THIRTY-NINE

THE OVERCAST SKY AHEAD CREATED AN OMINOUS SPELL OVER THE day ahead as Tomas and Meli made their way back to the farm. As it began to drizzle, Tomas was ever more conscious of his driving on the slippery roads. He was nervous at what the day would bring and so many things had to come together. Getting Meli back would be just the first step.

They had already placed the false Grail in the second cave for Tomas to find later with a witness, but the immediate concern was Berthe. There was no way that he would leave Meli to discover Berthe's fate alone and neither of them knew what to expect. Did she too die in the cave? Or maybe she was injured. No, they needed to do this together. As soon as that was done, he would need to return as fast as he could in order to orchestrate a lie.

Meli, looking as anxious as he felt, stared ahead, tensing at every curve on the mountain roads while he kept a constant watch in the back-view mirror to assure himself that they weren't being followed.

As they drove up to the farm, it was as if nothing had ever

happened. Snuggled safely into the landscape, the cottage looked the same. The kitchen light glowed warmly through the curtains and a curl of smoke spiraled lazily up from the chimney flue. It felt surreal, not at all matching the churning fear and adrenalin rush of what needed to be done.

The plan was to grab a few medical supplies in case they were needed, then head straight up to the cave. They exited the car and raced into the kitchen. Of all the scenarios that Tomas had imagined, what happened next was not one of them.

As they entered the kitchen, Berthe was quietly sitting at her usual place at the table, her tarot cards splayed out in front of her. A make-shift bandage had been wrapped around her left arm. A small blood stain had seeped through but looked to be no more than a graze from the bullet.

A heartbeat later, Meli was in her arms. Through the flow of tears, she cried out, "I thought you were dead!"

Berthe patted her back, soothing her as best she could with a, "There, there. It will all be okay." The entire time she looked at Tomas. No words were needed. *Well done young man.*

Looking out the window as dawn was rapidly approaching, Tomas broke the spell. "I need to get back to Montségur. There's still much to be done. You're sure you're okay, Madame?"

"Yes, I'm fine Tomas. But perhaps Meli and I could drive back with you. We'll be able to make our own way back, but I think it's important for Meli and myself that we be there at the citadel today. You can let us out before anyone sees us and carry on."

Tomas looked back at her arm, but Berthe waved him away before he could even ask the question. "I'll be fine, and no one will notice through my coat."

Tomas nodded his agreement. "Okay, but we must go now. I'll get the books from the trunk and check the fireplace while both of you dress yourselves warmly." Berthe stifled a smile.

Tomas had become a man overnight. *Good, because he's going to need to be in the years to come.*

Morning broke as they arrived back to the Montségur area. The defiant sky was gloomy and cold, streaked with endless cracks of light that stretched out to infinity. He parked at the base of the Pog, near a small graveyard and turned off the engine. It was time for goodbyes.

As he opened their door and helped Meli out, she shyly looked up and asked, "Will I ever see you again?"

Tomas lifted her hand to his lips and kissed her fingertips. "M'Lady, I am yours to command. Besides, I am now your guardian, remember?"

Meli smiled. "I'll hold you to that promise, Tomas Heinrich, Richter. Until then, M'Lord, we have work to do and don't forget the signal."

After helping Berthe out, he took both her hands in his own and smiled. "When this is all over, I'll be back, I promise."

"I know you will Tomas." She shrugged and gave a little grin. "It's in the cards."

Then, with a nod to them both, he got into the car and drove away.

———

Several hours later, a group of around forty people gathered at the base of the Pog. Having secured permission from the Third Reich to pay tribute to the Cathar martyrs, they were ready to start their ascent. The procession began in silence as a mixed group of men and women, young and old, slowly began the climb. A light drizzle left minute droplets on their hats and coats, headscarves and noses. Digging their hands deeper into their pockets, both Berthe and Meli bolstered themselves against the chill and joined the group.

Arriving at the "*Prat dels Cremats*", the group huddled together in tribute and prayer celebrating the lives of the martyrs of pure Christian love. Suddenly, the noise of an airplane engine cut through the silence and as everyone put their hands to their foreheads to look upwards, both Berthe and Meli quickly shared a smile before they too gazed up towards the fortress.

As they gathered in the crisp March morning air, a single engine plane, fitted with sky-writing equipment, circled the summit creating a huge Celtic cross in the sky before dipping its wings and continuing its journey. Tomas was safely on his way to meet with Himmler and present him with the artifact, where it would be placed at the castle of Wewelsburg.

———

That night, Berthe and Meli settled into the cottage and prepared themselves into starting a new life. After listening to BBC Londres, they talked until Meli could not keep her eyes open another minute. Exhausted and spent, she fell soundly asleep and dreamed.

She was back at Montségur, but this time she was not alone. She was surrounded by the spirits of past Keepers. Hundreds of both men and women glowed in shifts that shimmered of opals and colours as they joined together to support her. Their message was clear. She wouldn't be alone. Each one then proceeded to walk forward, reaching out to hold her hands. No verbal words were spoken, but rather a communion of minds took place where information, messages was transferred. These exchanges were a blur of pictures, emotions, names and always unending love.

At last in front of her stood her smiling Mamina, who held out her hand. Flashes of Meli as a baby, Sophie cradling her in her arms, Mamina and Pierre with love in their eyes, Mamina's heart full of love and promise. Squeezing her hand, Mamina looked deeply into Meli's eyes. "I couldn't be more proud of you, Meli."

Even in her dream, Meli knew she was crying. Tears streamed down her cheeks as they washed away the pain, the fear and heartache that bound her inside. Holding onto Mamina's hands, she didn't want to let go, but her grandmother was firm. Still smiling, she took a step back and faded into the mist.

The release was instantaneous. She felt as if she had been underwater, then in an enormous burst of energy, exploded to the surface. She felt clear, clean and powerful. She was no longer a little girl, but a confident young woman.

Waking from her dream, she reached for her amulet and scanned the room. In the corner was the slightest of shimmering, a swirl of a tiny star, enough for her to know that she wasn't alone.

The whisper that followed was like the gentlest of kisses on her cheek, like the twinkling of Sophie's eyes, or the sweetest of hugs that came after a tumble. "I love you, my beautiful daughter."

CHAPTER FORTY

A MONTH LATER, A LETTER ARRIVED AT THE COTTAGE ADDRESSED to Meli and postmarked from Paris as was dutifully noted by Henri Bouchard. He asked after her grandmother, but she merely continued with her excuse that she was out at the cave, in the barn, or not feeling well. Berthe was rarely discussed and assumed by the villagers to have been shipped to a work camp. Most expressed sympathy for Berthe, who was considered to be a resister, but there were still a few that sided with 'not rocking the boat'. It was those who could still cause her problems with the German authorities.

After he had left, Berthe came out from hiding in the front room and they opened it together. Inside was a small newspaper clipping. Huddled together at the kitchen table they read it together.

According to the German Ancestral Heritage group, founded by Heinrich Himmler, in early morning hours on March 16th, 1944, in the Ariege region of France, an amazing discovery was made.

In an undiscovered cave below where the Fortress of Montségur proudly stands, a false wall has been found and accessed by Lieutenant Wolfgang Koch.

Inside the hidden cavern was found the Cathar's most prized possession, a 1st century alabaster cup that had been kept safe in an intricately carved wooden box. This cup is widely believed to be the Holy Grail. Unfortunately, Lieutenant Koch fell to his death while rappelling down the cliff in what was a solo operation with the hope of finding another cave containing other artifacts. No books or documents have been found leading the researchers to believe that they had been hidden elsewhere or had simply never existed.

The cup itself was presented to Heinrich Himmler in a ceremony by Private Tomas Heinrich Richter, Lieutenant Koch's assistant, who flew the artifact back to Germany himself.

Both women hugged each other tightly and as Meli folded it back into its envelope, Berthe pulled out a handkerchief from her pocket to wipe the moisture from her eyes.

———

Over the next several months, the war continued in all its horror. Fifteen people were killed in a massacre at Frayssinet. There were the D-Day landings, the murder of 99 men by the SS near Limoge, and the horrific slaughter of 642 men, women and children killed at Oradour-sur-Glane. When would it end?

Every night they prayed, until finally Paris was liberated on the 25th of August 1944. It would take another year before the war would be considered officially over, but Paris was a start.

EPILOGUE

1955—Ten years later.

Tomas tossed his youngest daughter in the air, laughing himself at her four-year-old shrieks of glee while her older sister pulled at his leg begging for her turn to happen sooner than just 'you're next.'

Their mother, now 26, was in the kitchen looking out towards the hill where Mamina and now Berthe, were buried. A plaque had been placed, one for each of them including Sophie. One of Minoux's offspring, a fat white cat named Lancelot, Lance for short, brushed himself repeatedly against her leg, purring loudly to show his contentment.

She could hear Tomas and the children outside, laughing, giggling and their high pitch squeals as they thrilled to each new height. Had it really been ten years ago?

Now a history teacher, Tomas, with his impeccable French,

was accepted into the community, especially when his part in saving Berthe was made known.

After the war had ended, they admitted that Isabel had been shot by Lieutenant Koch, but only because she had been hiding Berthe. It was not revealed at the time, because Berthe was still in danger. No one questioned their rationale. Perhaps they were still numbed from the war, the lack of food, or the horrendous cost of human life.

No one had escaped unscathed. Even the years immediately after the war took their toll. Food and clothing continued to be scarce. As men returned home, their previous jobs had been filled by competent women, now widows, who themselves need to provide for their families. The transition years were not easy. Pointing fingers and placing blame was everywhere. After the liberation, the nation's fury turned to the collaborators and in a frenzy of anger and shame, more than 10,000 suspected collaborators were killed.

It was Tomas who made inquiries into Helene and Nicole. The story he reported wasn't pleasant to hear. After the death of Koch, Helene's money ran out, forcing her and Nicole to consider other sources of German financing. Considered 'horizontal collaborators', their picture was taken as they were paraded into the street and humiliated, naked, their heads shorn and bleeding. There was no trace of where they went after this. Despite everything, Meli hoped that they found their safe place. She also hoped that she would never meet up with them again.

The Kowalski family spent seven months at the internment camp until deported on the first convoy to Auschwitz from France. It wasn't known until later that Father Pelletier arranged for a family in the countryside to shelter the oldest daughter and was the one who coordinated her escape. She was the only one to survive. She was the twelfth child he was able to save.

As for Meli, she was content. That entire summer, she and Berthe had scrubbed the Banon cave until barely a trace of the blood stains remained. When she was able, the damaged barrels were replaced, as was the false wall.

Berthe had proved to be so much more than a family friend during those years. She was a valuable resource, Mamina, mother, sister and friend all rolled up into one soft hug of a woman. She taught her both ways to make cassoulet and didn't know what she would have done without her.

She was there when Tomas returned, a man in search of the woman he hoped she had become. And she had. They took on the farm together and she was grateful that Berthe was able to hold her firstborn in her arms before she died two weeks later.

They still had goats and chickens. She still made Banon, like her ancestors before her, and although neither little Alyse nor Lily had the mark, who knew what lay ahead. As she placed her hand on her blossoming womb, she smiled. There's always time.

She had published three books, 'The Key to Love', 'The Adventures of Amelie', and 'Charlotte's dream', which were well received. She was currently working on her fourth. For the most part, her dreams had stopped. She already knew who she was.

However, every now and then, a shimmer of light danced in a dark corner and beckoned her to pay attention, reminding her that she was loved. Meli always smiled at this. Looking around at Tomas and the girls, the cottage and the life they had created. Hmph…as if she needed reminding.

———

Don't miss out on your next favorite book!

Join the Melange Books mailing list at
www.melange-books.com/mail.html

THANK YOU FOR READING

Did you enjoy this book?

We invite you to leave a review at the website of your choice, such as Goodreads, Amazon, Barnes & Noble, etc.

DID YOU KNOW THAT LEAVING A REVIEW...

- Helps other readers find books they may enjoy.
- Gives you a chance to let your voice be heard.
- Gives authors recognition for their hard work.
- Doesn't have to be long. A sentence or two about why you liked the book will do.

ABOUT THE AUTHOR

Kate Riley is a professional business coach, facilitator and artist who is passionate about the 13th century. Her historical interest in this period was borne from an intense dream where she found herself in a besieged fortress disguised as a young man, surrounded by Templars and about to die. A voice strongly directed her several times to wake up and write down the word 'Cathar'. This dream began a thirty-year obsession, which has twice taken her to Montségur.

Ms. Riley's career has encompassed 20 years in the newspaper industry and another 18 years as a Business Coach. She currently lives in Innisfil, Ontario and is a Business Advisor for persons with disabilities across Canada.

www.katerileybooks.com

facebook.com/Kate-Riley-1704834233070805

ALSO BY KATE RILEY

Novels

The Last Cathar